A Romany Epistle

Taerith

by Rachel Starr Thomson

Taerith

Published by Little Dozen Press
Stevensville, Ontario, Canada
www.littledozen.com

ISBN: 978-0-9880613-7-8

Prologue

It was evening. The sun was beginning to sink behind the trees of Braedoch Forest, throwing its leafy depths into shadow. It was early spring and the forest was still newborn; winter's chill could yet be felt in the air at night.

On the eastern edge of the forest, the nine children of Isaak Romany were gathering together.

Their home was a small house of stone, composed of three circular chambers. In the central chamber a fire burned slowly, varying light dancing on the face of a tall man in a dark cloak. He waited for the nine to gather. His face seemed set in granite, as always; no hint of emotion, no whisper of affection for the children he had raised. He, Maeron Duard, was their guardian, nothing more. They did not care for him either. Though they had grown up in the house, they often chose to stay apart from it: they wandered the forest, worked in the woodshop, climbed the small mountains that overlooked their home in the north. They were not like others. Their life had been one of isolation. They knew weaponry and woodcraft, but little of humanity. They cared for each other and yet spent much of their time in solitude.

Their guardian was afraid of them. Once the clan of Romany had been strong and numerous. Duard's ancestors—druids and powerful, vengeful men—had cursed the clan nearly a century ago. In the succeeding generations, hardship, famine, and war had plagued them—helped along by the druids. At last, only Isaak Romany and his wife were left. They took their children to Braedoch and tried to live with them there. But Isaak was a powerful man of great personal force, and the few remaining druids feared that he would father a new beginning for the clan. They sent Duard to kill him. And he did. He killed Isaak and his wife, but could see nothing to fear in the children. Behind his face of stone there was perhaps a heart, for he kept them alive, and raised them.

But he feared them now. Alone, he thought, they could be no threat. But as long as they stayed together, the clan Romany might again arise.

*   *   *

Taerith Romany entered the yard on foot. He stopped a moment at the well and dipped a bucket of water, bringing it to his face in his strong brown hands. He drank, and with his hands still wet, pushed his dark brown hair back from his face. Taerith's was a solemn face, kind and possessed of a depth too great for his twenty-four years.

He stepped away from the well and looked pensively at the smoke rising from the round stone chamber he called home. His eyes, always thoughtful, had darkened with worry. Duard did not often call his charges together. Taerith looked down at his boots, oddly striped now from days of being alternately splashed with mud and washed clean by river water. He had been in the mountains a fortnight hence, camped out beside a shallow river, watching as multiple fishing poles, carefully selected from the surrounding trees, bent and bobbed over the water. He liked to fish. It was easier than hunting, a good deal less bloody, and afforded him time to think.

But his thoughts had been clouded, and now had come together in a threatening grey sky. He shook his head, as though he could shake them out, and giving his boots one last stamp, entered the house.

A few of the others were already there. They sat in the shadows, as far from Duard as they could get and still be in the room. Their guardian stood in silence by the fire. He surveyed them, keeping his thoughts to himself. As he had ever done. Taerith lingered in the shadows for a few moments, and then stepped to the edge of the light. He met his guardian's eyes, but did not speak. Moments later, Aiden, the eldest, joined him. Together they willed Duard's eyes to see only them, and leave the others to their own silences.

Duard waited until the last had arrived before he spoke. Then, slowly, he nodded, as though confirming that what he was about to do was right.

"You wonder why I have sent for you," he said. "I will not keep you waiting. The time has come for you to go."

Taerith blinked. The words were too sudden to sink in quickly.

"Braedoch is no longer home to you, nor are you any longer a family. You will each depart alone. You will have nothing more to do with each other from this day forward. You are not to communicate, and absolutely not to see each other. If you do, terrible consequences will follow—I am warning you now."

There was a shocked silence. Duard surveyed his charges with scorn.

"Make whatever preparations are necessary. You leave in three days."

Taerith spoke slowly, weighing the words on his tongue. "You are banishing us?" he said.

Duard's eyes met his with their familiar dark fire. "Do you question me?"

Some of the younger ones were already shaking their heads. Taerith's answer was almost a whisper. "No."

But he did… how he did. On the morning of the third day, as Taerith lifted his scant pack to his back and took a staff in his hand, he turned and looked back at the house with its slowly rising column of smoke.

"I question you, Master," he said. "And someday you will answer me."

The house did not respond; its lone occupant did not emerge. Taerith settled the pack over his shoulders, and walked away.

Chapter One

It was raining in the fields. Cold rain. Taerith stretched out his arms and raised his head, letting the rain hit his face and run down the bridge of his nose. He opened his mouth and gulped convulsively as the liquid trickled into his throat. It was good of the sky, he thought, to give him water. He had been at work with the other men, harvesting late corn, but the rain had put an end to the work for now. The fields were nearly bare anyway. Water puddled around his boots—held together now with string and patches—and turned the trampled furrows to mud.

There were a few other men left in the field; they drifted away now. They were migrants, men on the road who hired themselves out to the landlords to work the fields and bring in the last of the harvest. Taerith kept to himself; most of the others kept to themselves; they laboured side by side but did not know one another's names.

The work was finished. Taerith lowered his head and looked impassively at those who were leaving, then turned away and trudged back toward the road. This was not like other days, which had ended only to be born anew in the morning, once more to consist of labour in the fields. Work was really over now; the changing of the seasons was destroying his livelihood. He would go to the small nobleman to whom the land belonged and collect his pay.

When he had begun his travels, six months ago, he had hoped to find a new home, or a band of men to whom he could join himself. It had been a futile dream. Even those who banded together excluded him. Why, Taerith didn't know—he seemed to have something written across his forehead; the word—*Banished*—branded him.

But now winter was coming. He could not continue on alone much longer.

He paid his visit to the landlord and collected the last of his wages. Behind the haze of rainclouds, the sun was setting as Taerith again took to the road. He walked for miles through the darkening damp, until he found a small shelter, erected on a little hilltop not far from the road. Here he built himself a fire, wrapped himself in his cloak, and fell asleep.

He was awakened early in the morning by the clatter of wheels and the clop of hooves, and the sound of a wheezy voice muttering near his ear. He woke with a start and gained his knees in an instant, reaching for his sword. It was missing. Through the longish hair that fell into his eyes, Taerith looked across the fire into the face of a strange little man who seemed to have sprung up out of the sunrise. Grey, wizened hair floated around the little man's temples; his eyes twinkled, matched by the glittering of a gold earring that flared in the meagre morning light. He sat cross-legged with a grey blanket across his knees.

Taerith's hand searched the ground for his sword, and the little man chuckled—a breathless chuckle. He whisked the grey blanket aside and held up Taerith's sword, still in its scabbard, still attached to his belt, which was no longer around its master's waist.

"Looking for this?" the man asked.

Taerith froze, his muscles tense and his eyes watchful. The little man did not look like a threat, but he certainly held the upper hand… and the nearby sound of voices indicated that he had friends in the road. Unarmed and sleeping was no way to meet with bandits.

"Calm yerself, man," the stranger chuckled. "I'm no thief."

Taerith found his tongue, and spoke slowly. He was always careful to measure out his words. "I don't remember giving you my sword."

The little man hefted the sword. "Catch," he said. "I don't believe you're any more a threat than I am—but I like to be sure, before I give a man his arms back." He tossed it, and Taerith reached out and caught it out of the air.

"Thank you," he said, buckling it back on. "Would you mind telling me who you are?"

The little man drew a breath and rested his hands on his knees; he seemed to puff up like a swelling cloud. "My name is Findal," he said. "I am a man of the road."

"As am I," said Taerith, "though I would prefer not to be. My name is Taerith Romany." He held out his hand, and they shook across the fire.

"And what is wrong with the road?" Findal asked. "It has always treated me right well."

"It is likely to be cold in the winter," Taerith said, casting a glance on the lightening sky.

"True enough," Findal said. He narrowed his eyes and peered more closely at Taerith. "You have nowhere to go, then?"

"No," Taerith said.

Findal pursed his lips. "Well," he said. "Well. I will ask you no more, as you are evidently a man of few words. Will you break fast with us?"

Taerith stood, stretching his legs. His grey cloak fell around him. He reached down to help the little man up, and when he had done so, he saw that the man barely came up to his chest. "I can see no harm in that," he said.

"Good," the man said. He nodded, his eyes fixed on Taerith with obvious curiosity. True to his word, he asked no more questions. "Good," he said again.

The little man turned away from the fire. Following him, Taerith looked down the hill into the road, where he could now see the little company that had come upon him. There were several wagons in the road, pulled by merry looking little horses, and one magnificent red stallion was tied up behind one of them. This particular wagon was larger than the others, and enclosed; there were fantastic characters painted on the side in fading colours, and strange wild faces… and a unicorn. The other wagons were entirely ordinary: two closed, one open and filled with bales of covered hay. They had all stopped in the middle of the road and a small company milled around them.

Taerith was aware that they fell silent as he approached behind Findal, and as he stepped between the wagons into the makeshift camp, the strangers stopped what they were doing and stared. He tried not to stare back, and found that his easiest recourse was to cast his eyes on the dull brown earth. The strangers were not entirely easy to treat with indifference. They were dressed in strange, ill-fitting, weirdly sewn clothes; and the frames on which the clothes fit had a share of weirdness in themselves. Taerith could not help feeling that he had fallen in with something not quite human.

Rachel Starr Thomson 11

Findal hailed them all loudly, and with good, wheezy cheer. "Look alive, you all!" he said. "I've brought us a breakfast companion. There, Morris… bring us a little more firewood." As he spoke, he sat down by the fire, and beckoned for Taerith to do the same.

An extraordinarily thin, wiry man dressed in dingy red stepped away from one of the enclosed wagons with his arms full of firewood. He stepped lightly, as though there were eggshells beneath his feet, with an odd grace that Taerith found unnerving. The fellow threw the wood on the fire and then stepped forward and offered his hand. Taerith took it. It was smooth, and made him think somehow of a snake. "Morris Syve," he said. His voice was as thin as his body. He bowed his head slightly in greeting, and then retired to the fireside. He sat on the ground, threw one leg around his neck until the foot rested on the ground, and leaned on the misplaced limb. He continued to stare. Taerith averted his eyes, and watched as a short man with muscles so great they seemed ready to pop from every inch of his skin seated himself by the fire.

Taerith looked at Findal now, and the little man answered before the question could be asked.

"We are performers," he said. "Showmen. No stranger than many… more honest than most."

"I will eat and drink with honest men, wherever I find them," Taerith answered.

"Good fellow," Findal said. He pointed at Taerith with the blackened end of a stick he'd been using to stir the fire. "You could use a good eating, and a drink, from the looks of you," he said. "Where are you going, and where have you been? You need not hide anything from Findal… nor yet from his merry band."

The eyes fixed on Taerith from across the fire hardly seemed merry, yet he liked Findal, and felt that he could trust these people. In any case, he had nothing to hide. "I am come from the east," he said. "I have been traveling these six months, working in the fields as a harvester. I fear that work has closed its doors to me. As to where I am going, I hardly know. I follow the road."

"Then I'll tell you where you're going," Findal said. With his stick he dug something tightly wrapped from the embers of the fire, and set it out to cool. "You're going into a country where men and women like a good show, but will not pay too handsomely for it. It is not good land, not bad. A day more and you will be under the jurisdiction of Annar, king of these parts. He manages his estates well enough, and his people do not starve. He is in a good mood these days, as he is about to be married. So, we are going to perform for him, in hopes that love will make him generous."

Taerith took the food that Findal offered him—some sort of tuber, cooked nearly to mash—and tossed it from hand to hand. It was still hot. "He is a good man, then?" he asked.

"He's like his land… not good, not bad."

Morris spoke from across the fire. "We are grateful he is not his brother."

"Yes, yes," Findal wheezed. "Borden… now there's a bad piece of work, and no mistaking. Not one to give an honest man so much as a penny, not if he can stand on his head and whistle cheerily at the same time; not if he can teach a bear to dance."

"He lacks imagination?" Taerith asked, smiling a little at Findal's censure.

"He lacks anything that makes a man worthy," Findal answered. "I met him once, in court." He shook his head. "A bad piece of work."

"How far is the king's castle from here?" Taerith asked, as he unwrapped his breakfast and took a bite.

"Not two days," Findal said. "But we shall take three to reach it. We have an engagement in a nearer town. Will you accompany us there?"

Taerith looked up in surprise. He did not answer immediately, but looked around the camp a little more. Some way off from the fire he saw a woman step out of a wagon and call something to a boy who sat near her; the stallion who followed the wagons whinnied. Findal, waiting in expectation with his stick poised half in the air, had eyes neither unkind nor unwise. All in all, it was a more pleasant prospect than continuing down the road alone. He looked back at Findal. "I will," he said.

*　*　*

Four nights had passed since Borden, heir to his brother's lands, had slept. His soul was not easy at the best of times, but now he saw clouds on the horizon of his carefully planned future years. He was determined to stand on the castle parapet and stare them down, until they shrank and shriveled and dissipated before the force of his gaze.

The sun was sinking low over the fields that surrounded the castle. The falling darkness suited his mood. He made no move to go inside, down to human society, to the celebrations his brother was already holding. He was an old fool, Annar, drinking and blushing as though he were a young man in love, and not an old king waiting for a girl he had never met, who loved him no more than he loved her.

Borden watched for the convoy. It would come, with a carriage in its midst, bearing her who threatened everything. It would come, beneath the clouds. If he could have shattered it with a look, Borden would have. His eyes were always forceful; now, after days of brooding and nights without sleep, they seemed like the eyes of some old god, capable of turning an enemy to stone.

Yes, they would come soon. The bride and her retinue. And there would be more drinking, more foolish revelry, and then marriage. And a son would come to displace the brother who should have possessed the throne long ago.

The clouds were black indeed.

"My lord Borden." The voice was at his elbow, a thin, wavering voice. Borden turned on it, and his eyes burned into the stooped servant who waited nervously for him.

"What is it?" Borden asked, when the man's nerves had nearly reached a breaking point.

"The king calls for you," the servant said.

"The king," Borden muttered, and turned away. "I do not come at the beck and call of my brother."

The servant cleared his throat. "Please, sir," he said, "he requests…"

Borden wheeled around again. "What care I what he says?" he roared. "What is my brother? Tell me that, slave, and speak truth! What is my brother?"

"He is the king," the servant stuttered.

Borden caught the man's shirt sleeve, and spun him around toward the steps. He resisted the urge to kick the old fellow all the way down, instead releasing him with a shove. The man stumbled down the first few stone steps toward the courtyard, and was caught by the strong arms of a girl who stood, half-veiled in the shadows of the wall. Borden saw it, and bristled with anger.

"He can walk," he said.

The girl, who was considerably taller than the old man,

looked up at Borden's words but did not answer. She did not have to. Borden could see her eyes burning in the darkness, with nearly as much force as his own. She was angry with him.

"Come here," Borden said.

The girl hesitated a moment, and then lifted her chin and walked up the steps to the parapet. She faced Borden without wavering. She was tall, well-formed, and obviously strong. Her red-brown hair was tied back in a thick braid and partially covered by a green kerchief. She balanced a basket on her hip, full of laundry stained in Annar's banquets. A grey collar sat dully around her neck: mark of bondage. She had long been a slave in Annar's household, and Borden had noticed her before, in passing. She was remarkable for the way she carried herself: as much unlike a slave as a wild horse is unlike the broken nag that pulls a tinker's cart.

"You tell me," Borden said. "What is my brother? There is a tongue in your head."

She looked at him, and then answered slowly, "I know what you think him."

"Speak it," Borden said.

"You think him a fool," she said.

He smiled, and turned back to the wall. There was a balm in hearing the word from another's mouth. But the girl had not moved, and her presence had a power in it that demanded to be acknowledged. He turned a little and looked at her again.

"And what am I?" he asked.

"A tyrant," she answered, without wasting a moment on misgivings. "Who pushes old men down stairs. A bully who delights to hear his words sung back to him."

"You do not admire me for that."

"I have never admired you," she answered.

His anger at Annar had been for the moment slightly gratified; there was heat enough in his blood to boil up at another. She was a slave. He might demand opinions from her, but the discovery that she had any did not entirely please him.

"You speak out of place," he growled.

"And at your command," she answered.

The setting sun cast a glow over the girl's handsome features. Borden had seen her a hundred times before but never as an individual, and suddenly he wondered what manner of being lived in his house. She had a magnificence that belonged to queens, not to slaves. And she was angry with him… enough to answer him back and insult him, when he could do anything he liked to her and she could not defend herself.

"You obviously command your own opinions," Borden said. "What do you think of my brother?"

She swallowed, and looked away for an instant. Perhaps she was beginning to regain her calm, and with it, wisdom. But her words showed little discretion. "He does not deserve to be a king," she said.

"And neither do I?"

"No."

Their eyes met again, and a smile began to dawn on Borden's face, but it was not called there by any of the innocent pleasures that bring joy to others. "You're angry with me for abusing a servant," he said. "And you stand here and abuse me. I could cast you down the stairs just as easily."

She appeared to think it over for a moment, and took in his

brawny arms and broad shoulders; the iron cast of the face hidden behind his thick black beard.

"You could," she assented.

"What would you do if my brother tried it?" He half expected the answer, and wanted to hear it.

Her voice was low but she answered. "I would break his arm."

The smile broke free. He laughed. "You will not do well when a queen reigns in this house; you have too much spirit. Women can never abide to be eclipsed by one another."

"No more than brothers," the girl said. But now her voice had grown quiet; most of the fire had gone out of it.

"What is your name?" Borden demanded.

"Mirian," the girl answered.

Borden turned and looked out on the now shrouded fields. "You may leave," he said. He waited for her to reply, to thank him for dismissing her, but she did not. When next he turned his head, Mirian had gone.

The slave girl and all her powers of diversion gone, Borden fell again to thoughts of the future sweeping over the roads toward him. Every trace of a smile left his face as he meditated on the place his brother had now twice stolen from him. The weak should not rule over the strong. Borden was strong. The moon rose higher, and the still-heir of the kingdom sank down on his precarious position and quietly lost himself in obsession.

Chapter Two

Taerith watched from the wings as Findal's circus unfolded its strange and fascinating show. He had been with them now three days, and sat through twice as many performances. He knew now when to rush out with a bucket of water for the horses, which were transformed before an audience from cart-horses to dancers, with still other dancers upon their backs—Morris, who was as acrobatic on the back of a living thing as he was on the ground or in the air suspended from a rope or a wire, and Marta Grensloe, who had been a great beauty in her younger years and was still strong and good-looking enough to capture a crowd's attention when she stood upon a horse's back. Marta was out there now, her red hair done up intricately, looking too exotic for the good-natured matron Taerith knew her to be. Her little white mare was panting heavily, and Taerith scooped up the bucket of water from beside his feet and went out to meet them as they vacated the performing-ground in favour of Orlin, the small muscle-bound man who made quite a different use of horses—he was strong enough to lift one, and did so three times a week at least.

"You looked well out there," Taerith said as Marta led the mare to the bucket. The woman looked nearly as hot and thirsty as the horse, but she did not have the option of plunging her head into a draught. Breathing heavily, Marta nodded and beamed at Taerith, giving the mare a good pat. Her blue eyes were proud.

"She's a good little one," Marta said. "One of the best. Oh, Zhenya, there you are… thank you."

So saying, she took a cup of water from the boy who offered it. Taerith had hardly noticed Zhenya's approach. The boy could move with uncanny silence, considering that everywhere he went he limped severely on a crutch. He was young, no more than fourteen, and probably tall for his age, though he was so bent over his crutch it was hard to tell. His hair was a dirty brown, and fell into his eyes; his clothes were worn, but Marta kept them patched. There was a peculiarly starved expression in the boy's face, though his thinness seemed more a mark of his age than a proof of physical deprivation. Zhenya had no remarkable ability or weird physiognomy to make him of value to Findal's troupe; but they kept him, pitied him, fed him. Zhenya repaid them by doing every chore he could manage. Since Taerith's arrival the crippled boy had rarely been out of his shadow, though they rarely spoke to one another. Taerith liked him: he shared Zhenya's hunger. Young man and growing boy both understood that life held meaning, and that it was waiting for them to find it; both were quietly searching.

The mare was finished, and Taerith took the bucket away even as a roar went up from the crowd. Orlin had lifted some impossible weight of iron, and continued to add to his load. Findal's voice, endowed with astonishing volume and strength, drew the crowd's attention and bade them marvel at every feat. When his band was performing, Findal's voice lost all of its breathlessness; he wheezed the rest of the time, it seemed, because it took him so long to get his breath back after a show.

Marta smoothed down her dress and pulled pins out of her

hair as she stepped into the shadows of the tent where the animals waited when they were not in the center of attention. It was a smallish tent, but large enough to act as a stable; torn, patched, striped, and stuffy. It went everywhere with Findal and his people, and the multicoloured light produced by the sun's shining through it was already familiar to Taerith's eyes.

The red stallion, tied to a stake in one end of the tent, perked its ears up as Marta approached. Normally she would have given it a lump of sugar, but she was too busy pulling her hair down. "We're doing Findal proudly," she said, "finishing the season well. We will do a fine job before King Annar, though he will likely be too drunk to know it."

"How did you win an audience in the king's court?" Taerith asked.

Marta cast him a glance, her hair down now and cascading over her shoulder in red waves. "Findal is a master at making friends," she said. "He speaks so convincingly that everyone believes how great he is."

"And how great we are," said another voice, as a tall man entered the tent. He stooped and kissed Marta. "Findal never forgets his lovely rider, or the rest of us. You, now, Taerith—you'll soon be one of his bragging points. You're nearly one of us already."

Taerith smiled. He liked Randal, Marta's tall, sword-swallowing husband. Randal liked him also. After nearly six months of being an outcast, Taerith welcomed Randal's words—"one of us." He had no plans to stay with Findal, of course, and yet he couldn't quite imagine leaving. In three days Marta and Randal, Zhenya, Orlin, and Morris, even the horses, had become the closest thing to family that he had. And Findal, as Randal said, had already taken Taerith as one of his own.

"There is something you can do," Findal had said last night, "besides draw water, of that I am sure. We shall discover your talent and make you a part of us."

"I have sometimes written poetry," Taerith answered with a smile.

Findal had looked at him, frowned, snorted a little. "Something else, lad, something else. One cannot put poetry before a crowd."

Taerith suspected that, were he to stay, he would become another Zhenya. And there were things he could do—he could form wood, and work a blacksmith's forge, and be useful at fixing wheels and axles. He had nowhere else to go, and the idea of remaining grew more and more attractive by the hour.

They planned to move on that night, just after dusk. Findal's troupe did not normally travel after dark, but they had stayed overlong in the villages where they had found a welcome, and if they did not move when they could, they would miss the opportunity to perform before Annar. Findal counted on the king's drunkenness and fool's generosity to fatten the collective purse for the winter. Accordingly, when Morris had tied himself in knots and been tossed in the air by Orlin for the last time that night, the horses were hitched to the wagon and the small company moved out.

It was nearly midnight when they heard the sounds of a fight. Randal untied the stallion and rode out into the darkness while Marta waited with her lips tightly closed. He returned not ten minutes later, his dark eyes flashing. He reined up next to the board where Findal sat, on the front of the painted wagon. "Thieves," he said. "They have attacked a group of travelers."

"How goes the battle?" Findal asked.

"Badly," Randal answered. "For they are outnumbered. But I tell you the thieves are reckless… easily overcome."

Findal pursed his lips and looked down the road with a deadly gleam in his eyes. "Let us overcome them, then," he said.

Randal wheeled his horse around, ready to gallop to the battle ahead of the others, but Taerith stopped him by calling his name. "Take me with you." Randal nodded, and Taerith leapt from the wagon onto the horse's back behind the sword-swallower.

The stallion ran hard, and Taerith drew his sword as his blood began to pump. He was not afraid. He had never considered himself a great swordsman, but he compared himself to his brothers and sisters—and not one among the Romanys was a poor hand with weapons. Morever, in a fight Taerith was possessed of a deadly calm that made him hard to defeat, because he was never flustered, never distracted. He knew this about himself, and peered through the darkness to the whooping band of thieves, wishing he was already there to meet them.

His eyes were already adjusted to the darkness, as they had been riding in it for hours. He and Randal bore down upon the scene.

A lone carriage lay half on its side in the middle of the road, one of its front wheels snapped quite away from the axle. A horse was still harnessed to it; it strained at its load with frantic whinnies, but the carriage was caught in the deep ruts of the road and would not budge. It had evidently been the scene of a stand-off; the bodies of men lay strewn around it. Others, living still, were in the process of dragging a young woman out. She was not at all willing to go with them, and was doing her best to wrench herself from their grasp—but she was small, and fine, and they were great brutes.

Randal and Taerith rode up to the carriage without slowing,

and hope lit in the girl's face at the sight of them. "Help me!" she screamed. In the same instant Taerith had sprung from the stallion's back, and with one twist of his sword he sent the foremost thief's weapon flying away into the night. Another leapt toward him, weapon in hand, and Taerith beat him an instant. Another came, and Randal was there to meet him. Other thieves were also in the road, but they had no time to come against the invaders. Findal had arrived with Morris and Orlin, and all three shouted as they came like mad spirits of the night let loose.

The girl was left alone, and she sank against the side of the carriage and moaned. Taerith took hold of her arm and ran his hand gently down it, assuring himself that she was all right. "Are you hurt?" he asked. His voice was low and husky from the energy of the fight. She shook her head, her dark eyes avoiding him. The fight behind them drew a little closer, and Taerith all but pushed the girl back into the carriage. He followed her, and locked the door behind him, standing at the window with his sword drawn.

As the thieves did not immediately attempt to break the door down, Taerith turned his head back to his charge. She was a small woman, young, hardly more than a child, and very beautiful. Her hair was black as the night without, and her eyes shone like the stars. There were tears in her eyes, and they glistened as she fought to gain control of herself. She was not looking at him, though everything in her body language said that she knew he was there. If she could have become one with the carriage, she evidently would have.

"Who are you?" she asked. Her voice tremored, but Taerith heard a feeble attempt at courage in the questioning. His heart went out to her.

"I am not another enemy," he said, answering the question she had not asked. "My name is Taerith Romany."

She looked up at him. Her eyes were large and dark, set in a fine, pale face. "Lilia," she said.

Her voice was little more than a whisper, but it went to Taerith's heart like one of the arrows his sister Ilara used to shoot.

"Taerith!" shouted a voice from without. "Taerith, lad, where are you?"

Taerith leaned against the carriage door and felt for the handle in the shadows beneath the window. He could feel the tension draining out of him… tension he hadn't even realized was there. Findal was calling for him. He pushed down on the latch and the door swung open.

"I'm here," Taerith called, bending his head to step down from the tilted carriage. His eyes sought out Findal amidst the wreckage in the road. The little man was holding a torch high, looking about at the groaning wounded who lay all around.

Findal turned to answer, but Taerith had already gone halfway back into the carriage. Lilia was still sitting in the corner, looking like a frightened lamb. Taerith held out his hand to her. "Come," he said. "You are among friends now."

Tentatively she reached out and laid her slender fingers across his. He smiled, and led her into the open night. She looked furtively from side to side as she descended the broken step. Findal looked at them and smiled kindly.

"Don't be afraid, child," he said in his usual breathless tone. He nodded at Taerith with a fatherly crinkle about his eyes. "This is a good lad who's protecting you. You can trust him. Lean on him all you need to!"

He hardly needed to speak the words. Since she had taken his hand, Lilia had drawn closer to Taerith by the moment, and now was almost fainting on his arm. He held her up, and looked worriedly at Findal. "She needs to rest, Findal," Taerith said.

"Of course," Findal said. "Seat the child down. Any place is as good as another."

Nodding, Taerith looked over the site. There—Orlin had thrown a heap of debris into a pile, and it made a sort of natural throne. Taerith led Lilia to it and helped her to sit, chafing her hands anxiously. Zhenya appeared at his elbow with a drink of water, which Taerith gratefully took and offered to the girl. Zhenya's eyes met his when he turned to take the cup, and they were deep with concern.

"She'll be all right," Taerith said. "She's had a bad scare."

Behind them, Marta knelt down beside a wounded man and poked at him. A groan answered her, and she stood with her mouth grimly set. "We'll not move on tonight, Findal," she said. "Most of these men are hurt, and we can't load them all into the wagons."

Findal was making his own rounds through the wounded, with Randal close behind him. Taerith watched them for a moment, and nearly called out to tell Randal that the man to whom he was giving water was one of the bandits—an enemy. He closed his mouth before the words escaped him. The realization suddenly dawned on him that it did not matter one whit to Findal and his strange band of outcasts whose side the men were on. They were all wounded, they were all men. There would be no lines of distinction. And why should it not be so?

Lilia had by this time begun to recover her wits, and as Findal once again approached, she looked up at him with an expression of gratitude so touching that it made the old man falter in his steps.

"Well now, child," he said. "Tell Findal where you're going."

Lilia's eyes flickered down, to her hands, which Taerith still held—kneeling before her, he offered whatever strength he could. "To King Annar's wedding feast," she said.

Findal beamed. "And it is so!" he said. "Deus smiles down on us, for we are going the same way. You shall travel with us."

"I—" she began to say, and then stopped herself. She smiled at him. The smile had all the radiance of a midsummer moon, and Findal melted at the sight of it. "I would be glad to," she said. "Thank you."

She looked down at Taerith then, and her smile grew somehow sweeter. "And thank you," she said. She cast her eyes down with a low laugh. "I suppose I can take my own hands back now."

Taerith released her fingers instantly, and stood. Marta, who had paused to witness the scene, raised an eyebrow at him and said an enigmatic, "Uh-huh."

"Come, wife," said Randal, stepping and taking Marta's arm. "There is work to be done tonight."

Findal and his people fanned out into the crowd, and Taerith followed them half-reluctantly. Lilia remained seated, overseeing them like a dream of the night endowed with all the graces of fancy. Taerith knelt down beside a wounded man and tried to draw the man's eyes to his face.

"Can you see me?" Taerith asked.

The man groaned, but he nodded.

"Good," Taerith said. He looked up at Marta's call. "Bring them here," she was saying. "We'll treat them here, by the fire."

Taerith slipped his arms beneath the man's shoulders and legs, and with a grunt, he lifted him up and carried him through the wreckage on the road. A small fire was already blazing, testament to Zhenya's brilliance for the menial. The crippled boy looked up as Taerith approached.

"Bring him water, Zhenya, and wash his wounds," Taerith said. "You see where he is hurt." He drew back a ragged piece of the man's shirt as he spoke, exposing a deep gash in the shoulder. Zhenya fell to obedience immediately, and moments later Marta was there, soothing the man and administering some medicine of her own design. Taerith assisted the men in bringing the others to the fire, and then stood back, at a loss for what to do next. It was Randal who sent him back to the place his heart was hovering over.

"Marta will handle the wounds," Randal said, his deep voice falling quietly. "The girl should not be alone. She has been frightened. Go."

Taerith looked up at the tall sword-swallower, and wordlessly assented to the command. He turned to the place where Lilia sat, watching the proceedings and hugging her arm.

His heart leapt strangely as he approached her, and grew somehow as she looked up and greeted him with her eyes. He wondered suddenly why he had not gone back to her sooner.

The night lay before them, and he did not intend to leave her again.

Chapter Three

Celebrants had been pouring into the castle grounds since morning. Night had fallen hours ago, and still the lights of the castle looked down on the last holdouts of merriment and good-natured revelry. Given an excuse to be happy, the people took it—to the full. Those who had arrived sober were now drunk; some had fallen in the courtyard and lay insensible. *Just like their king,* Mirian thought with disgust. *I wonder if he's noticed that his bride has yet to arrive?*

She moved through the thinning crowd in the courtyard, balancing a basket full of bread of her hip. She focused her eyes on the kitchen door, sunken into the ground, and lifted her chin as she ignored the calls of those who had feasted too much already. She had been days in the kitchen helping make bread… months before that grinding wheat into flour. And for what? To prove once again that the land had a fool for a king.

Voices drifted down from the parapet around the castle, and a deep tone caught Mirian's attention. She slowed and looked up. Borden was there, above her, talking with a guard in the torchlight. The sight made her shiver for reasons she couldn't explain. She had half expected retribution after her strange confrontation with the crown prince—she knew how foolish she had been, but she had been angry. But he had done nothing to her. There had been no backlash; no punishment; no threats. Perhaps he was waiting until the celebration was over. The voices above fell silent, and Mirian picked up her pace again. Somehow she knew he had not forgotten.

A man was sitting next to the steps that led down to the kitchen. His hands and face were covered by sleeves and a cowl; he wore the brown robes of a priest. From his posture she thought he might be sleeping, but as Mirian approached he raised his head, startling her.

"Excuse me," he said in a low voice. "Might I trouble you for a crust of bread?"

She was in a rush to get inside, and he must have seen it on her face. "I've only just arrived," he explained, "and have not eaten in some days."

Mirian turned, half-involuntarily, looking over her shoulder for Borden. He wasn't there. "Come in, then," she said. "There's more in the kitchen."

The air in the kitchen was close and hot. The whoosh of cold air let in by the door as Mirian pushed through it cut into the room like a pathway. The room was full, and bustling. Merriment for the townspeople meant work for the servants and slaves who kept Annar's house. The priest followed Mirian in. She hefted the bread basket onto the table and motioned with her head for him to sit at an empty space across from it. She tossed him a small, brown loaf. "Someone'll feed you more if you need it," she said, and left him to attend to the work at another table. Two young girls were hacking at a mountain of cabbage. Mirian grabbed up a knife and joined them, attacking the work with vigour.

Behind her, the kitchen matron struck up a conversation with the priest. Mirian caught bits and snatches of it as she worked…

the priest's low voice somehow managed to travel under the sound of knives thwacking wood and vegetables.

"… a joyous occasion," she heard him say.

The matron answered, but her back was turned to Mirian and her voice could not travel through the thick air. Heat flared up as the woman stoked the fire in one of the ovens. A moment later she swung around, and her words carried. Her tone matched that of Mirian's mind: skeptical.

"… poor thing. Little more than a child herself, they say."

"And you say they have never met?" the priest asked.

"Why would they need to? The king only wants a son and heir."

Mirian grimaced. Celebrate though they may, no one had any illusions as to the real purpose of Annar's long-delayed match. An heir. Deus forbid Annar should raise the child himself—should create another as incompetent as himself. It would have been far better for Annar to die and give the kingdom to his brother. Borden was a hard man, but he had a right to be hard. He had been forced to watch his older brother waste responsibilities that Borden himself could have used well.

Mirian swept a pile of chopped leaves from the table into a basket and carried it toward the ovens, where a vat of thick stew was bubbling. She did not look at the conversers, but she could hear them clearly now. The priest was speaking.

"Strange that she has not yet arrived."

The matron had barely had time to say "Foreigners" in a disparaging tone of voice when the kitchen door banged open and Borden entered, sword at his side, eyes darkened. Three of Annar's soldiers followed him in.

"I am looking for the priest," Borden said. "I saw him come in here." As he spoke, his eyes fell on Mirian. She did not turn away, but neither did she answer.

"I am here," said the priest, rising to his feet. Borden turned from Mirian and accosted the priest. "You are needed," he said. "Come with us." He looked back up, and his eyes arrested Mirian once more. "You too."

The servants followed Mirian with their eyes as she set her work down and went out after the men, back into the cold night air and flickering shadows of the courtyard. Most of the drunks were gone—Mirian suspected that Borden had ordered them away. Horses waited for the men. Borden mounted with a single motion, and nodded at a gelding that waited, unadorned by the livery of Annar's stables. Mirian laid her hand on the saddle and prepared to mount. Behind her, the priest was slower to move.

"If I may ask, sire," he said, "what does this signify?"

"We have heard reports," Borden answered. "Devilry in the road. You may be needed to give last rites."

As Mirian swung herself onto the horse's back and helped the priest on behind her, she could feel the prince's eyes on her again. She forced herself to meet his gaze. It was inscrutable… he seemed to be examining her, judging her worth for some task. Whatever he had in mind, she was determined to be its equal.

Borden turned his heels into his horse's sides with a "Ha!" The band rode out of the courtyard at a gallop.

*   *   *

A rivulet ran through the fields near where the carriage had been attacked. Marta had sent Taerith down to it multiple times, and Lilia had insisted on being of help. Together they had carried buckets of water back for the wounded, until at last Marta declared them well saturated. Now they sat by the water, listening to it run over rocks and the roots of a few low trees, while the moon sailed high overhead. Findal's troupe had settled down for the night, and only the occasional groan or snore whispered its way down to the pair who sat by the river.

"I often sat by the river at night as a boy," Taerith said. "I would steal away when the others were sleeping."

Lilia moved a little; her skirts rustled in the night. It was too dark to see much of her, but when she looked up at the moon, its light was reflected in her eyes. "I sometimes imagined that I sat by a river," Lilia said. "And listened to the water singing. The song always made the moon cry." She turned her head and looked at Taerith. "Is that silly?"

"No," he answered.

They were silent a moment, and then she said, "I wish I could have really gone out sometimes. This is so lovely… I could only dream things like this. My uncle did not like me to leave my room. But I was glad… I slept in a very high tower, and the wind carried sounds and smells and feelings to me… so I had some real things in my dreams."

Taerith wished he could find something to say in reply. The contrast to his own childhood was so marked. He thought of his sisters and wondered about them… he had not known them well, though they were raised together. They had all had the freedom to roam.

"When I grew older…" he said, and cut himself off. "I stayed out longer. We all did. When I was twelve I stayed away a whole week."

"Weren't you hungry?" Lilia asked.

"Yes," Taerith said. "I tried to catch fish. But my skill then was poor… yes, I was hungry. But I learned."

"Did you stay by the water all that time?" Lilia asked.

Taerith nodded. He caught himself, and opened his mouth, but she must have seen his movement even in the gloom, because she responded.

"Why?" she asked.

Taerith smiled and looked down at his hands. "The river had so much to say," he said.

Once more they fell silent, and the lapping of the water was all that came to them. It was speaking as they sat, and Taerith strained to hear what it said. Did its gentle tones promise a future, or speak of a fading past? Did they hold some mournful prophecy? Moonlight glowed on the water, and Taerith wondered if the moon told the river what it could see in the faraway places whence the water flowed.

"And you?" Taerith asked abruptly, breaking the silence. "You are not in your tower any longer."

"No," she said. He heard her draw in her breath, and wondered what feelings stirred inside her. "Things do change. I am off to face an adventure."

"You have already had plenty of that," Taerith said.

"I confess, I do not long for more," Lilia answered. "But listen… the river goes on, and it does it so peacefully. I think it tells me to do the same. Bravely. I have never been very brave, but there were no dangers in the tower. Things change… so I will be different now."

Something was left unspoken, and Taerith yearned to know what it was. She rewarded him, in a moment, with a broken word: "Only…"

He leaned forward. She was looking off to the moon again, but she lowered her eyes to look at him. They were glistening… with tears or moondust, he could not tell.

"Only what?" he asked.

"I wish I was not alone," Lilia answered.

Taerith reached out and took her small hand in his. Her fingers closed tightly over his, like a child clinging to the one hand she knows in a crowd. He smiled, willing her to see the smile, and know herself cared for. "Tonight you are not," he said. "Perhaps you will not be again."

She looked down, and then smiled up at him. His chest tightened, and he determined that he would not let go.

They sat together, hand in hand, wordless through the night; they listened to the song of the river.

*   *   *

Zhenya had not been asleep. He was the first to hear the riders coming, and he woke Findal with a whispered, "Trouble!"

Findal rolled out of his bedding and took up a sword in the same moment, buckling it to his waist. His grey hair was wild from sleep, but his eyes were already bright and alert. "What is it, boy?" he asked.

"Riders are coming," Zhenya said. "Coming fast."

Findal kicked Orlin; Morris and Randal were already awake and gathering their weapons to them. "What is the hour?" Findal asked.

"Four hours till sunrise," Zhenya answered.

The men turned as one to the road, ready to meet whatever was coming. Marta was up, twisting her hair behind her. "Into the wagons, Zhenya," she said. "You'll not fight."

"Taerith is down by the river," Zhenya said. Marta opened her mouth to give direction when the riders galloped up. Their horses were fine and decorated in the king's own livery. Chief among the men was a strongly-built fellow, darkly bearded and well-armed. Findal laid his hand on his hilt but did not draw.

"What has happened here?" the man demanded. "Bandits… where are your prisoners?"

"You read the story wrongly," Findal answered with a slight bow of his head, "my lord Borden. It was my fine men and I who chased the bandits off in this same night."

"The carriage of a great nobleman lies wrecked behind you," Borden said. "Where is the woman it carried?"

Lilia's clear voice rang out. "I am here."

Every head turned to see Lilia and Taerith approaching. The young man's manner was guarded; his hand was on his sword, as though any minute he would spring to the girl's defense. But she laid her hand on his arm and said something quietly to him, and then stepped forward into the light of a torch Zhenya now held high.

Borden dismounted, and bowed his head. He took Lilia's hand and brushed her fingers with his lips. "My lady," he said. "We are grateful that you are unharmed."

"I thank you for your care," she answered. She looked up at Borden as he returned to his full height, and something in her voice faltered slightly. "Do I behold the face of… King Annar, ruler of these lands?" she asked.

Borden's lip curled slightly. "You do not," he said. "I am his brother, come to fetch his bride for him. We heard rumours of bandits in the road, and were afraid for you."

Lilia nodded and managed something of smile. "As you see, I am unharmed. These good people came to my rescue with not a moment to spare."

"Then, if you will, my lady," Borden said, "we shall take you the rest of the way to your new home."

He offered her his hand, and she took it and took a step forward. Then she paused, and looked back, seeking out Taerith among those who had helped her. There was a plea in her grey eyes—for understanding, for forgiveness. Back she turned again, to the sight of the retinue who had come for her.

"You see," Borden said, "I do not threaten you with the company of more brutes such as myself. This girl will help you to ride, and watch out for anything you may need."

Lilia took her hand from the king's brother. The young woman who stood holding the bridle of a gelding and looking down at her with veiled expression was neither friendly nor warm. She was tall, strong, and quite beautiful; obviously a slave, from her dress and the dull collar around her neck. Yet there was something in her presence that made Lilia feel very small and cowed. A priest stood next to the girl, and Lilia's heart answered to the kindness in his eyes. She almost wished she could travel with him.

Borden's voice shattered her hopes of riding with the priest. "Have you any wounded? Dying?" he asked Findal.

"It is possible," Findal said, "though we have done our best."

Borden nodded. "I have brought you a priest, to care for the dead. I presume we will see you all at the wedding feast tomorrow."

In answer, Findal only nodded.

The slave girl helped Lilia onto her horse, and the whole party rode away.

Chapter Four

Taerith's fist clenched as he watched the crown prince and his men ride away, Lilia with them. His face was impassive. A strange, half-stricken expression in his blue eyes was all that betrayed the presence of emotion behind his gaze. For ten minutes he stood and stared down the road, its mists clearing away before the coming morning. He took a step forward, and then halted in visible confusion. His hand went to his head and he groaned.

Findal stood a few feet away, looking on with sage eyes. "Wait, boy," he said. "Just a few more hours, and you ride with us. Unless you'd rather go the other way."

Taerith shook his head, and turned to meet Findal's eyes. "I'll go with you," he said.

Findal looked as though he wanted to lay a fatherly hand on Taerith's shoulder, but he restrained himself with an instinctive respect. "You keep your own counsel, then," he said. "It seems you always do."

Taerith looked back once more, tracing the steps he had taken when his shadow still covered Lilia with his protection—tracing them to the empty horizon. The sunlight streaking the road was stark. He wished the moonlight back again, falling over whispered words.

Marta had not bothered to go back to bed. She was making sure the wounded bandits and guards were as comfortable as they could be. There was no room for them in the wagons; the troupe planned to send others back for them. They would reach a small hamlet before approaching the castle, and hoped to procure help for the men there. Randal proposed to stay and guard them until help came, lest they fall victim to others as unscrupulous as themselves. Neither he nor Findal would hear of anyone else staying: the troupe was needed to appear in full splendour at Annar's castle. Besides, Randal's sword had dealt many of the wounds he now nursed. He took a strange pride in watching over those he had trounced.

Taerith did not say a word as he helped hitch up the wagons and prepare for the day's journey, but he worked with an intensity that made the others afraid to approach him. When Zhenya limped down to the river to fill a waterskin, he let his eyes wander over the bank. He wondered where Taerith and Lilia had sat— what they had said—if it was possible for men and women to fall in love in a single night. He dipped the skin into the water and reflected while the running water filled it. On his return, Taerith was mounting the red stallion. Zhenya handed the waterskin to him with his eyes full of admiration. The horse was a creature of the sun; Taerith a being of flint and forest. Zhenya's heart longed to enter into something of their spirit.

Taerith saw the look in the boy's eyes, eaten at the edges by the ever-present hunger in the thin face. He stretched out his hand.

"Will you ride with me?" Taerith asked.

Zhenya's eyes widened. "I cannot ride him," he said. "Sol is too mighty for me."

"But we would be together," Taerith said. "The strength of two, to pit against the might of one." He stroked Sol's neck as he spoke, fingers smoothing the horse's silken coat.

A smile broke suddenly over Zhenya's face, and he grasped Taerith's arm. In a moment he had been pulled up and was seated behind Taerith. Sol snorted and pawed the ground, impatient to be off. Zhenya maneuvered his crutch until it lay in the crook of his arm, one end poking out near his chin and the other resting lightly on Sol's right flank. From the head wagon, Findal drew breath enough to shout "Off we go!" They pulled away from the strange camp, leaving Randal with his long arm lifted in farewell.

In less than an hour they reached the hamlet, and Findal, Morris, and Orlin roused the populace with not a moment to spare—as much in a hurry to be off again for the castle as they were to send help to the bandits. Taerith watched them bang doors and loudly ring the bell in the square with misgivings. "They'll run us off," he muttered. Zhenya, whose hold on Taerith's waist had lessened as he grew accustomed to Sol's gait, replied, "They won't. Findal has magic in him. No one runs him off."

It was true. The initially irate villagers melted before the force of Findal's breathless urges and hyperbole, and within the hour a party had been raised to return to the field and bring the wounded back—the bandits to die or stand trial, as they would; the foreign guards to be nursed back to health. Something twitched in Findal's face as he heard the leaders say as much. "Well," he said. "And mind that you treat all men as men. I misdoubt some of you may find friends among thieves."

The speech was enigmatic enough, but even it seemed to strike a chord in the villagers. The leader of the men shot Findal a sharp look, and answered, "It may be."

Rachel Starr Thomson 41

More than two hours past; the troupe once again put to the road. The wagons could not move as quickly as men on horseback could have, and it was another two and a half hours before the castle hove into sight. A stone fortress, it rose from the only hill in the district, impenetrable and stern. The country around lay low and dark, forest and swampland surrounding a few fields where serfs produced most of the produce that fed the king and his household. The castle itself was surrounded by a high, turreted wall, and behind this rose three towers. One stood higher than the rest, and at the sight of it Taerith's face went ashen. He nudged Sol forward, and horse and riders flew past their companions. Findal watched them thunder past, and shook his head.

The road was full of travelers, heady with the atmosphere of celebration. Taerith urged Sol away from the road, into the fields, where his view of the castle was unobstructed and his mood unmolested. Suddenly he dismounted, throwing the reins to Zhenya, who caught them with a flash of worry on his face. Sol pranced under the boy, and Zhenya held on for dear life.

Taerith was not looking. He stood alone in the bare field, looking up at the grey walls and towers, lost in his own thoughts.

Zhenya let out a sudden yell, and Taerith turned in time to see the boy losing his seat. He rushed forward and caught Zhenya before he fell, propping him back up.

"Forgive me," he said.

Zhenya shook his head, but his eyes did not meet Taerith's. "Sol will not hold for me," he said. "Strength does not like weakness. I have learned that."

Taerith looked Zhenya in the eye. The boy's words had kindled something in his own eyes. "There is more than one kind of strength in the world," he said. "One may be weak in body, or in courage, and yet have a strength of imagination and virtue that makes mortals pale. Learn that, if you want a lesson."

Zhenya raised his eyes to the castle walls. "The wedding will be soon." He was not sure why he said it.

In answer, Taerith remounted. "Findal will be missing you," he said. Both knew he was talking to the horse. They rode back to the others just as the gates of the castle were raised to admit them.

*　　*　　*

Lilia stood in a gown of white, outlined by the grey stones that formed the edges of the tall window in the highest tower of the castle, looking down on the stream of newcomers to the feast. It seemed strange to her that they should all come to witness her marriage—she who had lived most of her life in high towers, kept away from the world and all its concerns. She tilted her head slightly as she stood, the fingers of her left hand resting gently against the stone, and tried to make out the faces and characters of people who were little more than moving spots of colour on the ground. Wagons and horses, men and women, freeborn and slaves.

A wind came in through the window, stirring Lilia's long black hair. Three maids had combed it until it shone. It fell in long tresses to her waist, the blue sapphires and deep red garnets the maids had fastened in it catching the faint snatches of sunlight that fell through the window. The wind was cold, but Lilia hardly noticed it. She had lived so long in high stone places that cold was as natural to her as moonlight, a part of the dreamworld that had always belonged to her.

She turned away from the window, and caught sight of herself in the mirror across the circle of the floor. She dropped her eyes a moment later and returned to the window. She was beautiful; she knew that. She thought—hoped—that her husband would find her acceptable. She feared his eyes more than the eyes of the gawkers who came by droves to the celebration, more than the cold dark eyes of Borden that had bid her no welcome though she would soon call him brother, more than the eyes of the bandits in the darkness who had threatened her with death or a worse fate only the night before. She feared Annar's eyes, because in them she would see love or indifference, and between those two alternatives hung the form and hue of her life to come. Once she knew, she would live with all the courage she could muster. It was the not knowing that strained everything in her.

She had not yet met Annar. When she had arrived in the dark hours of the morning he had not been there to greet the returning party. No one had told her, but she heard them: heard their low, mocking voices. The king had been drunk and would not rise long before the wedding. *I wonder,* she thought. *How much can you read in a drunk man's eyes?*

There were tears in her eyes. She was not sure how they had gotten there. She raised her hands before her face and let the tears fall on the white lace of her sleeves. Tears made such a small stain. Surely no one would ever see. Perhaps, after all, the tears would be for nothing.

Beyond the fields around the castle the dark fens lay, blotting out the landscape for miles around, criss-crossed by roads that were torn from the swamps and upheld by hard labour and pain. Farther away, Lilia could see the beginnings of the moors, and there, glinting under the sun's searching rays, the river. Grey-blue eyes appeared before her face: Taerith's eyes. She shuddered and turned from the window. There was a bed in the tower room; she made her way to it, and sat with her head bowed so that she need neither look at the world without or her reflection within. She feared herself just now.

A sharp rap at the door put Lilia's heart in her throat. She rose, smoothing her skirt with trembling hands. A thousand nights at home she had dreamed of a knock at the door and all that it could mean: the mysterious strangers, the legion of adventures that might ever wait on the other side. But the servant who entered, head bowed and voice mumbling and low, carried with her nothing of promise.

"You are wanted below, my lady," the servant said.

Lilia smiled at the woman, hiding her feelings as best as she could so the servant wouldn't feel uncomfortable. "Let me follow you," Lilia said. "If I try to find my way alone I will be lost."

The woman lifted her eyes to Lilia's face for a moment, but no emotion in them responded to the plea in the young woman's tone. She simply nodded and turned to go. Lilia squared her slim shoulders, picked up the hem of her dress, and began her descent from the tower.

Steep stone steps led downward in a sharp spiral, a close, colourless passageway that existed only to transfer travelers from one little world to another. Lilia had often thought of such passages that they did not have any claim themselves to placehood. They led to places full of memories, warmth or cold, horror or happiness, but they were only stretches of grey limbo without sympathy or character. But into what very different worlds they might lead! Her hand trembled as she reached out to steady herself on the stone. The servant woman did not look backward at her. Lilia had hoped that the woman's presence would make her feel a little less alone, but her hopes were as futile as the spiraling stairs were unflinching.

The descent took them down to the realm of celebration. From somewhere below Lilia heard shouts and cheers. Her cheeks coloured—she heard Annar's name in the chorus. He had presented himself to his people. She would be next.

The noise grew louder with every downward step. She felt faint, and tried to calm the fluttering in her stomach by smoothing the satin of her gown over it. At last they were plunged into it; they were on a level with the crowd; the new world was just on the other side of a wooden door. Lilia closed her eyes, drew a deep breath, and heard the creak of the hinges as the servant woman threw the door open. She stepped out into the open air, under the shadow of an awning.

Immediately the old woman was replaced by new attendants, young and fair, with their arms full of yellow blooms and their cheeks flushed and rosy. In their midst Lilia looked like a pale slender flower grown from the frost. The crowd hushed as she stepped out from the shade of the castle into the cold winter sun. They had formed a close-packed circle around a polished platform, built by the king's men at the entrance to the small chapel in one corner of the courtyard. The crowd filled the courtyard to its very edges. Young boys perched in the few trees that graced the ground, weighing down the branches like an awkward flock of adolescent cranes. Others had climbed the steps that led up to the castle wall, and used the stairs as precarious seats while guards patrolled the parapet above them. The rich stood nearest the platform, with military men and representatives of Mother Church, while the poorest tried to worm their way closer. Many stood outside of the castle walls altogether, and crowded the road.

Annar, sovereign of the castle and its varied lands, lord of fens and fields and moors, stood on the platform with his hands neatly tucked one in the other. He was a well-built man, not tall but broad-shouldered, yet his frame seemed slack next to his brother's. His neatly trimmed beard was heavily flecked with grey. It covered a face that beamed with pleasure now, but lacked any firm lines to tell its usual wont. He wore a suit of red and purple, trimmed with fur, and the crown on his head was lined with ermine.

The young, frail thing who came to meet him did not lift her eyes as she approached. He held out his hand and she took it, and dropped into a deep curtsey. He smiled, nodded, covered her hand. She rose and was drawn closer to her master. The voice of the visiting bishop began to drone out the wedding rites.

In the crowd, a thin boy leaned on his crutch and looked up at the faces on either side of him: one a woman's, matronly beauty bent in a compassionate frown, and one an inscrutable young man's. Neither of them had said a word and their silence was enough to drive Zhenya mad.

"Someone should stop it," he said out loud. He didn't think anyone else would hear him.

Marta nudged him. "Hush, child."

Taerith only turned and looked at him. Zhenya saw it in his eyes—he agreed. Taerith turned back to the ceremony, and the look on Marta's face stopped Zhenya from speaking again. He looked back up at the platform, the king, and Lilia. Her eyes were still cast down. Zhenya's heart went out to her. He knew what it meant when you didn't meet anyone's eyes… he knew what it meant when you didn't have any say in what happened to you. If he had had Taerith's strength, he thought, he would have leaped onto the stage and saved her.

Of course, if he had been Taerith, he would have loved her, and even though he was fairly certain Taerith did, the silent young man had said nothing of the sort. He wanted to ask him, but he bit his tongue. The bishop's voice rose above the crowd again. They were making their vows now.

And then Lilia faltered. Her eyes lifted and scanned the crowd. She was looking for someone. Her eyes met with another's in the crowd—Zhenya looked up; he was sure it was Taerith who spoke silently to her now. For a bare moment she smiled. In the next instant the question had been asked. Lilia turned her eyes to the man who held both her hands. The crowd grew dreadfully silent, and her voice could be heard—quavering a little, but clear. "I will," she said, and her doom was sealed.

*   *   *

From a distance the castle seemed to buck and heave with shadows in the torchlight. Within and without the walls the celebration raged, much as it had for days: drunk, heedless of much other than its own pleasures. Borden walked through the crowd and despised them all. They grasped at the king's marriage as an excuse for celebration, but they had no real cause to celebrate. The girl Annar had taken to himself would make no real queen. He knew a little of her—she was an oddity among women, brought up by a strange and reclusive father who kept his daughter locked away from the world, in the company of sparrows and a rare collection of books. She knew nothing of the real world, nothing of politics, nothing of harsh reality. She was beautiful, which was what Annar wanted, so she would sit as an ornament by his side until he tired of her.

Borden moved along the wall of the courtyard, his steps growing faster as he went. He had no where to go, but his thoughts drove him to keep moving. It was wrong—it was so horridly wrong. His brother had married a lovely misfit, and for all her unsuitableness she would likely fulfill her main duty: she would give Annar a son, so the damage wreaked by their family could continue on another generation.

A shout of laughter rose up from the crowd. In the center of the courtyard a group of performers plied their tricks. Borden leaned against the wall and peered through the mass of bodies to the gangly freak who twisted himself in a knot to the exclamations of the drunkards who looked on. A short, bald man with impossibly large arms hoisted the fellow in the air as though he was a feather and tossed him from one hand to the other. The crowd laughed and catcalled in appreciation. The circus had performed earlier for the king and his bride, who had disappeared an hour since. They continued now because the onlookers still loved them, and those with money to waste still tossed it to those who worked the edges of the crowd: a wheezy little man, a cripple, and a tall, good-natured sword swallower.

"Enough," Borden said to himself. "I grow weary of this foolishness." He turned to go—up the steps to the parapet, where he so often went to look over life and surmise its grim future, when a sudden clatter near the back gates drew his attention. He heard laughter and drunken shouts, but there was anger in some voices, and the sounds of a scuffle. He put his hand to his sword and ran to the gate, signalling several of his men to follow him.

He was not prepared for the sight that met his eyes. A gang of young ruffians were making their way into the gate, shouting and waving their caps, calling the attention of the crowd to a cloud of dust and confusion just beyond the castle walls. Borden caught sight of stamping hooves and a wildly tossing head, caught and bridled with a length of rope at which seven young men were straining, the foremost of them half laid in the dirt. Three of the white legs, thick with long grey hair that grew over the hooves, had been likewise lassoed. The animal neighed wildly and snorted; its white sides heaved with sweat and dust. The creature's head tossed again, and Borden saw the long horn glitter in the torchlight.

A unicorn.

"Here!" one of the young hooligans shouted. "We've caught us a gift for the king!"

"Fools," Borden said. He held up his hand, calling his soldiers up short. They had been about to run into the fray. "Let us see what they do," Borden said. The crowd had moved in all around, but they moved back skittishly as the young men managed to wrestle the unicorn in through the gates. There was a scream, and one of the ruffians fell heavily to the ground, his side slashed and bleeding copiously. One of his companions grabbed him by the ankles and pulled him out of reach of the stamping hooves.

Borden saw the victim's face as he struggled to his feet. It was ashen and angry. Likely he was the leader of the gang, and the unicorn had given them more trouble than they counted on—more the fools they, for any idiot knew better than to tangle with the untameable beasts. Breathing heavily, the young man snatched up a spear from a guard who stood close by.

"We'll have its head, then!" he shouted.

He drew his arm back. In the next instant, Mirian had snatched the spear from him. She snapped the spear in two and turned on the lad. "What manner of beast are you?" she demanded. "Let the creature go!"

The ruffian's face grew angrier still. He was still bleeding, and he stood clutching his side and trembling. His face shone; he had been drinking.

Mirian's words galvanized the crowd. They had been too drunk and too shocked to act before, but when the voice of sense fell on their ears they recognized it. Many of them raised their voices in assent. "Let it go… free the beast!" Unicorns, rare, beautiful, and unpredictable, were held in a kind of awe half-sacred and half-superstitious. They were said to be the harbingers of disaster, or of luck, or of otherworldly interference. The sight of the unicorn, lashed and lassoed, standing within the gates of the castle with its sides flecked with sweat and blood sobered the crowd. Some of the boys who had clung to the ropes ensnaring it drew away now. Others surged forward, blood running hot, to take their places. The circus performers had by now come to the scene, and they took it upon themselves to drive the more hot-headed of the crowd back again, away from the unicorn.

And then a boy stepped out of the crowd: the cripple who had solicited money for the circus. He held a bucket of water and a sponge, used for horses many times before. Without a word he limped toward the unicorn. He was a thin waif, Borden thought, with a curiously fearless expression on his hungry face. He ignored the young hooligans who reached out to stop him—they did not touch him, for his circus fellows were quick to stay their hands. The unicorn stood panting as the boy approached. It snorted, and for a moment it seemed as though it would rear up. Instead, it plunged its nose into the bucket and drank deeply. The boy hesitated a moment, and then laid his hand on the creature's blood-streaked mane. There were tears in the cripple's eyes as he stroked the unicorn's neck.

Borden fought to keep a sardonic smile from his face. Something mythic was happening between boy and beast—they were bonding. It happened once in a lifetime, and ruined any hopes the ruffians had for making a glorious martyr of the unicorn. The creature would be tamed now. It would belong to the circus. If anyone tried to separate it from the boy, it would die. So all of the effort the fools had put into dragging the beast to the castle in the hopes of making themselves heroes and mighty hunters had gone to increase the power of a traveling circus to attract passers-by and their coins. It served them right.

Apparently the same thing had occurred to the gang of ruffians. Most of them had relinquished their ropes and gathered around their leader, whose angry tone could be clearly heard though his words were thick with pain. Borden sank back into the shadows and sought out the bloodied warrior's face. His eyes were dark with anger, and they were fixed on Mirian. One by one, the eyes of the gang turned to the same place: Mirian, who still stood at the fore of the crowd, her hair blazing under the torchlight, her stance tall and proud as ever. They were angry. They knew better than to tangle with the unicorn now: it had a boy to protect, and would be three times as fierce as it had been before. Besides, the crowd had taken the unicorn's side.

But Mirian stood alone, and they would hold her responsible. After all, had she not wrenched the spear away and chided the leader of the gang as though he were a child, the unicorn would not have had a chance to bond.

Borden's hand tightened on the hilt of his sword as the young men slowly gathered around Mirian, but he did not draw it. He wanted to see what she would do. He told himself that he would not let her be abused too harshly—he wanted to see her blaze to life in her own defense, and best them all.

One of the ruffians reached out and shoved her. Her eyes flared up and she shoved back. One of them grabbed her by the hair; she drove her elbow into his stomach and threw him to the ground gasping for breath. They began to attract the crowd's attention now. Light glinted off of a knife blade. Borden started forward.

The young man raised his knife just as Mirian was occupied with two others who tried to hold her down. Borden's heart suddenly beat faster, and he broke into a run. He needn't have. A young man stepped out of the crowd and grabbed the knife-wielder's wrist, twisting it until the boy dropped the knife with a yell.

The young man held a sword in his hand. He came to Mirian's aid with the flat of it, and drove off her assailants. Borden's eyes narrowed. He had never seen the fellow before. He was tall, but not remarkably so, well-built and strong, but not more than other men. His hair was dark; there was something of flint in his face. He raised his voice and addressed the ruffians in a clear, strong tone.

"You will put down your weapons," he commanded, "and leave the girl alone."

"She's a meddling slave," the bleeding leader spat. "We've a right to teach her a lesson."

The young man's eyes flashed with anger. He seemed to get his words out with effort. "You have no right," he said.

The leader of the ruffians laughed. He scoured the crowd with his eyes, and they grew uncomfortable. Many of them knew him; he was a leader among the common people, young as he was. "Will you stand for this?" he said. "A slave accosts me, and I'm not to have vengeance. What will you say when the beasts of burden turn on you?"

The young man's face grew pale with anger, but he contained it marvelously. Mirian did not speak; she was watching her rescuer intently. Borden saw that she was favouring her right arm; she might have been hurt in the scuffle. The young stranger took in the effect of his opponent's words on the crowd and realized that he might not win by appealing to their better natures. They were unsettled by all that had happened, and were prone now to assert themselves as lords over something—over Mirian, as nothing else presented itself to be abused.

"You will not touch her," the young man said. "She is the queen's personal attendant. Would you anger your king on the night of his wedding?"

Borden let go of his sword hilt. The crowd was bested, ruffians and all. He smiled as he stepped out of the crowd. Mirian's eyes went to him immediately. There were words in her eyes, and he wanted to hear them—but not now.

"You heard the stranger," he said. "Be off with you, all of you. Go back to your celebrations, and leave the queen's maiden alone." His dark eyes bored into the leader of the gang, who still stood clutching his side, livid and frustrated.

"Get yourself home," he said. "Tend to that wound, and count yourself lucky—the beast might have killed you."

The leader bobbed his head in obeisance and limped away.

Borden held out his hand to the young stranger who had come to Mirian's rescue. "I am Borden, the king's brother," he said.

The young man took his hand at the elbow. "My name is Taerith Romany."

Borden's eyes narrowed as he looked the young man over. "Yes," he said, "I recognize you now. You were among the queen's rescuers."

Something flickered in Taerith's eyes, but he covered it well. "I had that privilege, yes," he said.

"You must enjoy coming to the rescue of hapless women," Borden said. He saw the way Mirian stiffened, and enjoyed it. He looked at her, sported with her for a minute as she fought to hold her tongue. "Go on, girl," he said. "Make yourself presentable. Your rescuer has given you a fine position, and you'll take it. The queen will have need of you tonight. Go! Report to the head steward."

Mirian gave him one last resentful glare and turned on her heel. Taerith and Borden watched her go.

"They had no right to treat her that way," Taerith said. "She seems a brave soul."

Borden nodded. He held back the words on the tip of his tongue and said instead, "I do not pretend to account for the ways of the world—why she is a slave, and others are not."

Taerith gave him a curious look. The crowd was dispersing around them, leaving even the sight of the unicorn and the cripple for another day. The members of the circus had gathered around the bonding pair, who still stood close together.

"You ask these questions?" Taerith asked. "Not many do."

"It is simpler to take life for granted," Borden said.

"Do you hold with the practice of slavery?" Taerith asked.

Borden laughed, a low laugh. "Bold questions you ask, but I give only guarded answers."

"You are wise, then," Taerith said.

Borden raised his sword arm and gestured toward the circus. "You traveled with them last night," he said. "Are you among the company? You hardly look like a freak."

Taerith coloured slightly. "They have been good to me," he said, "but I have not settled my way."

Borden almost surprised himself with the words that came from his mouth. "Stay here, then," he said. "Join my guards. You have a clear head and a strong arm; we could use you."

Taerith visibly started. Borden tried to puzzle out the emotion in the lad's face, but he could not. Taerith, in his face and voice, gave answers that were careful to reveal nothing.

"Think on it, at least," Borden said. "Surely it will be several days before your friends move on."

Taerith nodded. "I will," he said at last. "Thank you."

The courtyard, on Borden's orders, had nearly cleared. The crown prince nodded in satisfaction and turned to make his way to the wall at last. Just as he began to mount the steps, he looked back. Taerith had joined the circus performers, and together they were crossing the courtyard. The unicorn walked behind the crippled boy, docile as a lamb, and Taerith walked by the child's side. He was silent.

Strange boy, Borden thought. Inscrutable the stranger was, but Borden was sure he knew one thing already—Taerith would stay.

Chapter Five

Taerith walked beside Zhenya and the unicorn for a few minutes, then turned back to the scene of the fight. It occured to him suddenly that someone might follow the slave girl into the house and make trouble for her—if their hearts were pounding as strongly with adrenaline as his was, they might not easily give up. Some of the young fools still lingered, but none made a move toward the door. For a moment he considered going through it himself: he had seen the girl favouring her arm; she was hurt. Yet he knew, from the way she had carried herself, that she would not welcome his intrusion. Borden's voice came suddenly from behind him. He too had returned to the scene.

"What possessed you to make a lady's maid of that one?" the crown prince inquired. "Sooner a Fury's housewoman."

"I thought only to help her," Taerith said. "I did not think you would make my words reality."

"The revel will not end for several more days," Borden answered. "To act as the queen's property will keep her safe until the ruffians depart. You think quickly."

The torn, scuffed earth and bloodstains on the ground alone testified to the struggle of minutes before. Taerith blew out a breath of air as he regarded the door again. He wondered what sort of gift he had sent Lilia. He lifted his gaze to the castle towers, and concern quickened within him. How did she fare, the beautiful, lonely bride of the morning? Shouts and laughter interrupted. He turned on his heel abruptly, and plunged into the crowd.

*   *   *

Mirian shook as she walked; the blood pounding through her veins threatened to overwhelm her with every step. The servant's corridor through which she walked was largely deserted; all were occupied elsewhere, as she ought to have been. She stopped suddenly and pounded the wall with one arm, and then sank down against its cold stone. She drew her other arm in, cradling it. It ached, dully at first, but with a pain that built with each passing moment. The pain joined the cacophony of her thoughts, half-drowned by emotion. She wished the young man had let her alone—she might have defeated them all—she might have killed them. Or perhaps, as was more likely, their numbers would have overcome her and they would have beaten her within an inch of her life.

Even in that, there might have been some release… some *freedom*.

Tears, angry and unwanted, blurred her vision and slipped down her face. She brushed them off with her sleeve and buried her face in the crook of her elbow, resting on her knee while the other arm throbbed.

Faces and shouts seemed to whirl around her: the bloody horn of the unicorn, the enmity of their faces. For a moment she had done something significant. For a moment she had challenged the sort of idiot power she hated so much, and it had turned back to fight her, and nothing had stood between them. Her tears grew hot and threatened to spill forth in sobbing earnest. The moment of freedom was gone. The exhilaration of justice was snatched away. She sat in the narrow slave hall, still in bonds, still under orders—a lady's maid. The thought was repulsive to her.

Blood and emotion pounded in her ears and she did not notice the approach of soft feet. In a moment fingers touched her shoulder, and she reacted swiftly, jerking her head up and pulling away with a sharp defensive instinct.

She recognized the man who stood before her: the priest. His bearded, gentle face showed only a little surprise at the violence of her reaction.

"I apologize for startling you," he said.

"No," she said, hastily wiping her face with her sleeve. "You've a right to be here as much as I." She turned her face away from him, and made no other move.

"Is there anything I can do?" he asked. He seemed hesitant to ask, but unable not to. She grimaced.

"Nothing," she said. "You are absolved of your priestly duties."

"Forgive me," he said, seating himself on the floor beside her. "I did not ask because it was my duty."

She waited a minute, and when he made no move to go, she turned her face back to him. She had gained control of herself now; there were no more tears. The throbbing in her arm still distracted her, but the adrenaline rush was gone, and anger took a back seat to the annoyance of dealing with his presence.

"Is there something you want?" she asked.

He chuckled a little, eyes on the stone floor. It struck her as incongruous that he should laugh when surely, her maidenly plight seemed dire indeed. He had come upon her crying like a frustrated child, and had apparently been nonplussed by the fact. "I know what you did outside," he said. "It was a courageous and just thing. I have come to sit in the company of a heroine and wait until she needs something."

"Don't worry," Mirian said. "I have been well rewarded."

He didn't seem to hear the bitterness in her tone. "Yes," he said, "you have. You will serve the queen herself."

Mirian stood abruptly. "I was not made for housework," she said. "She will very soon replace me, if she knows anything. Excuse me. I have to report to the steward."

She swayed a little on her feet for a moment, and then stalked off down the corridor. The priest stayed behind and watched her go.

The stone passage took her to an inner room where the Chief Steward of Annar's house, a tall, stoop-shouldered man called Grey, presided over the workings of the household. He was there, with his sharp-tongued, sharp-eyed wife, as Mirian had expected him to be. She bowed her head in deference as she entered his presence, and ignored his wife with all her might.

"Master Grey," she said. "I am sent by Lord Borden."

"Be quick with your business," Mistress Grey said. "We haven't got all night."

Mirian did not look in the woman's direction, but kept her eyes on the weary husband. He regarded her with a question in his eyes. "And what message do you bring?" he asked.

"That—" Mirian bit the word off, and tried again. "That I am to make ready to serve the queen, as her personal maid."

Mistress Grey forced herself into Mirian's line of vision: a thin woman of average height, silver-haired, face tightly drawn across high cheekbones and a narrow forehead. "That is my business," Mistress Grey said. "You will deal with me. Queen's maid? How did you ever manage to gain such a position?"

The pain in Mirian's arm was getting worse, but she set her jaw against it even as she kept her eyes from flashing too much in the mistress's direction. "Believe me," she said, "I do not want it."

Mistress Grey reached out and grabbed Mirian's injured arm suddenly, pushing her toward the door. Pain shot up from the elbow, and Mirian bit back a gasp. She clenched her teeth and allowed the woman to propel her toward another servant's passage and a long set of stairs. Mistress Grey shoved past Mirian into the lead as they ascended the stairs, up to a high tower. At last they reached the top, and Mistress Grey nodded to a room. "That is the queen's room," she said. "It is vacant at the moment. Start your duties by making it ready for her. Your quarters are below, on the landing we just passed. You will share the room with two others, who have already been serving the queen well. Clean yourself up before the queen sees you, and in all matters, girl, hold your tongue."

Mirian shot Mistress Grey a look, and said through clenched teeth, "I am holding it."

The woman drew herself up, and regarded Mirian with a look of utter contempt. She reached into a pocket and pulled out a key. "To the queen's room," she said. Mirian stretched out her open palm and Mistress Grey dropped the cold bit of iron into it. "Your duties begin now," Mistress Grey said, and took herself away down the stairs with a disdainful swish of her long skirts.

Mirian shivered as she looked down at the key—the tower was cold. She wondered why the queen had been assigned to such a place. Slowly she unlocked the door and pushed her way into the small room where the king's bride would lodge. It was sparsely but tastefully furnished, framed by dark purple curtains over a window that let in a draft, cold and shadowed. There was wood in the fireplace, but the hearth was clean of ashes. There was no sign that other servants had been here before her—serving the queen well, as Mistress Grey had claimed. As best she could with her arm still throbbing, Mirian started a small fire and did what she could to make the room a bit homier. Warmth would help more than anything. She watched the flames lick at the wood for a few minutes, approving of its propensity to grow quickly. She came to herself a moment later: the queen might return at any moment, and she should not find her here.

The passageway outside the door was likewise cold and dark, and Mirian found herself leaning against the wall as she descended to the servant's room below. The door was locked against her, but after she knocked an old woman opened it—greeted her coldly, and pointed to an empty corner of the room where Mirian could make do with a blanket and a cushion to rest her head. The other women were servants, not slaves, and both decades older. Mirian knew her place. She lay down in the corner without complaining.

She tucked her arm in as close to her body as she could. It felt cold, and she needed it to warm up. She closed her eyes, and images jumped up unbidden: the unicorn, the fight, her moment of glory. A tear fell on the stone floor beneath her, though she did not want it to, and hardly acknowledged that it had.

*　*　*

The bright colours of Findal's tent glowed richly under the torchlight in the far corner of the courtyard. Taerith made his way through the drunken huddles to the flap of the tent, and ducked inside.

Randal and Marta stood, side by side, leaning over the side of the stall they had erected for Sol. Sol himself was staked in the opposite corner, ignoring his oats with a curiously humbled, nervous air. Marta turned at the sound of Taerith's entrance and motioned for him to join them.

On the far side of the stall the unicorn lay, its flanks still heaving. Its head was tucked in to nuzzle the boy who had curled up against its side and whose hand slowly stroked it. Taerith smiled as he took in the expression on Zhenya's face—wonder lost in the deeper emotions of love and care. Equally did the beast seem absorbed in the boy. Taerith's heart went out suddenly to the scene. He opened the gate, and ignoring Marta's warning hand, went in and knelt at Zhenya's side.

The unicorn looked up, but it made no move. Taerith felt the tension in his own body as he knelt: the deadly, unpredictable power of the creature was palpable in the air. But Zhenya welcomed him with a smile as he continued to stroke the unicorn's side.

"You said," Taerith said in a low voice, steadying himself with a hand on the strawed ground, "that power does not love weakness. There. Nature has made you a liar."

"It has done so kindly," Zhenya answered.

Taerith nodded. Tentatively he reached out and touched the creature's flank, turning his hand and running the backs of his fingers down the hot white fur.

"Magnificently," he agreed. "I will always remember you, Zhenya, as one chosen by strength."

Concern flickered across Zhenya's face. "You're not leaving, are you?" he asked.

Taerith sighed, stroking the unicorn once more before rising to his feet. "I don't know," he whispered. "Say nothing."

Zhenya nodded, his dark eyes following Taerith as he brushed himself clean of dust and straw and rejoined Randal and Marta outside the stall. Marta was glowing. She had loved Zhenya before, in her own way, but somehow the unicorn had made of the cripple someone who inspired greater affection than he had before.

Randal turned away from the scene and raised his eyebrows for Taerith's attention. "A drink?" he asked. "It's free tonight."

Taerith acquiesced, and together the two stepped out of the tent, Randal bending low under the folds of the cloth. The courtyard before them was alight, heaving with laughter, glowing with ale. Randal secured them each a mug full, and the two men walked together, swords buckled at their sides, disdaining to join in the other men's games and conversations.

"It is a merry celebration," Randal said, nodding to the crowd. "Still, I shall not be sorry to leave it."

"And when will that be?" Taerith asked.

"In a day or two, when the peasants have run out of coppers and the king out of hospitality. Perhaps sooner—that unicorn may mix things up a little."

Taerith only grunted in response.

"You're very quiet," Randal said.

Taerith smiled. "You show how little you know me. I am seldom anything but quiet."

"Ah," Randal answered, lowering his ale, "but you are trying to convince me that there is nothing on your mind, and I do not believe you."

Taerith raised his mug and took a drink. They stood silently for a minute, and Randal's expression changed in the silence—

taking on the solemnity of his next words. He hesitated over them as he gave voice again.

"I think I should tell you that I don't believe Lilia is safe here."

Taerith looked up sharply. "Why do you say that?" he asked.

"The bandits talked amongst themselves; I listened," the sword-swallower answered. "Annar is not a popular man. It seems his chief virtue is his childlessness. The bandits weren't after money. They wanted to prevent Lilia from ever giving her groom an heir."

Taerith let the words sink in. They were cold, unyielding words.

"The men who attacked the carriage are in prison, but they are not alone in their animosity, or even in their strategies."

There was silence again, in which the crowd's merriment filled the space between the men without welcome.

"I thought you should know," Randal said finally.

Taerith nodded. "Yes—thank you." His mind swam as he stepped away from Randal.

Stay. Borden's offer blew like a northern wind in the inner storm that built up in him. Stay. To what end? For a moment he had told himself that Lilia might be his, that the kinship he felt in talking to her might make a new home for him. But that hope was gone; he dared not entertain it. She could not be his. And yet… and yet, in a very different sense, he might still be hers. His fingers tightened around his sword hilt as he walked away, hardly even remembering that Randal was there.

The crowd around him seemed suddenly rife with enmity. He had not heard the mutinous whispers before; now he heard them on every side. Yes, even the peasants mocked when they spoke of Annar. And some mocked with a darker tone of enmity; some threatened as they drank the king's wine. He heard Lilia's name on the night breeze and he thought his fingers might snap the hilt.

Who would protect her if he did not stay? Annar seemed perched on a throne of straw. Taerith had taken his character in the moment he saw him: there was no courage in the man, no wisdom, no self-sacrifice. Would Borden watch over his brother's wife? Perhaps… and yet, Borden had held back when the ruffians had threatened the slave girl, and if a man's heart did not move him to help one woman, why should it move him to help another?

There is a very great difference between helping a slave and guarding a queen, Taerith told himself. He kept walking. His heart argued back that there was no real difference at all.

Stay.

Taerith stopped suddenly. He had passed out of the castle gates. He stood in the deserted road, under the moonlight. The towers of the castle rose high above him. The wind played an eerie tune in the stony heights. He turned and looked back, through the open gate to the warm colours of the circus tent, billowing slightly in the breeze. He thought of the crippled boy who rested in the strength of the unicorn. For what seemed like the hundredth time since he had come, he raised his eyes to the topmost tower, and thought he saw Lilia through the stones: looking out over the fields and fens like a crippled bird whose dearest and most fearful desire to was to fly.

He bowed his head. The pain in his chest tightened. How *could* he stay?

How could he go?

Chapter Six

Mirian rose before dawn and slipped down the stairs, the stones cold on her bare feet. The muscles in her feet and legs were stiff; her fingers half numb. The elbow of her wounded arm seemed frozen in position; she moved it as much as she could, ignoring the resulting ache. She pushed the outer door open and darted across the silent courtyard, stepping carefully past a drunk who lay, dead or unconscious, near the stables where Mirian had been wont to sleep in past days. Inside, she dug out a shawl and threw it over her shoulders, bending down to wind strips of cloth around her feet. She blew a lock of long hair out of her face as she finished tying the ends of the ragged strips, wincing as she moved the fingers of her sore arm.

Back outside she went, just as the first light of the sun began to touch the castle stones. The towers rose, high and stern, above the rift in the stone wall where Mirian made her passage to the fields. The furrowed ground was colder than the air, but welcoming as the dirt sank beneath her toes. She walked with her face lifted, eager for the first true glimpse of sunrise. Her thick braid had begun to come out as she slept, and she loosened the last of it now, letting her red-brown mane blow free, ends waving with the fringe of the brown shawl.

A lone tree grew in the middle of the field, bent, twisted, and gnarled. It was there that Mirian hurried. She had nearly reached it when she stopped short. Someone was there. The rising sun outlined his figure: his back was turned to her. He was a young man, by the thickness of his dark hair and the strength in his shoulders and arms, but there was something in the way he stood that made him seem old… almost ancient, like the tree beside him. Mirian tried to make a noise and alert him to her presence, but something caught in her throat when she tried. Her mind was tense as a greyhound: too many times as a child she had imagined that the tree might resurrect the ghosts that dwelt at its roots. The presence of a stranger in the faery light of dawn unnerved her, and for a moment her feet wanted to flee.

He turned, a little slowly, still unaware of her presence, and his blue eyes opened a little in the surprise of finding her there. It took a moment for Mirian to make out his face with the sun in her eyes, but when she did, she recognized him immediately. It was the young man who had come to her aid in the fight with the unicorn. From the rumpled state of his grey clothing and the melted frost that damped his boots, Mirian guessed that he had spent the night in the field. From the corner of her eye she noticed that his sword was in its scabbard, leaning against the tree trunk. She resisted the urge to cock an eyebrow: it was foolish of him to put his weapon where he could not reach it.

"Good morning," he said. His voice was low and a little curious. She inclined her head awkwardly, avoiding his eyes, and said nothing.

"Have you nothing to say in return?" he pushed.

"I am a slave," she answered.

"You had plenty to say last night," he said.

"I was angry last night." She looked away and mumbled, "I always talk when I'm angry."

He had moved closer, and was probing her face in a way that demanded she look at him. Self-consciously, she did. It was frustrating, being in this position. What was he doing camped beneath her tree, anyway?

"You're not angry with me, then?" he asked.

There was something in the friendly tone of his voice that loosened the tension she felt, and something sparked in her green eyes. "I could be," she said.

He folded his arms across his grey tunic and smiled. "I thought I had done something. You are containing your annoyance well, but I know when a woman is not pleased with me."

He was a handsome fellow—Mirian grunted in what was nearly a sarcastic laugh. Of course he did.

"I have sisters," he said.

"Oh." She moved toward the tree, taking her eyes away again, avoiding him. She didn't want to talk. She wanted to be silent, and let the old ghosts speak in the silence. The tree was her place to think, to be still, to brood—to be entirely alone. She reached out and laid her hand on the familiar grooves of the tree bark, then turned and leaned against its trunk, letting its low hanging branches shield her against some of the wind. Her clothbound feet slipped naturally into the crooks of the gnarled roots beneath her. The young man's sword was leaning against the trunk just beside her. She blurted out suddenly, "You should keep your sword close to hand, when you're outside the walls."

The young man looked at the sword and frowned a little. "I don't like to sleep with it," he said. He stood regarding her for a moment: a woman cradled in the arms of a tree, almost as strong as the tree itself. The newborn sunlight glinted on her grey collar, its fire dull: not like the fire he could see in her soul, even if it was dampened beneath a cloak of awkward obeisance.

He noticed suddenly that she was holding one arm bent, and memories of last night's altercation sprang suddenly to mind. He took a step toward her. "Are you hurt?" he asked. "Your arm…"

She covered her elbow immediately with her other hand and said, "It's fine."

"I know a little about healing. If you would look me look at it…"

Fire suddenly flashed in her eyes. "Keep away," she said.

He stopped. "All right," he said. He ran a hand through his dark hair in a gesture of helplessness, and pointed at his sword. "Will you hand me that?" he said. "I should put it on, I suppose."

She looked at him suspiciously for a moment, and then reached down slowly with her good arm and took hold of the sword's hilt. It was heavy in her hand, but well-balanced, and she resisted the urge to test its way through the air before she handed it to him. His fingers touched hers as she did, and she withdrew quickly. As he buckled his sword on, curiosity got the better of her.

"Who are you?" she asked.

"My name is Taerith Romany," he said. "I am a stranger in these parts."

"That's clear enough," she said. "Why did you sleep by my… in the field all night?"

"I needed to think," he said. "Castle walls are too confining." He smiled suddenly. "Is this your tree? I think that's what you were about to say?"

Mirian bit her lip for a moment, and then said, in a guarded tone, "Yes."

"I think you are a very different sort of slave," he said. "Though I haven't met many."

"I was not meant to be a lady's maid," she blurted. From the expression on her face he knew she hadn't meant to say that.

"And that is why you could be angry with me?" he said. "I'm sorry. I was trying to protect you, and it was the only thing I could think of."

"I…" she stopped a moment, and then started again. "I suppose I should thank you."

"I suppose you're welcome," Taerith replied. After a moment he asked, "Do you have a name? Don't worry, I won't tell anyone in the castle that you're a landowner, or that you were talking to me."

She smiled in spite of herself, and said, "My name is Mirian."

He smiled back, and suddenly she jerked away from the tree trunk and started to half-walk, half-run back to the castle. "It's getting late," she called over her shoulder.

He raised his hand in farewell. He watched her go, seeming to disappear into the side of the castle wall. He fingered the hilt of his sword thoughtfully; his touch was weighted down, slow with sadness. He turned to view the castle wall again. Twice now he had watched the slave girl go at the command of others, against her own will, against her desire. He sat down at the roots of the tree, feeling a little guilty. He had ruined her morning plans, whatever they had been.

His eyes scanned the brightening sky as he thought. *Her whole life is a banishment,* he thought. *How can anyone ever be at home where they are under the control of forces they cannot be in harmony with?* He clenched his fist suddenly, and touched his brow with his knuckles. Badly he wanted to know freedom—choice—the power of knowledge and control. They had never known it, the children of Isaak Romany. Only when they left home and wandered in Braedoch Forest had they held the illusion of being their own. They had only to come home to remember that other forces shadowed their lives; that another power controlled them. Maeron Duard, their guardian, had watched them with a strange malice even as he raised them.

And then the banishment… and instead of becoming free, Taerith felt more bound than ever. He had not chosen to be here. He did not know what he wanted now. Something else was pushing his life, and he did not know where.

He rose and wandered in the field, letting his booted feet sink in the furrows. He strode back and forth and in circles, and it occurred to him that all his pacing was nothing more than a bitter metaphor for his own life. Suddenly angry, he stopped and dropped to his knees on the soft earth. He looked up to the sky and shook his head. Empty skies… there were no answers there.

Suddenly a movement caught his eye. Something was flying in the air above, just beyond a wisp of cloud that the sun was slowly burning away. At first he thought it was a gull, but as he slowly began to rise, hope stirred in him that it was one of Wren's falcons. His sister's first letter had reached him some four months ago: a feeble pushing against the power that bound them.

The bird came a little lower, and as it did, the white wisps of cloud seemed to gather around its wings, curling and dancing about its feathers with a ghostly clinging. Taerith froze as the cloud began to grow, outlining the bird and then seeming to become part of it: suddenly the bird was growing. Its white cloud-wings shone, not with the sunlight, but with a strange otherworldly glow that seemed to come from within the creature's wings. In moments the wings had grown till they blocked out the sun, and all Taerith could see was a great expanse of feathers across the sky, and the shining form of the bird at their center. His eyes grew wide and his legs seemed to lose all strength as he sank back to the earth: and then, with a beat of its wings that reverberated in his ears, the bird swept down and folded its wings on either side of Taerith.

The great feathers blocked out everything: the fields, the castle, the sun itself. Taerith found himself enveloped in warm darkness, and a voice spoke: stronger and clearer than the echoes of the wing-beat:

"Peace," it said.

Something that had been binding Taerith's chest seemed to break, and weeping freedom filled him. He crumpled to the ground, face pressed against his arms. Something soft and light and warm brushed his cheek—a feather.

It was gone. The warmth disappeared, replaced by the crisp chill of early morning. The rich darkness was snuffed out in an instant: morning sun in a blue sky replaced it.

Taerith scrambled to his feet and looked to the sky again: yes, there was something there… flying… fluttering. It came down and lighted in the tree, and he looked at it in disbelief. It was nothing but a dove… a small white and grey creature with nothing abnormal in its appearance or its manner.

He looked up to the sky again: the dove itself was nothing. Something had perhaps used it to get his attention, but that Something had a life of its own, and did not need to remain within the bands of any earthly creature.

"Deus," Taerith said. At the sound of the name his whole being was flooded with yearning. His heart leapt with freedom. He shook his head, trying to comprehend. "Who are you?" he asked.

There was no answer. Taerith discovered that he was smiling. He had read, in the old manuscript his father had given him as a child, that Deus, the Great God, would sometimes touch a man. Taerith's mind raced back through the crumbling old pages. *Only-Wise,* the Romanys had called Deus. Could He, then, give wisdom in a touch? It must be—for Taerith felt that he knew something now, though he could not put it into words. The world that had been a hauntingly confused tangle for so long would straighten itself. The beginnings of the straightening were there in his mind.

And *peace.* The word spoken had become a tangible thing inside him. He turned and regarded the castle, and knew what he would do. He strode toward the castle.

He needed to find Findal.

*   *   *

Findal was hard at work packing up the tent and other supplies. He turned at Taerith's approach and huffed, "Taerith! Good, good. Lend Randal a hand; good lad. We be pulling out."

"I'll gladly lend a hand," Taerith said, taking hold of a cord and helping Findal tie the flaps of the tent down as he spoke. "But I'm afraid I won't be going with you."

Findal halted without looking at Taerith; his fingers faltering with the cords. He sighed, and turned his grey wispy head. "Sad to hear it, I am," he said. "I had hoped you were becoming one of us."

Taerith swallowed a bit of a lump in his throat. "I'm sorry to disappoint you," he said. "You've been family to me. It's been some time since I had one."

74 Taerith

"Still keeping your secrets to yourself?" Findal asked. "Yes, of course. What's a past between friends anyway?" The old man's eyes were glimmering, but as something occurred to him, his gaze sharpened. "But I do have a mind to speak to you about the future. I don't want to judge, lad, but tell me: what keeps you here?"

Taerith looked up at the sky, his fingers still tying knots in the cords. "Borden asked me to stay and join the guard…" he said. He wasn't finished, but Findal cut him off.

"You're not staying for the sake of the prince. You like him no better than I do."

Taerith smiled and looked at Findal with a hint of reproof. "I haven't made up my mind about him," he said.

"It's about the queen, isn't it?" Findal asked.

"Yes," Taerith told him.

"Lad," Findal said, "I'll not see you stay and get yourself into trouble. It was one thing when she was just a pretty stranger to rescue, but now…"

Taerith interrupted him gently. "She'll never know I'm here," he said. "I am a man of honour, Findal. I'll honour the king as I do his wife."

"Then what…?"

"She didn't choose to come here any more than I did," Taerith said. "But now we're here, and I see a way that I can be of use to her. She needs someone to… to love her, Findal. Not to possess her and not to fall in love with her, but to make it his business to see that she's cared for. I mean to be the one. From a distance."

Findal shook his head. "I think you're not choosing an easy way for yourself," he said.

"I have not chosen my way at all," Taerith said. "But I begin to believe the forces behind the choosing may not be evil after all."

"Well, my boy," Findal said, "if ever you need a home on the road again, just you come asking after Findal. You'll always be welcome with us."

Taerith nodded. The others had begun to notice that something was happening, and they gathered behind Findal now: Randal with his arm around Marta's shoulders, strange Morris and bulky Orlin. Only Zhenya was missing… still with his unicorn somewhere, weakness delighting in strength.

Findal stretched out his hand, and Taerith grasped the extended arm. "Thank you," he said. He raised his eyes. "Thank you all, for everything."

Chapter Seven

Taerith watched Findal's wagons disappear into the darkness of the fens with a curious constriction in his throat. A short-lived family, they had been—but a family, nonetheless. Zhenya had found him just before they left.

"I'll not forget you," the boy had said, leaning on his crutch.

"Nor I you," Taerith answered. "We shall meet again, Little Brother."

Zhenya smiled a faint, crooked smile at the name. He reached out an arm and Taerith grasped it, hand to elbow. Zhenya looked up and whispered, "Take care of Lilia."

"I'll do my best," Taerith had whispered back.

The words echoed in his mind now. Behind him, the castle loomed like a malevolent presence. Yet something rose up in him to meet it—something winged; something wild. He turned to face its grey walls. Lilia was somewhere behind those stones, and with her, his future.

The last vestiges of the celebration were still going on as Taerith entered the gates, but they were more distasteful than ever to him—newly alone, he had no desire to strike up an acquaintance with the last few drunks to remain. His eyes sought out some refuge in the courtyard, or better yet, the powerful form of Borden, whose command he now lived under. Instead, his eyes lit on a figure who was familiar for some reason he could not remember: a priest, who sat beneath his cowl looking out at the world from a shadowed corner of the yard. Almost without thinking, Taerith found himself striding toward the man.

The priest looked up at Taerith's approach. "Ah, the stranger. Well met," he said. His voice was mild, as was his face beneath its sandy, close-cropped beard.

"Stranger no longer," Taerith said. "I have joined Borden's guards."

"Well, then, I am glad you have not yet reported for duty," the priest said. "I wanted a word with you. You have the look of man whom Deus has touched. Please, sit… I cannot offer you more than a patch of ground, for I own nothing in this ungodly place, but it is a friendly patch of ground for the moment."

"It is that," Taerith said, seating himself on the earth beside the priest. "Who are you? And where do you come from?"

"My name is Joachim," the priest said. "I am a subject of Hosten, the mightiest lord in the Five Kingdoms, and your nearest neighbour to the east."

"The Five Kingdoms?" Taerith asked.

"Do you know so little about the land where you now serve?" Joachim asked.

"When I had a home," Taerith answered, "it was far from here."

"Ah" Joachim said. He looked down at his brown robe for a moment, then lifted his head and explained, "Corran, the kingdom where you now reside, is the farthest western edge of an alliance made by five kings. They stand together, lest any one of them be swallowed up by larger kingdoms in the south. It is not always an easy alliance, but it has worked. If it was not for his fellow kings, your lord Annar would have been annexed long ago—or overrun by barbarians in the north. My lord Hosten protects him from the latter evil."

"Did you come here to celebrate Annar's wedding feast?" Taerith asked.

"No," Joachim said. "Annar's affairs are not so important to the neighbouring kingdoms that they would send an emissary— even one as poor as I. I came to deliver a message. And you?"

"I hardly know," Taerith said. "My wandering brought me here, and I believe I am to stay here… I confess I understand little of the path that has led to today."

Joachim smiled. "We are both men sent by God," he said. "I knew you had the mark of Deus on you the first time I saw you, standing as the queen's defender."

The memory came back to Taerith in a rush: Joachim had been the priest with Borden when the prince had come with his guard to escort Lilia to the castle.

"I don't know what you saw," Taerith said. "If Deus has touched me—and I believe perhaps he has—it was not so long ago as that."

"That was hardly long ago," Joachim said, chuckling. "But Deus chooses a man long before the man knows he is chosen."

"Chosen for what?" Taerith asked.

"Only you can answer that," Joachim replied.

A shadow fell across the men, and Borden's deep voice cut through the morning air.

"There you are, lad," the crown prince said. "Get up, and come report for duty. You have much to learn, and not much time in which to learn it." Borden raised his voice as he spoke, so that all within the courtyard could hear him—soldier and sot alike. "We have just received word that the lord Hosten will visit us in half a week's time. When he arrives, he should see a show of strength that will not embarrass Corran, or its lords." His voice dropped to a tiger's purr as he spoke the last three words. Taerith rose immediately, conscious of the priest's eyes on him as he left.

Taerith walked a pace behind Borden as they strode across the yard to the guard's barracks: a narrow, long-running series of rooms built into the side of the castle's northern wall. Men jumped to their feet as Borden entered.

"Look sharp," Borden shouted. "All of you, on your feet. Make me proud to be your commander!"

He need hardly have spoken. Despite the harshness in his voice, Taerith saw the pride in Borden's face—and it was well-deserved. The barracks were spotless; the men dressed, fit, and apparently ready for anything. If he had been nervous about joining Borden's guard, Taerith felt his unacknowledged fears go out of him. These were good men following a commander they respected. Anyone could have seen as much.

"Emmet," Borden said, calling one of the men out. "Ride east. Find our lord Hosten and greet him in the road. Find out how many he brings with him, and how long he plans to stay. Jonas, take your men and troll the borders. I don't trust our neighbours. If they are bringing any surprises, I want to know."

The men in question nodded, barked out orders to a few subordinates, and left the barracks. Borden planted himself in the middle of the floor with his arms folded across his chest.

"Kardas, we will need meat. Take your boys and hunt it down." Borden turned to Taerith suddenly. "Can you hunt, lad?"

"That I can, sir," Taerith answered.

"Man or beast?" Borden asked.

"Beast, if you will allow me," Taerith answered.

"Very well," Borden said. "You are under Kardas's orders for the present." He turned his eyes away, dismissing Taerith from his thoughts as he continued. "Tridian, find last night's trouble-makers and lock them away. I don't want a repeat under King Hosten's eye."

Something else seemed to occur to him, and he turned his eyes back to Taerith, who had crossed the room to join the slim, dark young man called Kardas. "You two had better come with me," he said. "Master Grey knows better than I the needs of the day."

* * *

Master Grey, chief steward of Annar's household, was bent over a long list of provisions in the kitchen when Borden burst in on him with two men in tow. Grey looked up with a dogged expression on his face. The look on Borden's face warned him to silence.

"Going over the stores?" Borden asked.

"Yes, my lord," Master Grey said, laying the list down with a dignity that said he was annoyed but willing to be long-suffering.

"Good," Borden said. "I have come to offer you the services of our fine young hunters. We have guests on the way."

Grey's weathered face blanched. "Guests?" he asked.

"King Hosten of Moralia," Borden said. "He will be here in

three or four days' time. You will make ready for him—a feast."

"My lord," Master Grey said, "we have just celebrated. The stores are low…"

"Which is why I have brought you hunters," Borden interrupted. "Tell them what you need and they will do all they can to get it for you." He lowered his voice and leaned across the counter toward Grey. "I know this is not what you wanted to hear from me today, old man. I did not want to hear it either. But you are no fool—you understand that we must put on a splendid feast for Hosten."

"Does he come with a large party?" Grey asked, swallowing whatever it was that he wanted to say.

"I don't doubt it," Borden answered.

"It is not to be—" Grey stopped in the middle of his sentence. He nodded unhappily. "The servants will revolt," he muttered. "So much work to be done, and they are already worked to the bone from the days past."

"Be glad my scouts learned of Hosten's approach when they did," Borden said. "I have no doubt he meant it to be a surprise."

Borden stepped back and ushered Kardas and Taerith forward. Master Grey knew his business, and it was a matter of minutes before he had handed them an extensive list of meats. Kardas took the list without a word, though Taerith thought he saw a comment brewing under the hunter's silence.

"Will that be all?" Kardas asked.

"Yes," Master Grey said, all but wringing his hands. "Yes, it will have to do."

Kardas nodded and, on silent approval from Borden, withdrew. Taerith followed him out into the morning air.

"There is not this much game left in the fens," Kardas said. "Not at this time of year."

He said nothing more, and Taerith abstained from questioning. The other men assigned to the hunt were making preparations. The two men went to join them.

In the kitchen, Borden continued to tower over the steward as he clapped his hands and began to issue orders for preparation. When every servant within earshot had been thrown into a whirl, the harried old man turned back to his prince.

"Was there something else you wanted, my lord?" he asked. His tone was wheedling: displaying obeisance while begging to be left alone.

"You have a slave in this house," Borden said. "She does not act like a slave."

Grey averted his eyes to his list. "Mirian," he said, fussing with something on the table.

"That's the one," Borden said.

"Has she offended you?" Grey asked. "She is wild, my lord, but she works hard, and the altercation last night was after all in the best interests of…"

"I'm not here to attack her, or to attack you for failing to keep her under," Borden said. "Stop defending yourself; it's embarrassing."

Grey fell silent.

"Well?" Borden asked.

"Well?" Grey echoed, looking genuinely lost.

"Who is she?" Borden asked. "I know her name—but where does she come from?"

"Don't you know?" Grey asked. "She has been here since she was born." His voice quieted, genuinely subdued for the first time since the conversation had begun. "She is the last of the old family, my lord."

Borden looked sharply at the steward. When he spoke again it was slowly, as a man who is threading thoughts even as he speaks. "I understand—from my men—that she has something of a feud with your wife."

"The mistress objects to her spirit, my lord," Grey said.

"Be that as it may," Borden said. "Mirian has been installed as the queen's maid. It was on my orders. I want her there, Grey. She is not to be removed from the position except on my orders. Do you understand?"

"Yes, sir," Grey said.

"She does have spirit," Borden said, half to himself. "You say she was born here? Who raised her? That task would have fallen to you and your wife, would it not?"

"Her own mother raised her, till she was six or so," Grey answered.

"Did she learn her spirit from her mother?"

Grey did not meet the prince's eyes, but his voice took on that strangely subjected quality once more. "Her mother was a broken woman, my lord, as she was meant to be." He cleared his throat. "After she died, the child raised herself. My wife did her best by her, but she couldn't handle her—even then."

The steward raised weary eyes to Borden's face. "I don't know what you have planned for the girl, but…"

"Speak what you want to say," Borden said.

"She's a good girl," Grey said finally. "Treat her kindly."

Borden's mouth twitched. He turned to leave, then said over his shoulder, "I have no other plans, Master Grey. I leave you to your kitchen, and wish you success in readying the house. Our visitors will not be forgiving if you fail, steward, and neither will I."

Master Grey nodded as Borden left, his face as close to a picture of martyred misery as it could be without losing dignity.

*   *   *

Mistress Grey met Mirian on the landing below the queen's room. She cast an eye of disapproval on Mirian's windblown hair and rags, lip curling as she took in the silver tea-tray, laden with the queen's breakfast, which the slave girl held in her hands. She pursed her lips while Mirian waited for her to step aside and let her pass, her eyes challenging the woman even in the silence.

"I do not understand why the prince would choose to cast his pearls before swine," Mistress Grey said at last. Mirian cast her eyes down as the diatribe continued. "You are a disgrace to this house. When I think of how happy your mother would have been to see you so honoured… and you so uncaring!"

"Why should I feel honoured?" Mirian asked. Her voice was low, husky. The shadow of the old tree still hung over her head, holding the promises and hopes of years long past tangled in its roots. Her mother—poor, foolish, defeated woman—seemed less a part of Mirian's blood than the ancestors buried beneath that tree, who had died defending their home with a passion that Mirian remembered in dreams and in nightmares and felt, when she awoke, pounding through her veins. Yes, her mother would have been happy to know that her daughter served as a slave in the place where her fathers had reigned. But it took so little to make her happy.

"She'll be waiting for you," Mistress Grey said, not deigning to answer the question. "Pray that she's still asleep and does not know how late you have been in coming."

Mirian did pray it, in the way of fleeting thought, as she mounted the last few steps to the heavy wood door. There was no sound from the other side, and she pushed the door open and entered.

The deep purple curtains had been opened, letting in the morning sun. It streaked a pale path over the stone floor, passed through the drapery over the bed, and fell on the pale face of the young woman who lay, eyes closed, with her slight hands resting on the coverlet. Dark hair fell over the girl's shoulders, whitening the skin of her neck and shoulders. Mirian stood a moment and looked at her: Annar's wife. How much harm would she do the kingdom before she did them all a mercy and died?

Mirian turned abruptly away, laying the tray and its contents down as quietly as she could. The queen must have awakened earlier, for no one else would have opened the curtains. For an irrational moment she considered drawing them again. She seemed to be in the room with something already dead. Surely the queen would not stir again to welcome the sun, or ever to shut it out. Mirian finished arranging the items on the tray, and turned. The illusion was broken. Lilia's grey eyes were open, and fixed on her.

"Thank you," she said. Her voice was soft and young. Mirian felt something in her hardening against its sweet tones. The thought of this child sitting by Annar's side sickened her… union of weakness and foolishness, it could only mean ill for the people.

Mirian nodded in recognition of the queen's words, and forced herself to speak. "Is there anything else?" she asked.

"Yes," Lilia said, speaking hesitantly. "I rode with you the morning I came here, but I did not learn your name."

"It is Mirian. I am… yours to command, my lady."

Lilia tried to smile but failed at it. She turned her face away, as though she would hide if she could. Mirian was aware that she was intimidating the queen of Corran, her mistress, and she hated the newcomer for it. Didn't she understand that they needed strength?

"I don't…" Lilia began, and then tried again. "I shall have to meet the king, when he calls for me. I don't know what there is to—that is, I don't know what to wear, or how to present myself. You will help me?"

"That is the usual practice," Mirian said. She could not keep the dry edge out of her voice, though she tried her best to speak softly.

"Thank you," Lilia said again. She tried, with a bravery Mirian did not recognize, to meet the slave girl's fiery eyes, but could not withstand the burning in them. She lowered hers again and played with the stitching on her coverlet. She was trembling, from somewhere deep inside, and she fought to keep the tremour out of her voice. "You may go for the moment," she said, quietly. "I will call for you when I need you."

Mirian left the room, and Lilia looked up to the sun that fell toward her in white rays. She closed her eyes and let the rays wash over her, over the thick blankets and the white drapes that hung over her bed; over the thin lace-embroidered gown that lightly graced her shoulders, over her hands. She turned her palms up slowly, as though she might receive something from the morning light. She stood suddenly, and went to the window. Across the field, a group of riders was galloping away. One of them turned and looked back, and even at such a distance she thought she recognized him.

Taerith. Could it be?

In the cold of her tower room, Lilia smiled. She had imagined him, of that she was sure, and yet in the imagination she was not so entirely alone. She was no longer trembling as she turned away from the window.

Chapter Eight

The earth beneath Taerith's feet sank as he crept over it, the boggy reek of the mud rising to meet the close darkness of branches that hung down from old, spindle-rooted, thick-trunked trees; dripping long strands of black leaves. He had gone with Kardas and the others north from the castle, plunging into thick forest over ground that sank lower and lower until it became an alien world of water and wood, haunt of creatures that rooted and wallowed and showed themselves but rarely; the haunt, too, of stranger, more dangerous things: of unicorns, and nightmares.

Kardas, it seemed, had the blood of a hound in his veins. He led the hunters deep into the swamp on the trail of an ancient stag that had not migrated with its tribe, staying on it long after dogs would have lost the scent and become bewildered in the mud and water. They were close now, and Kardas had directed them to fan out and come at the creature from every side. They would circle the stag rather than cornering it; lessen the chances of someone being injured. Taerith's heart grew heavy as they closed in. Between him and Kardas was a silent understanding: there would not really be a fight. The stag was retreating into the heart of the swamp to die. Whatever its life had been, it was over now.

Taerith clenched his jaw even as he rubbed the ashen spear in his hand with his thumb. He had always disliked hunting.

He stepped ankle-deep into a pool of water and slime, but he kept his eyes focused on the gloom ahead. He could hear the stag's heavy breathing now. It had sprinted only minutes before, but must have smelt the others closing in.

Just ahead, the trees widened into a small clearing, and in it Taerith caught a glimpse of movement. For an instant he saw it, standing tall, the stark bone of magnificent antlers rising from the grizzled old head. Its red fur was slick with mud and matted on its legs and flanks; its head and the long hair of its neck were greying and ragged. The stag's sides heaved; it was tired and fearful, yet there was no panic in the creature's eyes.

Lordly one, Taerith thought toward the stag, *you have lived long to end like this.*

From the trees beyond the stag a man suddenly appeared: one of the hunting party. And then others could be seen shifting in the undergrowth, and Taerith caught sight of Kardas emerging from the shadows, spear lifted. The stag leaped away from the man nearest him with a tremendous splash, hooves churning the water to a foaming white, and the first spear flew. It came neither from the hand of Kardas or of Taerith, and it pierced the stag's hide just above its right front leg. Taerith moved as he watched, spear raised, body tensed to finish the kill or spring to the defense of one of his fellow hunters. But a second spear flew, and still the ashwood remained in Taerith's grip.

The stag raised its head suddenly and bellowed. The sound filled the clearing and made the water tremble all around.

It was over quickly. More spears, and the men moved in; there was a quick flash of a sword, and the stag lay dead in the muck.

The men gathered round and began to make it ready to take back to the castle. Taerith raised his eyes from the bloody scene. Kardas stood directly across from him.

Both men still held their spears in their hands.

They fell in beside each other on the trek home. Both carried meat on their shoulders, from the stag and a few birds they had taken down catching the deer's trail. "I hope," Kardas said under his breath, "that Hosten is happy with his supper."

They walked in silence after that, both exhausted from the day's hunt and aware that it was miles back to the castle. Taerith watched Kardas curiously as he walked: something in his lithe, terse movements made Taerith feel as though the young man beside him was not entirely human. Part beast he may have been, sired by some mythical creature. In the perpetual twilight of the swamp, such a story did not seem implausible. But if he was a predator, he was not one to give way to bloodlust. Kardas had not wanted to bring the stag down any more than Taerith had.

On the edge of the swamp they passed through a village. Taerith could smell fresh water and ale in the air; he became aware, suddenly, of how dry his mouth was. One of the hunters approached Kardas.

"We are thirsty," he said. "Let us stop here and rest a while. Have a drink and a bite to eat." There was a public house in the village square, from which the sounds and smells of life emanated. The scent of smoked meat suddenly reached Taerith's nostrils, and his stomach knotted at the smell. They had been working long and hard.

Kardas looked at the man for a moment, almost as though he had not heard him. The burden he carried appeared too much for his limbs; he was as tired and filthy as any of the rest of them. But he shook his head.

"Only if you are able to pay for it," Kardas said.

"We are the king's men," the hunter protested. "We are entitled…"

"If these people are not hungry now, they soon will be," Kardas said. "Let them not say we took anything from them that we did not have to."

He looked at Taerith, his expression still half-distracted. "I think it will be a lean winter," he said.

To Taerith's surprise, the hunter did not push the issue further. He nodded, sniffed, and tightened his belt with a look at Kardas, but he went back to his load without another word and shouldered it.

With no protest beyond grim mouths and grunts, the other men followed suit. Kardas took the first step toward the castle, and Taerith fell in just behind him.

"Here, my lords!" A voice from the public house stopped them in their tracks. They turned together and beheld a brawny man standing in the door, an apron tied about his waist. "Lord Borden's hunters, are ye not?"

"We are," Kardas answered, taking a step toward the man. For all his size, the tavern keeper moved back as though uneasy at Kardas's approach. Taerith thought he saw a glint of fear in the man's eyes, even as his hearty tongue made the presence of fear seem not only implausible, but ridiculous.

"You are all hungry," the man said. "Come in. Dine, drink, the lot of you."

92 Taerith

The hunters' faces remained straight, but Taerith caught their subtle eagerness as they looked toward Kardas and waited. His eyes were narrow with thought. He slowly shook his head.

"No," he said. "We have no money."

The innkeeper seemed more uneasy than before; Taerith could it hear it in his voice now. "It is my gift," he said. "For the prince's men."

The hunters were muttering now, casting unhappy glances at the dark features of their young leader—features which were settling into a stubborn cast Taerith recognized. He had see it before in his brother Aiden. It was the look of one who knew he was right, and it was always followed by a clash—for others inevitably took convincing. He took a step nearer Kardas and said in a low voice, "Perhaps we might accept a drink only."

Kardas looked at him, and though he did not smile, Taerith saw that Kardas had understood his suggestion for what it was: mercy to the men; peace to their leader. He nodded and turned back to the innkeeper. "We accept your offer of a drink," he said. "No more than that."

The innkeeper stepped aside, satisfied, while Kardas's hunters converged on the inn door. Their mood had changed in an instant, from unhappy cooperation to cheer.

Taerith was last through the door, with Kardas only a few paces behind him, but just before the tavern's noisy dim closed in over him, he saw a hand clap down on Kardas's shoulder and heard a voice intone, "Greetings, my lord Half-Blood."

Taerith drew his hunting knife and was back on the street in an instant. Three men stood around Kardas. They held no weapons that Taerith could see, yet their expressions were unmistakably threatening. The chief of them, a tall, stocky man with a half-shaven head and a dull wine-coloured cloak, drew his hand back from Kardas's shoulder. He glowered at Taerith with such displeasure that he almost expected him to hiss.

"Who is he?" he asked.

"I am a loyal servant of the prince," Taerith answered. Kardas stayed tense and silent. He seemed ready to spring, and Taerith found himself trying at once to watch the three men and to decipher some sort of instructions in his companion's dark eyes. That they were in danger he did not doubt. The air was charged with it. The men were between him and Kardas, a geography he did not like. He took a step closer.

"Put that knife away, boy," the leader said. In the same instant, one of the three pulled a knife from somewhere and lunged at Kardas. The young hunter threw his arms up just in time, grabbing the man's wrist with both hands and wrenching it aside with incredible strength. The assassin's forward motion bore them both to the ground, where Kardas struggled to draw his own weapon while fending off his attacker.

Taerith moved to his aid without a lost heartbeat, but the third of the strangers met his advance with a sword drawn from beneath his cloak. Years of training in Braedoch—sparring both with his brothers and with the unpredictable dangers of the wild—served Taerith well. His reaction was automatic; he needed only a second to prepare himself for attack. By the time his assailant was on him he was more than prepared. He sent the man's sword spinning into the street. Face dark with anger and flushed with action, he raised his knife, fixed his eyes on his assailant, and hissed, "Get out of here. Go!" The man turned and ran.

It was over. Kardas was picking himself up out of the dirt; the wine-cloaked leader and his crony had vanished. Breathing hard,

Taerith offered Kardas his hand and pulled him to his feet. The young leader brushed himself off and looked after the runaway with a narrowed eyes. Some of the hunters emerged from the tavern, asking questions that neither Taerith nor Kardas bothered to answer.

"Who was he?" Taerith asked, quietly so that the other men did not hear.

"Meronane," Kardas answered, all but spitting the name. "The foul priest of Engnor."

"What did he want with you?" Taerith asked.

"To slit my throat and send my gutted carcass back to the lords of Carron," Kardas answered, wiping dust from his mouth. It was flecked with blood from the fight. He turned and looked at Taerith, dark eyes glinting like slick black rock. "You have not heard of the Narrow Path before, have you?"

Taerith shook his head, sheathing his hunting knife as he did so. He folded his arms and waited for Kardas to continue.

"Meronane is a rogue priest," Kardas said. "He brings killers with him where he goes, for he has sworn to break his holy vows of peace only to take the lives of Annar and his family. Deus has told him that the Heavenly Kingdom must be established here in Corran, and Meronane himself will hold the throne until a more heavenly comes to take it."

"It would seem that Annar holds that right, as Corran is his throne," Taerith said.

"It would," Kardas agreed, "if Annar were not the devil incarnate. Deus told the priest that, also. And Borden is his chief demon. Meronane and his followers call themselves the Narrow Path, for Deus has said that no one will enter the kingdom except through them."

"Your pardon, my friend," Taerith said in a low voice, "but Deus has said nothing of the kind."

Kardas inclined his head in a gesture, not of agreement, but of admittance to a possible point.

"What is being done about this threat?" Taerith inquired.

"Too little," Kardas answered. "Meronane is a master fox. He hides himself well. His following is small; Annar does not see much threat in it."

"And Borden?" Taerith pressed.

"Has bigger threats to worry about," Kardas said. "The Path may be a lot of bloody badgers, but Hosten is a wolf."

Kardas looked Taerith over with an appraising eye. "It is a cruel and ruthless country you have come to," he said. "If you had not already joined us, I would have advised you to keep going."

"What about you?" Taerith asked.

Kardas smiled. "This world will kill me someday," he said. "I stay where I may sink my teeth into it first."

"In Borden's service," Taerith said.

"I am not free with my loyalties," Kardas said. "The world has treated Lord Borden much as it has treated me. He has earned my loyalties, and I am content to serve him."

Without another word, Kardas bent down and picked up his load again. He whistled loudly, and the hunters emerged from their rest and began to follow their leader back to the castle.

Neither Kardas nor Taerith had taken a drink, but if they were thirsty they hardly felt it.

*　　*　　*

Lilia watched the sun set from her high window. Her stomach was knotted with hunger, but she hardly noticed it.

Annar had not called for her. Not once.

Birds were circling the top of the tower: around and around, dipping and soaring, cackling to each other in the evening light. Far below, in the courtyard, people mingled and called like the birds. She wondered what they were doing—what kept them so busy even at this time of night. Perhaps they were preparing a feast for her husband.

She turned away from the window abruptly. What would it be like, she wondered, to be remembered?

Her fingers brushed the remains of the breakfast tray Mirian had brought her while the day was still more than another disappointment to fade into the grey of the past. Mirian. She could call for Mirian… it would break the silence.

She half-smiled to herself even as the thought passed through her mind. When had silence ever bothered her? There was no comfort in Mirian's presence; the tall servant girl frightened her. The birds outside grew louder; squawking; fighting; flapping. No, she would not call Mirian. Besides, what use was company that came to you because it had to? She missed her old companions: books. Vellum and ink; words and their worlds; gorgeous illumination. Her father had told her once—oh, yes, sometimes he had spoken to her—that not many people had books. He told her that she was the most fortunate of women because she could read. And it was true. More true with every passing day; with every passing hour. Her father owned three books, and they had become her doorway to the world and its ideas and ideals; the place where she met the thoughts of others and delighted in recognizing herself. They were the only abetting of loneliness in a life that had hardly dared hope for a day that was not lonely.

And now life had changed, and she lived with people, not paper. Her husband was a king. Why, she asked herself as she moved away from the window, had she stayed all day in her room? She was the queen.

They do not want me, she told herself. *I have felt it.*

And yet, she was the queen. There was a world beyond the tower. She could smell it. Now and again its sounds came up through the floor, with the smells of bread and manure and life haunting the echoes.

Her hands were at the latch of the door—it was not locked, this door, not like every other door she had known—and then she let herself out, and her feet were on the stairs. She moved lightly, quietly. Her steps were uncertain but her heart grew with every step. Hope lit her way. She was out, free, and searching for something outside of captivity. Perhaps she might find something to take back with her. Her heart was pounding and she hushed it. *The door was unlocked,* she told herself. *You are free to walk in this place.*

Shadows lay throughout the castle, but torches blazed in the halls and larger rooms. The servants were hard at work: scouring, preparing. They watched Lilia with veiled eyes as she passed, and looked down when she tried to meet their glances. Some eyes were not so veiled, but there was no friendliness in them. Lilia's steps faltered, and suddenly she wished she was back in the tower. At least the birds did not meet her approach with so much frozen diffidence.

"My lady." The deep voice came from behind her, sending her heart into her throat. She whirled around. Borden stood behind her, the expression on his face one of displeasure. She was dwarfed by his stature, and she flushed as she lowered her eyes from his. "What are you doing here?" he asked.

"I… I only…" She tried to speak, but words would not come.

"Where is your attendant?" Borden asked, searching the shadows behind her with his dark eyes.

"I am alone," she said. With great effort, she lifted her head again. She was in a lower hall, and there were people all around. They were staring. Listening. The flush came back into her face.

He lowered his voice a little, but it still seemed to echo off the stone walls. She flinched as he spoke. "You should not be wandering alone," he said. "It is not seemly… or safe. Don't you know that you have enemies in this kingdom?"

"This is my husband's castle," Lilia said quietly. "I thought…"

"You thought wrong," Borden said. "Tonight, it may be safe. But more strangers are coming. What would you do if you ran into an enemy?"

She cast her eyes down and said nothing. He lowered his voice further, raking her with his eyes. "You're not even properly dressed," he said. "I gave you a servant. Use her."

He turned on his heel and walked away from her. The servants pulled themselves out of their momentary pause and returned to work, and when Lilia lifted her eyes again she found that no one was even acknowledging her presence.

"My lord," Lilia called after him. Where the courage to call had come from she wasn't sure, but there it was. She could not go back to the tower with nothing but shame to take back with her.

Borden turned, eyes flaring. The anger in them startled her, but she swallowed fear and said, "I wanted… is there a book in the castle?"

The question caught Borden off guard, and for a moment he simply stared at her. Then he opened his mouth and said, "No. We are men of the sword and of the aleskin here. If you want books, find a monastery."

And he was gone. She sighed—what else could she do?—knotted her fists, and started the long walk back through the castle's strange corridors, back to the stairway and her place of exile.

The foreign priest Joachim, sitting in the corner of the hall, watched her go. In pale grey she looked like a ghost walking the halls. "Or a dove of peace," he said aloud. "But no one will hear the message, will they?" He looked down, eyes moistened with sympathy, and stood suddenly. He had time.

He had just enough time.

*   *   *

Borden found Mirian in a corridor from whence she had watched the whole encounter. He could not decipher the expression on her face.

"Why weren't you with her?" he asked.

"She did not call for me," Mirian answered.

"You are her maid," Borden said back.

"But not her keeper. She has not called for me since this morning. I followed her to be at hand when she does call; is that not enough?"

"No, it isn't," Borden said. "She won't call for you; she is ignorant, and she is afraid." Half to himself, he muttered, "She cowers when I speak to her."

Whatever Mirian wanted to say in return, she kept it behind closed lips. Borden charged on.

"Annar needed a woman strong enough to make up for his weaknesses," he said. "He made the wrong choice. I am as disgusted with them both as you are. Any other day of the year, the queen may walk herself right onto a gallows if that's what she desires. But not now. Surely you have heard the news—Hosten of Moralia rides upon us even now, and he must not find us weak. Not in any way."

Mirian looked away, still holding her tongue.

"Look at me," Borden commanded. She did.

"Keep the queen in hand," Borden said. "When she must appear, see that she carries herself decently. As much as you can, keep her hidden away."

"She is the queen," Mirian said, finally looking directly at Borden. "She is not under my control."

He was silent for a moment, and then a slight smile played at the corner of his mouth. "Why not?" he asked. "The strong always control the weak, and you and I both know which of you is stronger."

He began to turn away, and added, "In any case, you are under my orders. Your hand is mine in this. I want her controlled as a rider controls his horse."

"If I overstep my authority, I must answer to the king," Mirian said. "Not to you. He could have my head if he wants it."

"You will not even need my protection," Borden answered. His eyes went back to the hall where Lilia had stood. "Do you think she would complain? I am not asking you to break a horse, Mirian. I am asking you to control one that is already broken. Do not give her time or space to gain her own head; do not give her freedom." He spoke slowly, pronouncing every word with deliberation. "Our allegiance with Hosten is a very complicated dance. One misstep, and we will all pay for it."

He turned away, leaving Mirian looking after him.

Chapter Nine

Mirian entered Lilia's room the next morning without knocking. The young queen turned from the window with startled eyes, but she did not question the intrusion. She wore only a simple shift. Her grey overdress, little more regal than a peasant's garb but made of good enough cloth, was draped over the end of the bed. Apparently she intended wearing it again. Mirian ignored it, striding across the small room to a chest of stained oak, its corners overlaid with gold. She threw it open, filling the room with the spicy scent of perfume and wood. Rich colours greeted her: queen's clothing, specially chosen and fitted for Lilia before her arrival, dresses in deep red and forest green, mulberry and a gorgeous blue so dark it was nearly black. Mirian fingered the blue dress, almost reverent of its softness. Lilia had been looking over her shoulder this whole time, but now she turned and took a step closer.

"Are those mine?" she asked.

Mirian looked at her almost with disbelief. "Have you not even opened this yet?"

Lilia shook her head. "I thought… well, it was closed."

"You are at liberty to explore your own room," Mirian said. "You're not a slave."

"I—" Lilia began, but the sight of Mirian's slave collar cut her short. "Oh," she said.

Mirian pulled the dress from the chest and let its long folds fall to the floor. "From now on," she said, "you get dressed every morning. That's the first thing. If the lords of the castle call for you, you're not to come down looking like a villager."

"I'm sorry," Lilia said. "I didn't know I had any choice."

Mirian stared at Lilia for a moment, then nodded. Without a word, she started to help her on with the dress. Lilia let herself be handled, as compliant as a child. Several times she seemed about to say something, but Mirian ignored her. She started fiercely on the laces, only gentling a little when she saw Lilia wince as she pulled one too tight.

There was a brush on the table, and Mirian reached for it. Lilia held up a hand and stopped her with a soft, "I can do that."

Mirian turned from the table and yanked the bedding up on Lilia's bed. She was smoothing it out when Lilia said, "Thank you."

Mirian nodded without looking up.

"You haven't always been a lady's maid, have you?" Lilia asked.

Mirian looked up and sighed in irritation. Lilia stood in the sunlight, the blue in her dress deep and rich in its rays. Her hair was darker still, and likewise made gorgeous by the sun. Her skin was paler than ever, and her grey eyes were almost pleading—for something Mirian didn't want to recognize. She pursed her lips and answered, "I am a slave. The queen should not talk with me."

Lilia turned away abruptly. She took the reprimand as Mirian had expected she would: silently, without protest. She was like a doll: responding to everything that pushed her without fighting back.

Mirian tucked the last stray bit of bedding in and went to the door. She turned and looked at Lilia's back, bowed head and slumping shoulders, frail white hand resting on the stone by the window.

"Call for me if you need me," Mirian said, and left the room. She let the door close behind her, slowing it with her hand so that it wouldn't jar. She frowned. Something was making her unhappy—guilt pricked at her. She didn't care. She started down the stone steps, telling herself she only needed a glimpse of the sun and some air.

Mistress Grey met her halfway up. Mirian felt her spine go stiff as iron and her emotions straightened in the same fashion, unhappiness fleeing behind the instantly erected wall. Mistress Grey looked at her like a snake at a trapped rat: hateful, but just wary enough to keep its distance.

"Your queen was down here yesterday wandering like a kitchen maid," she said. The snake struck.

"I'll do my best to control her next time," Mirian answered.

"Don't talk back to me, girl," Mistress Grey said. "You do your work, and do it well. If the queen shames us in front of Hosten, Lord Borden will have your head."

Mirian almost smiled: the rat had teeth of its own. For the first time in her life she felt a measure of power over Mistress Grey. "Lord Borden may not see things your way," she said.

Mistress Grey narrowed her eyes. Her voice dropped to a hiss. "Don't think I don't see his eyes following you," she said. "But don't you get any ideas. I know the world better than you do, girl. Don't you start thinking his attentions a good thing."

Mirian tried to answer, but her tongue strangled every word before it could leave her mouth. Her face was hot; she was blushing, and she hated it. She hated Mistress Grey for it.

For a barely perceptible moment something new came into the mistress's eyes: bitterness, but a new kind of bitterness. "I don't know why I bother trying to warn you," she said. "I should let him eat you alive, for all the good you've ever done this place."

Mirian's eyes glimmered through her sulk. "Shall I tell him you said that?" she asked.

Mistress Grey stabbed once again, but this time all the venom was in her eyes. She turned away and stalked up the stairs.

Mirian looked after her for a moment. When she started her descent again, her legs were weak beneath her. She stumbled as she walked, and found herself half-leaning on the wall for support. Angry tears were welling up in her—why was she crying? Why? She had never cried as a child. She didn't want to cry now. She staggered into the sunlight like a drunk, throwing her hand up to shade her eyes.

Her shaded gaze was met by the return of the hunters. Kardas was leading them with the antlers of a great stag tied to his horse's flank. The new one, Taerith, rode almost beside him. All of the men were weary and filthy, but they had meat with them. Meat enough to lessen the threat of Hosten: meat enough to make a show of wealth and hospitality. She watched them unload their horses until she realized that Taerith had seen her and was coming toward her.

He smiled as he approached, even as she looked for something else to fix her attention on. She shifted uneasily, but resisted the urge to bolt.

"How is your tree?" he asked, bowing his head slightly as he came within speaking distance.

The confounded tears started to rise again. She cleared her

throat. "I don't know," she said. "Lady's maids don't get outside much."

He seemed slightly troubled. She noticed that much, as she forced herself to look at him. Why did she feel guilty in his presence?

"I hope your lady is well," he said.

"I'll tell her you inquired," Mirian said, half expecting the words to scare him off. There was something beneath the surface of his words that she recognized as dangerous: an obstacle in the flow of water. He frowned slightly at her words, but his tone did not change.

"Please don't," he said. "I would rather you didn't mention me." He peered at her, as though he was waiting for her to speak on her own. She didn't.

"She is well?" he pressed.

"Well enough," Mirian said. "She is the queen."

He smiled again. "And I am a hunter," he said. "You are a slave. What does that mean? It makes us neither well nor poorly."

The other hunters were finishing their work, and Taerith began to turn back toward them. "I should help," he said.

Mirian nodded. Was he waiting for her to agree? He unnerved her—talked to her as if they had some understanding. She felt chided. Suddenly her own words sounded empty and childish in her ears. She looked up. The tower stretched above her. Lilia was probably still by the window.

A deep voice boomed across the courtyard: Borden, greeting his hunters. She watched as he emerged and greeted first Kardas, then the others; gripping them by the arm and talking earnestly with them. If he looked her way he would see her.

She slipped inside before he had the chance.

*   *   *

The horn of Hosten sounded over the fields and roads as the king of Moralia approached. It vibrated in the castle walls and made the shadows of evening tremble. The wolf was coming.

Borden stood on the castle wall and looked out on the road that stretched before him. The sun had half-set, draping the road in dusk. The lights of Hosten's caravan announced that he had a large entourage with him: dozens, perhaps scores, of men: more than Annar had to man his entire castle. It was a deliberate show of force, intended to cast Annar's weakness in his face. Borden was determined that the attempt should not succeed.

He left the parapet, calling for his horse as he descended. "To me!" he bellowed, and his guards took up the call. He stroked his beard impatiently as he waited, while around him his men gathered, leading horses, lining up in formation. Kardas and Taerith held the reins of their horses side by side. They made a strong pair: one all darkness and power, the other intelligence and diplomacy. Borden beckoned to them.

"You will ride at my back," he said. "You others, ride three abreast behind them wherever the road allows."

He turned to Master Grey, who stood waiting with two of the household servants. "All is ready, steward?"

"Indeed, my lord," Grey replied.

"Honour Hosten as you have never honoured my brother," Borden said. "Much depends on it."

"I understand," Grey said. Borden trusted that he did.

They rode out into the dusk, torches dark. Borden would signal when it was time to light them. He hoped to catch Hosten off guard, though there was little chance of doing so completely.

It was a dry, cold night. The wind in their faces as they rode smelled of snow coming.

Taerith smelled it. Weeks ago it would have concerned him for himself—he had been on the road then, nothing but a vagabond with little hope or shelter. Now it worried him, but not for himself. Horse hooves on the road kept a steady beat in the otherwise still night. The last hints of sunlight had disappeared. Taerith held tighter to the reins. In the darkness beside him he thought he could hear Kardas's horse breathing and shaking its head.

It had been Kardas's refusal to allow his men food at the tavern that first told Taerith something was wrong. Since then, the signs had been everywhere. The already-lean faces of the commoners who came to the castle. The barely-concealed fear in the steward and his wife as they bid the servants prepare a feast for their visitor. They did not fear Hosten—they feared the feast itself. Winter did not bode well for these people in the best of times, but this year, Annar had taxed their stores beyond discretion for his wedding feast. Now Borden taxed them again to feed the visiting king.

The smell of snow in the air was the smell of starvation and suffering.

The sound of hooves and voices, jangling tack and wagon wheels reached through the darkness, first seeming to swell from their own ranks and then clearly signalling the presence of others. A moment later the glimmer of torches became visible as Hosten's party rounded a bend in the road. Borden lifted his hand—Taerith could barely make out the motion in the scant moonlight—and commanded, "Lights!"

Rachel Starr Thomson   109

Taerith reached for the torch bound to the side of his saddle. Beside him, the noise of striking flint was accompanied by sparks, and Kardas's torch flared to life. They lowered their torches so the heads touched, and Taerith's blazed up in return. He dismounted and ran to light the man behind him. Flame birthed flame, and soon the column pocked the darkness with orange light and the drifting outlines of smoke.

Borden still held his hand high. The riders came to a halt behind them, reining in their restless animals.

"We wait," Borden said. His voice carried to Taerith and Kardas but not beyond them. "When he is twenty paces off, ride to my side. We will greet him together."

They made no answer. Borden knew they had heard, and would obey.

Hosten had seen them. They heard shouts from the other party, relayed back through its ranks long and loud enough to indicate at least forty riders, with horses and wagons. Borden's fifteen did not flinch at the sound, anymore than their leader flinched. The newcomers slowed in their approach, ascertaining who it was that waited for them in the road. They came into sight: forty men at least, all alike in the torchlight. Borden raised his hand and beckoned with his fingers, urging his horse forward at the same moment. Taerith and Kardas moved as one, riding to either side of their leader.

Five horses broke from the approaching column. In the center a huge man rode astride a grey warhorse. Before him, even Borden looked small. The man wore rich furs, yet there was nothing either soft or luxuriant about him. His long golden beard was streaked with grey: piercing eyes were hawkish in their power, even in the darkness. In height and girth he was a bull, and like a bull, it was all muscle and power and unstoppable force. He rode up with two warriors on either side of him. Borden spoke first.

"Welcome, my lord Hosten."

Hosten raised a hand in greeting. "Well met, Lord Borden. Where is your brother the king?"

"He prepares for your arrival," Borden answered.

"You are as grim as ever, I see," Hosten said. "Short answers and hidden meanings, eh?"

Taerith shifted uneasily. Hosten was considerably older than Borden; as he drew closer that became clear. Yet the condescending note in his voice sounded more like a challenge than anything else.

Hosten's eyes left Borden to quickly assess his men. He gave a half-snort at the sight of Kardas and beckoned to someone behind him. "We took the long route here, and brought you a gift from the north," he said. A man rode up behind him and handed him a sack, tied shut with twine. Hosten laughed as he hoisted the bag up.

"Heads of the northern devils we protect you from," he said, and threw the sack into the road.

Taerith's stomach lurched and he looked away, dreading lest the bag should come open. His eyes went to Kardas, who watched the progress of the sack with stony interest.

"They're troubling the border early this year," Hosten said. "They'd be snarling at your heels already if my men hadn't cut them down like the dogs they are."

The sack still lay in the road. Borden, distaste written on every feature, turned to command Taerith to pick it up. Kardas anticipated him. Before a word could be said, he dismounted and picked up the sack. He bowed to Hosten, who watched him with an expression that was both amused and hostile. Without a word, Kardas turned again and mounted, tying the sack to his saddle.

"We will escort you the rest of the way to the castle," Borden said. He had hardly acknowledged the sack, and he did not look at Kardas now. "Feasting awaits you."

"As it should," Hosten replied. He smiled and waved his hand. "Feasting shall always accompany a wedding, eh, Borden? A joyous time for all of you. For all of us."

Borden nodded curtly. "Indeed," he answered.

He turned his horse, and galloped ahead. His men parted the way for him and then fell in around the newcomers, riding in pairs. Taerith reined toward Kardas, but the young man dug his heels into his horse and galloped ahead.

Chapter Ten

"They're coming!"

The call descended from a watchman on the wall. They were ready. Bread, ale, savoury meat; scoured floors and clean bedding; everything was ready. The castle gates burst open and Borden rode in, fast, his best men behind him. He dismounted and handed off the reins.

"Where is my brother?" he roared.

"Patience," Annar answered. The people of the castle, made more numerous by villagers and farmers conscripted for the occasion, parted as their king came forth. His hair and beard were neatly combed and trimmed; his ermine robe richly brocaded. Borden's lip nearly curled at the sight of him. His young wife was on his arm, pale and trembling, dressed in a rich blue gown. Borden's eyes sought Mirian and found her among the king's attendants, dressed like a lady's maid but uncowed. Her eyes were on him—no, not on him now, but on Taerith. Taerith stood just behind him.

"You ride like a bearer of bad tidings," Annar told his brother. His tone was mildly reproving; like one who spoke to a temperamental child.

Borden bowed. "Behold," he said. "King Hosten approaches."

Even as he spoke, the first of Hosten's retinue entered the gates. They rode in tall, proud lines and turned to form a square, pushing the people of the castle back. In their wake Hosten came. The castle lights set warhorse and tawny master aglow. He came to a halt with his men crowding in behind him. He looked down on Annar and did not dismount.

"Greetings, king of Corran!" the Moralian bellowed. His eyes, made sharp with years of greed, rested on Lilia. "And greetings to the king's wife."

Lilia kept her head up as Hosten dismounted. He approached them like a lion in his pride: took her hand, bent, and kissed it. Her hand shook but not, she hoped, too badly. Hosten turned from her and extended his arm to Annar.

For a moment nothing happened. Borden cursed under his breath. Annar had not missed Hosten's subtle disrespect. He looked the king over now, regarded the hand of the mightiest of the Five Kings as though it were a fish.

Abruptly, Annar took a step forward. The kings clasped elbows in greeting. Borden watched them, all too aware of the uneasy quiet of the crowd. Hosten's men still sat astride their horses in formation, as though they were keeping back a mob.

Borden raised his hands to the kings, a practiced smile marring his face. His eyes nearly bored a hole in his brother as he spoke. "Let us go to the feasting, my lords."

*   *   *

Annar sat behind his board, hanging over his ale cup with shining face. Hosten sat on his right hand amid the wreckage of supper; Lilia at his left. She had hardly touched the fowl laid before her.

"These are good times for my kingdom." Annar bragged. "There has been much feasting here of late."

"Good times in truth," Hosten answered, his speech stronger and not so slurred as Annar's. "Tell me, man, how long until you produce an heir to inherit all this wealth?"

The sweep of Hosten's arm took in the hall, the servants and slaves who lingered about the tables, the men who ate little that their guests might eat much. From the far left corner of the hall, Kardas glowered at him. He was seated, with Taerith and the rest of the Borden's guard, at the end of a long table. Annar's answer was too slurred to be heard through the din of the feast, but they saw him to turn to Lilia as he spoke, and the king's whole table burst into laughter.

Taerith watched Lilia intently. He trusted to the crowd and commotion to keep him hidden. He saw and felt her discomfort; her downcast eyes and flushed cheek spoke eloquently… and there was something else. She looked exhausted, almost sick. The king's laughter ended Taerith's tolerance. He stood and looked over the heads of Hosten's soldiers to the shadows where the servants hovered, looking for Mirian. He found her quickly. She was standing in the far corner behind the king's table, arms folded, eyes fixed on the men before her. Disdain was written plainly on her face: she would shrivel them with her disrespect if the power was in her to do so. Taerith pushed through the crowd, making his way beyond the torchlight to the wall where Lilia would not likely see him. Hosten's men paid him little mind. He turned briefly and saw that both Borden and Kardas were watching him go, but he did not bother to stop and explain himself.

Mirian looked away from the objects of her disgust just long enough to catch sight of Taerith striding toward her. She turned herself a little, almost as though she would ignore him. He saw her discomfort but pressed in anyway.

"Can you get her out of here?" he asked, his voice low.

"What, the queen?" Mirian asked.

"She's ill," Taerith said. "Look at her."

She didn't meet his eyes. "The king will not be pleased if she leaves now."

He was silent, willing her to look up. She finally did. "Don't you think they've laughed at her long enough?" he asked.

"I—" Mirian looked away again. The table was back in uproar; drunk, laughing, disgusting. Taerith caught the way she looked at them.

"She's going to be sick if you leave her there," he said.

Mirian nodded. "Go back to your men," she said. "I'll do something."

Taerith managed a grim smile. "Thank you."

"Go," Mirian repeated. "Why are you still standing here?"

Taerith answered her with a nod and began his way back to the board where Borden's men feasted. His feet moved unwillingly. It galled him to send Mirian to do what he wanted to do— what the king or his brother ought to be doing.

"What are you about?" Borden demanded when he reached the board. His voice was low but urgent enough. It caught Taerith off guard.

"The queen is ill," Taerith said. "I asked her maid to take her away."

He looked through the crowd and saw that Mirian was at Lilia's elbow, bent over so she could speak into her ear. Lilia still seemed half-distracted, but he saw her nod even as Annar roared a question at the slave girl. Mirian shot an answer back with only a little bristling; Taerith smiled in spite of himself. Annar was too drunk and too slow of mind to notice his own slave stiffened when she spoke to him.

"What her slave does is none of your concern," Borden said. "Nor is the queen."

Taerith looked back at his leader. "Your pardon, sir," he said. "She is my queen, and a woman at the mercy of merciless men. I thought she was all of our concern."

For a moment he thought he saw Borden go red beneath his beard, whether with anger or shame he couldn't tell and didn't guess. But the crown prince regained himself quickly. "You're right, of course," he said. "She should be removed from this farce before my brother makes a greater fool of himself."

Taerith inclined his head in assent. "I believe Mirian has already taken care of things."

Borden looked up. The queen's chair was vacant. In the shadows behind the dais, Mirian was escorting her from the room.

* * *

It was late at night before Taerith saw Mirian again. The moon had risen high above the castle tower, and Taerith sat warming his hands by a small guard fire in the courtyard. He was alone. Emmet, one of the older of Borden's guards, was on watch with him but had chosen to take his place near the quarters where Hosten's men were garrisoned. He did not expect trouble from them tonight, but if it arose the old soldier was confident of his ability to handle it.

Mirian stepped from the wall into the moonlight, unaware of Taerith's eyes on her. She hurried across the courtyard toward the stable. He rose as she came, heading her off without a word.

She gasped when she saw him. "Do you always skulk in the shadows like that?" she asked.

"The stables may not be to your liking tonight," Taerith said quietly. "Hosten brought many men with him; some sleep in there."

He saw her shoulders slump a little: she was disappointed. She started to turn away, but something occurred to her and she whirled back to face him. He was unprepared for the fire in her expression.

"I did what you wanted tonight, in the hall," she said. "Don't expect me to do it again."

"You did what you should have done," Taerith said.

"Don't patronize me," she said. "I may be a slave but I'm no lower than you are."

He blinked in the darkness. Words came slowly. "Do you think that's why I approached you?" he said. "It doesn't matter to me that people call you a slave."

She bit her lip. The moon was bright enough for him to see it. Something was tearing at her, and it went deeper than the resentment he'd seen in her before. It flashed upon him suddenly that the emotion she wrestled with was guilt.

"Tell me what you're thinking," he said.

She looked away.

"Tell me," he pressed.

"She is the queen," Mirian said. "She ought to be strong; we need so much from her. It's not right that I should bully her."

"Then don't," Taerith said. "Lilia is weak, Mirian, in very many ways. And you are strong."

"You sound like Borden," Mirian muttered. He chose to ignore the comment.

"I've watched you with her. You resent her; you use your strength like a stick to beat an erring child."

"What else am I supposed to do?" Mirian snapped. "I don't want her as my responsibility."

"Nor is that what she needs," Taerith answered.

"Then what?"

There was silence for a moment as a cloud passed over the moon. The air was cold; Mirian shivered and pulled her shawl around her shoulders.

"Be her friend," Taerith said. "Lend her your strength, don't beat her with it."

Mirian turned away. Her head was bowed. Her voice reached him, muffled. "I can't."

"Then you're not as strong as I thought," Taerith said.

Mirian straightened her shoulders, pushing down the lump in her throat as she looked up at the moon. Something snapped in her and she turned suddenly, but Taerith was gone. He had returned to his fire.

*   *   *

They stayed.

Days and nights they stayed, past a weary week. Hosten settled in upon the castle like a great boar wallowing in Annar's scant mud.

Taerith attended the feast every night. Kardas was always there, watching Hosten and his men—waiting for something with sharp dark eyes. Borden stopped sitting with his men and took his place at the head table, where he watched jealously over Annar's every word. Lilia appeared at her husband's board every night, to be shortly spirited away by Borden or Mirian. Once she was gone, Taerith retreated to the kitchen.

It was hot there, despite encroaching winter, crowded and frantic. Master Grey himself oversaw the work. Steam and flour made the air thick and mingled with sweat and salt to create an odour that lay under everything, even the scents of meat and bread and dried fruit.

Fifteen days had passed, and Taerith drew Grey aside in the corner of the kitchen.

"Tell me what harries you so," he said. "You are worried; I can see it."

"Hosten will ruin us," Grey said, just loudly enough that the nearest cooks could hear him. His voice was ragged. His usual discretion was half-lost to the harsh demands of desperation. "Our stores will not last two more days."

Taerith saw the faces that turned up at Grey's words; the hands that kept kneading and stirring with the grim determination of a man who hangs himself. "Perhaps the winter stores—" he began.

"These are the winter stores," Grey snapped. "What Hosten and his marauders eat was to have fed our mouths through the winter."

Taerith's stomach sank. The servants kept working. He saw a woman blink away tears that mixed themselves with the bread dough beneath her hands. "Were the provisions so few?" he asked.

Grey lowered his voice a little now. "Annar's wedding feast was ill-timed," he said. "The year's yield was poorly; much of our harvest has already gone to Hosten in tribute, for he keeps our northern border." The steward's thin hands tore at the borders of his apron as he spoke. "He should not have married, not now. Lord Borden foresaw this and told…" he trailed off and bit his lip. His fingers still worked almost convulsively, but defeat had replaced his anger. He shook his aged head. "We shall feed the boar two more days," he said, "and then we shall all starve together."

Taerith stood alone as Grey moved away, still shaking his head. Someone opened the outside door, and a blast of cold air reached him. He started. Urgency gripped him; Grey's words shot energy through him. For a moment he thought he saw his sisters among the women who worked in the kitchen: his family, facing starvation. From somewhere deep in his memory he heard the rushing river and stirring trees of Braedoch Forest: home to fish, home to game. He could already feel the hunting spear in his hand. He made for the door, pausing to lay his hand on the shoulder of the woman whose tears no longer fell into her baking.

"Don't be afraid," he said, and passed into the night.

The Great Hall was still lit: light poured from the high windows into the courtyard. Laughter burst from it, but the sound brought no cheer. Into the corridor, up the stairs Taerith rushed. He re-entered the hall and searched for Borden. He was seated at the king's table. Taerith did not pause. He made his way through the rows of soldiers. He had nearly reached Borden when the voice of King Hosten halted him.

"We will take the men out tomorrow for a fine hunt," the king boomed. "My soldiers are spoiling for a kill."

Borden was uncharacteristically hesitant in his reply. "There is little game left, my lord."

Annar cut in. "There is plenty," he said. "Well, plenty enough.

Most have moved south, it is true; but there are enough left to sport with. It is a fine idea. I have not been on a hunt myself in some time."

Taerith bent down to Borden's ear and said, "My lord, we need that game for ourselves."

Borden ignored him, not bothering even to look in his direction. "Very well," Borden said. "My own hunters will lead you out."

"My lord…" Taerith said, more urgently this time. Borden stood, turning his broad back to him. His voice echoed in the hall.

"Kardas, stand up!"

From the far end of the hall, Kardas warily stood. "You will lead these fine men," Borden said. "If anyone can find the last of the game, you can."

Hosten's voice cut in, sealing the certainty that weighed down Taerith's stomach. "Will a half-breed northerner lead us?" he said. "You have a fine sense of humour, Borden. It is good, it is good!"

The hall dissolved again into the chaos of conversation and half-drunken laughter. Borden stalked away from the head table. Taerith followed him out into the corridor.

Borden turned on him. "You are bold to approach me at the board," he said.

"I forgot myself," Taerith said. "We are badly in need of food, my lord… for the castle."

"We will have it," Borden said. "There is food enough in the villages."

Taerith began to speak, but Borden silenced him with a raised hand. "You will go with my men to collect it," he said. "If Grey's whining is correct, you should start tomorrow."

Chapter Eleven

Emmet led the men. For a moment Taerith had feared Borden would place *him* in command. Bile rose in his throat at the very idea. The village air was cold, stingingly acrid with smoke. The smell burned in his nostrils as he dismounted quickly and took the little stone-lined path to the cottage door. The wood of the door was old and cracked. He rapped on it. First to the door—the others waited behind him, on foot, grim and already weary. The morning had been hard on them all.

But they didn't hate this—not like Taerith hated it. That was why he went to the door first. To tell the villagers, somehow. To take their anger on himself; do penance. To show mercy if he possibly could. Emmet had been first at the last door, and his rough lack of compassion made it all worse.

The door stayed closed. Taerith rapped again, and as he did a boy stepped around the corner of the house. He was fifteen, maybe sixteen. Gangly but tough. He had a mallet in his hand.

"Go away," the boy said. "There's nothing here."

"We all have to pay taxes, lad," Emmet shouted from the gate.

"It can't be helped," Taerith said.

"We've paid," the boy insisted. He took a step closer, and Taerith began looking for the best way to wrest the mallet from the boy without injuring him. "We paid at the end of the harvest!"

"It wasn't enough," Taerith said. He kept his voice calm, tightly under control.

"It's never enough!" the boy cried, raising the mallet half-unintentionally. Two of Emmet's men sprang forward, but Taerith had his hand on the tool's handle before they could reach the door.

"Where's your father?" he asked. "Let me speak to him."

"Go ahead," the boy said, casting a glance over his shoulder. "He's in the graveyard."

Taerith closed his eyes for a moment, his fingers still tightly wrapped around the mallet handle. The boy did not pull away from him. He was studying him; watching Taerith's reaction to his words.

"I don't want to rob you," Taerith said. "Let us take what we came for; it will be better for you."

The boy shook his head, longish brown hair falling into his eyes. "We'll starve. How's that better?"

"You won't," Taerith said. His voice was too low for Emmet or the others to hear him. "If I have to bring you my own rations every winter, you won't starve."

The boy's body relaxed a little. He looked suspiciously at Taerith, then at the men.

"My mother," he said. "She's got to eat, too."

"Just let us take what we need," Taerith said. His throat was tight. Already he was mentally calculating how far he could make his own rations go—how long he could survive while feeding two others. "Don't make the men impatient with you."

He let go of the mallet. The boy lowered it. He stepped back, then turned toward a small outbuilding six feet away. "Here," he said, half-sullenly but loudly enough for Emmet to hear. "You can see what we have."

They entered into the dim dust of the building. Stores of winter corn were laid up in patched baskets. Straw was laid over cabbages and potatoes in a recess in one corner of the floor, and from the ceiling dried strips of meat dangled—goat, Taerith thought from the smell. A squawk and clatter arose from the far corner of the barn as the men began to untie meat from the ceiling and heft baskets of corn onto their shoulders. Emmet cast his eye on the few hens and a rooster that were penned in there. He nodded toward the corner.

"Take one," he told Taerith.

Taerith's stomach sank even as he followed Emmet's instructions. Too many autumns spent laying up food for the winter with Aiden and Arnan rushed back to him. There was so little here—such a long winter in the waiting.

The boy stood in the door and watched them with his arms folded. Taerith thought he trembled a little as the men began to exit. With the scrawniest of the chickens held firmly in hand, he passed close by the boy.

"You did right," Taerith said. "You warded off worse suffering than this."

The boy looked up at him. There were tears in his eyes, and shame behind them. But hope kindled there, too. *Man of the house,* Taerith thought. *Dare hope that you've done well.*

Taerith tied the clucking chicken to a board in the wagon they pulled behind them, and it settled in among barrels and burlap bags with a few other rattled hens. Their raid on the village had produced precious little, yet as Taerith mounted his horse and looked back at the house with its cracked door and dirty, smoking chimney, all he could think was how much they had taken. He burned the house into his memory. He'd be back that winter—back with anything he could provide.

But the next house… and the next… you couldn't feed a village on one soldier's rations.

They started down the road, the wagon creaking behind them. Homes grew thicker as they approached the center of the village, and children ran alongside them. Singing. Chanting something. Taerith's heart grew heavier as he caught the words.

"Curse the king, curse the queen, let the harvest run away."

Emmet glared at the children but said nothing. The others hardly seemed to notice. Taerith missed Kardas—not that the taciturn young man would have said anything, but somehow he knew there would be something in the dark hunter's eyes worth reading.

The day was only half-over.

*   *   *

Lilia watched Mirian as she bustled around the room, stoking the fire and beating at the dark purple curtains as though she would drive the dust from them by force and intimidation. The queasiness in Lilia's stomach rose and she swallowed convulsively, trying to keep it down. From the height of the sun it was nearly noon, and she had not left her bed. Annar and Hosten had left on the hunt early that morning, so she had not been wanted.

She was glad of it. She tried as hard as she could to be a credit to her husband, but Hosten unnerved her and left her feeling exposed and shamed every time she raised her eyes or opened her mouth. Every day spent in the foreign king's presence made her feel weaker.

Mirian turned and looked in Lilia's direction, hunting for something else to do. The slave girl had said fewer words this morning even than usual, and Lilia was almost amused by the look on her face. Normally she would have been cowed by Mirian's evident disdain, but today she was too tired to be intimidated.

Too tired… watching Mirian work was making her tired.

Mirian noticed Lilia's eyes on her. She folded her arms, cocked her a head a little and said, "Is there anything you want me to do?" she asked.

"Yes," Lilia said. The word came out low and muttered, though she hadn't meant it to. She swallowed again. "Sit down. You're exhausting me."

"Sit—?" Mirian began.

"On the bed," Lilia said, waving her hand at the coverlet. "Just sit."

Mirian looked around her, and then moved to obey. She sat down awkwardly, as though she was afraid of breaking the bed, and folded her hands in her lap. It was a posture entirely unlike Mirian, and it made Lilia laugh.

"Why are you laughing at me?" Mirian asked, eyebrow askew.

"You weren't made to sit still, were you?" Lilia asked. "You look like you don't know how."

Mirian started to answer and bit her tongue. An instant later she sprang to her feet and turned her back on the bed and its occupant entirely.

"You haven't eaten breakfast yet," she said.

"I don't want it," Lilia said.

Mirian turned halfway back. "You should eat," she said.

"I don't think I could keep it down," Lilia said.

"Are you sick?" Mirian asked.

Lilia shook her head. Loose strands of black hair fell across her pale cheek, and she brushed them back. She moved her hand as though it weighed too much, and dropped it back to the sheets. "I'm tired," she said. "Feasting makes me tired."

"Sitting at the feast makes you tired," Mirian said. It was suddenly dawning on her that she had not seen Lilia eat in days. "You cannot be said to feast yourself. What have you eaten since Hosten's arrival?"

Lilia's eyes were closing. She was falling asleep. "A little," she said, and then fell silent.

Mirian stood in the light of the window, staring down at the bed and the sleeping girl in it. For the first time she was just that—a girl—not a queen or an enemy, but a girl who needed looking after. Taerith's words echoed in her ears: *Lend her your strength.* Something smote at Mirian's heart, and whether it was guilt or concern she couldn't be sure.

She stood another five minutes, just watching the queen as she slept. Convinced at last that Lilia would not awake for some time, she picked up the empty coal bucket next to the fireplace. As she straightened up with it, pain shot through her arm at the elbow. She flinched a little as she passed through the door. The arm had nearly stopped bothering her, but the pain was back now—whether irritated by the growing cold or something else, she wasn't sure. There were bandages in Master Grey's keeping; she would seek him out and see about wrapping her arm.

She was rounding the last bit of staircase when she nearly tripped over the man: an unfamiliar man of average height and build, skulking at the bottom of the steps. He took in her collar with a glance, and anger darkened his face. "Watch your step, slave," he snapped.

She nearly snapped back. Instead, she took him in with a cold glance and demanded, "What are you doing here? These are private quarters."

He took a menacing step closer to her. "Why do you think I would answer the likes of you?"

Her eyes blazed in response, and she drew herself up with such presence that the man took a step back again. "I am the queen's personal attendant," she said. "You will answer me, or answer to her."

"I'm a guest at the feast," the man said. His voice was still surly, still threatening, but Mirian heard the loss of confidence beneath it. "The night was cold; I found shelter where I could take it."

"You cannot take it here," Mirian said. "Get out."

The man's lip curled, and he spat on the floor at her feet. Without another word, he stalked off.

She watched him go, frowning. The pain in her arm was nearly forgotten, but her hand wandered to the elbow and she found herself rubbing it without thought. Suddenly, warm fingers closed over her arm. She whirled around, ready for anything.

Borden stood behind her. A smile lurked on his lips. His folded his arms as he took in her stance: not a deer ready to flee, but a panther intent on a fight.

"Well done," he said.

It took her a moment to find her voice, but she found it. "He was lying," she said. "I've been up and down these stairs twice this morning; he did not sleep here."

"Do you know who he was?" Borden asked.

"No," Mirian answered.

"So for all you know he might have been some new king, and all our alliances destroyed by your tongue."

"He was no king," Mirian said.

"You know commonness when you see it?" Borden said. "You should, as you are hardly common yourself, are you?" He lowered his voice, and it sounded in the darkness like the voice of some devil. "You are ten times the queen Lilia will ever be."

She stared, unable to find words to answer him.

"Do something about your arm." He brushed past her in the closeness of the corridor. "My brother will return soon, and I think you will have duties then."

*　*　*

The hunting horn announced the return of the men from the hunt. The priest sat in the courtyard shadows and watched them. Kardas, Borden's dark hunter, rode behind Hosten's riotous men. Joachim could feel the young man's animosity from where he sat. It was natural, he thought, that men should sense the tide that had turned against Hosten. It was natural that they should despise him, for soon there would be nothing left of him worth honouring.

The thought was not a pleasant one. Joachim clutched his bundle closer, fingers running over the smooth cloth wrapped tightly around it. He watched the men dismount. His eyes fixed on Hosten. He stiffened when Hosten looked his way, but no recognition showed in the king's eyes.

The courtyard smelled of sweat and blood. Servants helped the hunters unload their trophies—only a few deer, thin and old, and many birds—and took the horses away to be brushed down and given water. The men laughed, joked, celebrated their prowess in stealing the country's last few resources. Joachim lifted his eyes to the far side of the courtyard, where the young stranger called Taerith left the soldiers' quarters to speak with Kardas.

The sun set. The courtyard emptied of men. The lights of the feasting hall were lit; voices began to call from it into the cold night. Still Joachim sat, stroking his bundle, waiting.

Finally he judged it time. He rose and slipped through a servant's door, into a corridor that led behind the feasting hall. A slight smile tugged at his lips as he heard footsteps coming the other way. He had hoped to intercept her. He stationed himself by the door to the hall and waited.

Lilia appeared, dressed in a gown the colour of purple-red wine. The slave girl, Mirian, walked just behind her. Her head was bowed; an uncommon posture for her, so she did not see the priest at first.

"My lady," Joachim said as he stepped out of the shadows. Lilia's startled eyes greeted him, but she seemed unable to find any words. He smiled. He stepped forward and pressed the small bundle into her hands. "A gift," he said. "I hope it may keep you company."

A puzzled frown on her face, Lilia slowly pulled at the twine that held the cloth close to its treasure. The material fell away, and she gasped.

In her hands was a small book, no thicker than her palm, bound in dark blue leather. She looked up at him, and there were tears in her beautiful grey eyes.

"Thank you," she said. "Where did you—"

"It doesn't matter where it came from," Joachim said. "A priest has access to such things. It is yours now. Care well for it."

Lilia pressed the book to her heart and nodded, trying to smile. "I am grateful. I wish I could show you how much."

Joachim smiled at her again, and bowed slightly. "My lady's tears are thanks enough," he said.

Mirian's voice sounded low from behind Lilia. "The king will grow impatient," she said.

Lilia half-turned toward her slave. She nodded, and brushed away her tears with the back of her hand. "Yes," she said. "I am sorry. We'll go in now."

Joachim stepped away from the door, bowing as the pair passed through it into the light and noise of the feasting hall. The door closed behind them and he stared at it for a few minutes. "Not yet," he said to himself, quietly. Then he turned and walked away, toward another corridor, another end of the hall.

*   *   *

Borden looked up as the queen entered. Her hands were low; clutching a book against the fabric of her long, deep red skirt. He frowned. Why she had brought such a thing to the feast was beyond his powers of deduction. He lifted his eyes past her, to Mirian who walked with an unusually subdued air. As Lilia lowered herself into the wooden chair at Annar's side, seating herself with her usual attitude of near-flight, Mirian retired into the shadows behind the table.

Hosten was drinking already, tearing pieces of venison from the hunters' catch. His booming voice overpowered the table. The braggart was detailing his battles in the north. Annar hardly responded. He was put out about something. Lilia's knuckles were turning white as she wrapped her fingers around the book in her lap and kept her eyes turned down.

Borden listened to Hosten and watched Annar with some worry. Hosten liked an audience; he might turn angry if Annar didn't pay him more attention.

"Your meat grows worse by the day," Hosten said, jokingly waving a haunch in the air.

"You have eaten all the best," Annar said. The words sounded pulled from a sulk.

"Come, my lord," Hosten said. "You are not so impoverished."

Annar picked at his plate. "My people will feed us. Still, you have decimated the hunting."

"With your permission, of course," Hosten said. He forced some humour back into his voice. "Surely you are not afraid for your stomach, Annar? When has the time of reckoning ever come upon you?"

"It comes upon you now, my lords."

The voice echoed from the back of the hall. A man stood there, cowl thrown back from a sandy, bearded head; a priest with unusual fire in his eyes. He walked forward, unheeding of those who tried to stop him. He approached the board, stopping only feet away from it, and pointed his finger at Annar.

"This time next year your throne will sit empty," he said. "Lord Deus has sent me to tell you. You have robbed your people and brought great injustice on this land. Therefore God will bring judgment upon you. All of your plans shall come to naught, for you will not live to see them carried out."

He turned to Hosten, and the fire in his eyes flared higher. "As for you, mighty king," he said, "in future the dogs will tear at what remains of you, for Deus has seen the craft with which you would plunder others, and He will plunder you."

Hosten's face twisted with rage. Annar still sat dumb, but dark: a smoldering cloud seemed to have come into his face.

"Fool of a priest!" Hosten growled. "I warned you, man, not to come into my sight!"

The priest lowered his pointing finger, but he did not flinch at the threat implicit in Hosten's expression. "I heed not the warnings of those who do not heed God," he said.

Hosten turned on his host suddenly and roared, "Give me a sword! I will have the blackguard's head!"

Borden stood before he knew what he was doing. "Be calm, my lord," he said. He glared at Joachim. "A loose tongue may not justify murder. Take him as prisoner instead, to face justice in your own country."

"Who are you to tell me what to do?" Hosten exploded.

"He is my brother." Annar stood. He was only inches from Hosten, and the look on his face sent Borden's stomach plunging. No. Not now. He could not be such a fool.

"My brother," Annar repeated. "And you are our guest. A pretty guest! You come and you drink all my wine and you eat all my meat; you brag and you boast, and you bring scum like that into my kingdom!" He pointed at Joachim as he spoke. Heat rose in his face as he pushed the words out past the liquor that thickened his tongue. "I am sick of you, mighty king. Get out of my house."

His finger was still pointing at Joachim. He turned his head and followed its line, exploding when his eyes fell on Joachim again. "Borden! Remove the man. Put him away."

Borden did not move, but two of his men came from the back of the hall and seized Joachim. The priest made no move to ward them off, and with a nod from their leader the men shoved him out of the room. Borden's eyes stayed on his brother and the king of Moralia. His stomach churned.

"You insult me," Hosten said.

"Somebody should," Annar slurred.

Hosten's hand tightened around the wine goblet in his hand until Borden thought he would snap the wood. "I go," the king said. He stood. "Your tribute, King Annar—I have increased it."

"Increase it all you like," Annar returned. "What's that to me? Find your tribute somewhere else. I won't pay an ox like you another farthing."

Hosten's eyes glimmered. Whatever tempest was brewing within him, he held it inside. Borden wasn't fooled. There was pleasure in the king of Moralia. His plan had worked.

"Then know for certain," Hosten said, stepping away from the table, "that everything you own will soon be mine."

Annar merely looked up at the king. "Why are you still here?" he said. "I told you to get out."

Hosten held up his hand. Two of his servants rushed to his side, handing him his cloak and sword. He buckled the weapon on and swung the cloak around his shoulders. Slowly, he took one last look around the feasting hall. He nodded in satisfaction. Reaching into a pouch at his waist, he pulled out a silver coin and tossed it to Lilia.

"To the queen," he said. "The only thing of value in this Godforsaken kingdom."

His eyes swept from Lilia to Borden. "I leave you the northern borders!" he said.

In a moment he was gone. His soldiers followed him, some silent, some jeering. The king, his wife and brother, and a handful of servants and soldiers were all that remained in the hall.

Lilia's hand left her book. She stretched her fingers across the table and picked up the silver coin, examining it with a puzzled air as though she could not focus her eyes on its surface. Borden nearly exploded. He reached out and knocked the coin from her hand.

"Don't you know when you've been insulted?" he said. "Would that he had taken you with him!"

Lilia looked up at him. For a moment her eyes focused on his face, but he could not decipher the expression in their grey depths. Annar reached out and touched her shoulder, and she shuddered slightly at the touch. As Borden watched, her eyes rolled back and she slipped from her chair to the floor.

Annar looked down at his motionless queen. He was too drunk to know what to do. If he had been sober, Borden would have been sorely tempted to thrash him. The ramifications of Annar's temper had only begun to insinuate themselves in his brother's mind.

Mirian pushed forward suddenly, moving chairs out of the way and nearly elbowing the king aside. She crouched down beside Lilia and gently lifted the queen in her arms. She stood, strong and tall, and her eyes rested first on the king and then on Borden. Without a word, she turned and left the room, Lilia's head resting on her shoulder, slender arms hanging down.

When they were gone, Borden turned to face Annar and the wreckage of all he had worked to preserve.

Chapter Twelve

Mirian waited with her back to the cold stone wall outside Lilia's room. She started each time someone came in or out, servants bearing jugs of steaming water, rags, and strong-smelling broth. At last they all trooped out again, single-file through the narrow passage to the stairs. Mistress Grey came last of all, iron keyring in hand.

"To think of you," she snapped. "Tending her every hour and never even noticing. I don't know whether to call you blind or stupid."

"Call me both, then, and be done with it," Mirian answered. She held out her hand, and Mistress Grey placed the key to Lilia's room in it.

"Mind my instructions," she said. "And for God's sake ask for help if you need it."

Mirian closed her fingers over the key. "Yes, ma'am."

Mistress Grey gave her a sharp look. Mirian did not react to it, and Mistress Grey turned to go. When the last footstep had died away on the stairs, Mirian gingerly pushed open the door.

Lilia looked up from the bed. Mirian moved automatically to the window, then thought better of it and left the curtains alone.

She turned abruptly to Lilia.

"When will the baby come?" she asked.

"Late in the summer, Mistress Grey tells me," said Lilia.

Mirian nodded. She reached into her skirt pocket and drew out the book Joachim had given Lilia in the hall before the feast. She held it out as though she expected Lilia to come take it, then stepped across the room and laid it on the table next to the bed.

"I was afraid that the king would destroy it, so I… I went and found it first," Mirian said.

A slow, solemn smile turned up the corners of Lilia's mouth. "Thank you," she said. "And for carrying me here… thank you."

Mirian turned deep red. "Who told you about that?" she asked.

"Mistress Grey."

Mirian turned away. "It was my job."

Lilia laughed—a clear, bell-like laugh that rippled in the pool of Mirian's embarrassment.

"Not just any lady's maid could have carried me up all those stairs," she said.

Mirian wheeled around and snapped, "Oh yes, they could. You weigh about as much as a gnat."

The words struck them both as so ludicrous that each saw the other swallow a laugh. Lilia's expression grew solemn again.

"I heard Mistress Grey chastise you in the hall."

Embarrassment again. Mirian flopped into the chair next to Lilia's bed and folded her arms, eyes cast down and brow stormy.

"She shouldn't have," Lilia continued. "I told her not to."

The thought of Lilia giving orders to Mistress Grey hardly registered with Mirian. Her guilt suddenly welled over.

"I deserved it," she said. "To watch you growing weak and ill and not recognize that you were with child… I'm a fool."

"I didn't recognize it myself," Lilia said.

Mirian looked up at her, startled. "What did you think you were, dying?" she asked.

"Yes," Lilia answered. She chuckled a little and rested her hand on her still-slender belly. "And all the time there was life growing in me."

Mirian hardly heard the last comment. She turned and faced Lilia, leaning forward, her voice low and intense.

"You thought you were dying?" she repeated.

Suddenly there were tears in Lilia's eyes, but she smiled through them. "Yes," she said.

Mirian's voice was thick as she spoke, as though she needed to choke something down but couldn't. "People only die of broken hearts when they give up," Mirian said. "You're not that weak."

"How do you know my heart is broken?" Lilia asked.

Mirian's own eyes were instantly awash with tears, but they stayed there, shining in her eyes, refusing to fall. "I'm sorry," she said. "I should have helped you."

"Even though slaves don't talk with queens?" Lilia asked. She reached out suddenly, and took Mirian's hands and pulled them toward her, sitting up and leaning forward as she did. "I know I'm only a queen," she said. "But if you'll speak with me… and touch me sometimes like this… smile… I'd be so grateful."

Mirian's fingers tightened around Lilia's small white hands until she thought she'd crush them, and she forced herself to loosen her grip. She stood abruptly. Lilia still held her hands, like a pleading child. She turned her grey eyes up.

"Grateful," she repeated, "and Deus himself will bless you for it."

Mirian nodded, and somehow through her tears she smiled. "You should sleep," Mirian said. "You've been too weak. Rest now."

Lilia released her hands and laid back, closing her eyes with a hint of a smile on her face. Mirian stood watching her until the young queen fell asleep.

She turned away at last and moved to the window. Brown fields stretched out to the borders of the forest. North. Vaguely she knew that trouble would come from the north. Hosten had promised it.

The tears through which she saw it all condensed suddenly and traced damp trails down her face. She could still feel Lilia's weight in her arms; the small hands clinging to hers. An image had burned itself in her mind and it rose before her now: she saw herself, carrying the queen away from the hall. But the image blurred, even as her chest began to heave with emotions she resolutely shoved down; she saw others, carrying another woman, a dead woman, away… her mother.

For an instant she was a little girl watching again. A tiny sob burst from her. She clamped her mouth shut, clenched her fists, turned from the window as if she expected to face an enemy. No one was there but Lilia, still sleeping. She turned back, leaning on the stone of the window.

Someone was riding across the fields toward the castle. Two men, riding like the devil was on their tail. From the height of the castle she couldn't see the way their horses frothed, but in her mind's eye she could.

*　*　*

The watchmen knew them at once and ordered the gates opened. They didn't slow up until they were nearly there; then they pulled their horses to a high-stepping, nervous walk, and rode into the courtyard. Borden had already been called. He strode up to the first rider and said,

"What news?"

The man was covered in dirt and grime. He wiped his forehead and answered, "There's been a raid at Esktown. Crops are gone; a lot of people… gone."

"It's too soon," Borden said. "Hosten only called his men off yesterday. Esktown is too far south."

"We caught two of them still in the town. We brought their weapons back; you can see for yourself. It's northerners."

Borden cursed. "The swine. He must have called his men away from the border weeks ago. He knew Annar would give him a reason to do it."

He turned his back on the messengers and ran the figures in his mind. How many miles of borderland… what number of barbarians beyond it… how far they would likely come for plunder. He cursed again.

He turned back to the messengers. Others of his men had gathered in the courtyard. They stood watching him, silent and grim, arms folded. Above them the sky was grey and clouded; snow was coming in earnest.

"Gather what you need," he said.

"Sir?" Emmet asked.

"We're going north. All of us. When they attack again we'll be there to meet them. Hosten thinks we aren't strong enough to defend ourselves. Prove him wrong, and I'll stand with you."

The men nodded. They turned away, all except a few who waited. Emmet approached Borden and clapped a hand on his shoulder. Borden nodded, and Emmet stepped back and headed for the stables.

Kardas remained, looking up at his leader through smoky eyes.

"I believe in your loyalty," Borden said.

Kardas nodded. There was no trace of light in his face, nothing but deeply-meant conviction. "You have no cause to fear it," he said.

"Taerith?" Borden called, looking toward the last remaining man in the courtyard. Taerith approached quietly, waiting until Kardas had disappeared into the soldiers' quarters before he spoke. "Is it wise to take all the men away?" he asked.

"We need every one," Borden said. "The greater show of force we can give the marauders, the better. Once we've beaten them soundly once or twice we can send some of the men home. The northerners are deadly, but they're primitive, and they don't act as a group."

"There are home threats," Taerith said.

"There's nothing else to do," Borden said. He had nearly raised his voice, and immediately he looked apologetic. "I'm sorry, Taerith." He fixed his dark eyes on the young man. "Can you kill a man?" he asked.

"If I must," Taerith said.

Borden nodded. "I believe you. I want you to fight beside Kardas."

Taerith raised an eyebrow. "To spy on him?" he asked.

"No, to fight with him," Borden repeated. "I told him I trusted his loyalty, and I meant it. The others may not. Best he fights beside a man he can trust."

"Yes, sir," Taerith said. He bent his head. Borden couldn't account for the sorrow in Taerith's face, or the conflict he saw there.

"Work it out, whatever it is," he said. "We need you with us entirely, not with half your heart left here."

Taerith smiled an odd, crooked smile. "That is a hard request," he said. "I am not even all here. Pieces of my heart are strewn in more places than you know."

Borden's voice was softened as he issued his final order. "Pack up, poet. We leave tonight."

"My lord?" Taerith asked as Borden began to walk away.

"Yes?" the prince asked, turning.

"What has happened to the priest?"

"The poison-tongued prophet?" Borden asked. Taerith nodded.

"He is in the safest possible place," Borden answered. "Look down."

*   *   *

There was a dungeon beneath the castle. It was both dank and chill, though not cold enough to keep out the vermin. Taerith could hear them skittering away in the darkness as he descended the staircase: a long, steep descent that seemed to have been carved from stone and yellow mud. Guards sat at the bottom of the stairs, playing dice beneath the glare of torches. They looked up, startled, at Taerith's approach.

"I want to see the priest," he said.

One of the guards pointed down a rectangular corridor with his knife. "Down there," he said.

The corridor was black as pitch, and Taerith ducked his head as he entered it. He reached out and touched one of the walls; sticky cobwebs met his fingers. The corridor—more of a tunnel really—stank. Of what, he wasn't sure.

Toward its end, the corridor suddenly widened and led off into two different directions. Faint light glimmered from the left, and the rustle of straw indicated that someone had moved.

"Joachim?" Taerith called.

"I'm here," the priest's voice came back.

Taerith took the left path four steps, and a cell began to take shape in the gloom. Iron bars separated it from the corridor. Joachim was sitting within, leaning against the wall on the opposite side. Taerith could just make out the form of him, robed and hooded. The cell was squarish and roughly formed, with clay and rock walls that swept far higher than the dungeon level. High above, nearly at the ceiling, brick-sized apertures let in a little light and air.

Taerith reached into his shirt and pulled out something long and thin and wrapped in a rag, which he tossed through the bars. It landed near Joachim's feet. The priest leaned over and picked it up. "Thank you," he said.

"It's not much," Taerith said.

Joachim untied the thin cloth that covered it, and pulled out a piece of iron that had been shaped to a point. He looked up, and in the measly light Taerith thought he saw a twinkle in the priest's eye.

"Thank you," he said. "There's so much clay in these walls, this will serve me very nicely."

"I thought you might keep the dates with it," Taerith said. "Or write hymns in the wall."

"Or prophecies," Joachim said, his voice at once deep and laughing—at himself, Taerith thought.

"Why did you do it?" Taerith asked. "You knew it would send you here—and bring us trouble."

"Has it brought you trouble?" Joachim asked. "I'm sorry for that."

"You didn't answer my question," Taerith said.

"I did it because Deus sent me," Joachim said.

"So you said."

"And you, boy? Deus touched you, too. I saw that in you."

"I thought Deus had sent me here," Taerith said. "To help protect… Lilia. But I'm leaving now. Borden calls us to the borders, and I pledged to serve under him. I'm not sure what to do."

Joachim shifted in the darkness, shuffling the damp straw beneath him. He held up the iron pen, studying it in the dank light. "What do you know about Deus, Taerith?"

Taerith was quiet a long moment. "That he has wings," he said.

"Then," Joachim said, "like the eagle, He sees more than you do. Trust that He will not stop watching over you and over Lilia. Go, fulfill your pledges, and don't fear. That is my advice. There is little purpose in fear."

From above, the sound of horses neighing drifted into the cell. Taerith looked up. "We leave tonight," he said. "Be well, friend."

"And you," Joachim responded. "I will pray for you."

Taerith was quiet again. He began to turn away, then stopped and said, "Pray for us all."

*   *   *

Taerith joined the soldiers in the courtyard. The snow was beginning to fall, swirling down on a light wind that promised to freeze the night and make their ride an arduous one. He had wrapped his feet in cloth before booting them, and his cloak was wrapped around his shoulders and fastened with a thin iron clasp. The wind blew in his hair, chilling his ears. He twined the reins of his horse around his fingers as he watched the others mount.

Borden shouted an order, and Taerith mounted. The horse surged forward with its fellows; with a rush and pounding of hooves, they were away.

From the shadows, a man watched them go.

He smiled to himself. When the courtyard had been empty five minutes he walked into the center of it, then turned and looked up at the high, narrow windows of Annar's feasting hall. "The time has come," the man said. He cast his eyes up further, to the tower where the queen—the queen, with Annar's heir forming in her—slept. His smile was frozen, and it eroded like ice under the night wind.

Wrapping his cloak around himself, he left the courtyard and the castle behind him. The few servants who patrolled the walls, slack and unpracticed compared to Borden's now-absent guards, did not even see him go. Down the road he wandered, till he reached an inn in the nearest village.

The man entered the dining hall, moving through the smoke and dim lighting toward a corner where sat a man in a wine-coloured cloak.

"Greetings, Father Meronane," he said.

Meronane looked up at him, his eyes flickering in greeting. He said nothing.

The man's voice dropped nearly to a whisper as he took the seat opposite the priest. "Borden has removed his men," he said. "They go north to combat the barbarians, who have already attacked at Esktown. And there is more—the queen is with child."

Meronane nodded. "The devil has spawned," he said. His voice was deep, solemn like a funeral bell. He stood, his tall form blocking out the lights that smouldered on the wall behind him. "We will give the people time," he said. "The barbarians will slaughter Borden's men even as the villagers starve. Hunger will teach them to regard their deliverers well."

In another corner of the room someone was singing—a girl, a server in the tavern, who carried only scant fare to her customers and mockingly spilled out her words in explanation. Meronane smiled at the sound. The words were indistinct through the dull tavern clamour, but he had heard them sung often enough in the town.

Curse the king, curse the queen, let the harvest run away.

Annar had given them the people's backing. Hosten had given them opportunity. The priest's band would show themselves strong when the time came to attack the castle. But it was Meronane himself who would put an end to the king's line—forever.

Chapter Thirteen

Annar paced. The servants kept out of his way. He fretted—Borden galled him every day, but he was necessary. He had always been necessary. Once or twice in the week since Borden had gone, Annar's wife tried to comfort him. He sent her away and ceased calling for her. Rarely was he allowed so much luxury to be sullen, and he wished to take it.

"What is this swill you give me?" he asked, looking up from his plate to the face of his steward. Master Grey's face was a carefully arranged mask.

"There is nothing better, my king," he said. "The servants eat—"

"How dare you tell me what my servants eat?" Annar shouted. "I am the king! You will do better than this."

Master Grey nodded. He summoned a lesser servant with a flick of his fingers, and the man came and took Annar's plate away. "As you say, my lord," Grey answered.

Mirian was in the kitchen when Grey and the flustered servant entered it.

The cook nearly exploded at the sight of the returned dish. "It's not good enough," Grey said.

"And what am I do to about that?" the cook asked. "You show me a better bird, and I'll cook it—he should be grateful he's eating fowl; the rest of us—"

"I know what the rest of you are eating," Master Grey said. "Salt it. Dress it up a little differently. Just so he doesn't recognize it when we take it back."

Master Grey caught sight of Mirian, preparing a tray.

"How is the queen?" he asked.

"Holding little down," Mirian answered.

"No surprise," the cook said.

"At least she's trying to eat," Mirian said. Her voice was low. Grey regarded her for a moment, aware that her eyes were on her work so she did not see him. Something had changed in her—it was barely perceptible, but the change was there. The image of Mirian carrying her royal charge through the servant's quarters and up the stairs came back to him, and the steward found that a smile tugged at his weary mouth.

Mirian picked up her tray and left the kitchen, her skirts swishing around her. She walked with such a purposeful stride—such an air of command, as though she intended to get the breakfast down Lilia and keep it there. Not for the first time, Grey wondered how the slave girl had become what she was. The henpecking of his wife had not crippled her—the near-imbecility of the girl's mother had not been passed on. *The old family is in her still,* Grey thought. He blinked and looked away, to the platter the cook was thrusting under his nose. The same anemic chicken, dressed in a thick sauce made of stewed prunes.

"It will do," he said.

Mirian pushed her way into Lilia's chamber, laying the tray

down beside the wakened queen and crossing to the window to dash the curtains open. It was a clear day: blue and sun-filled, and Lilia smiled in the rays that suddenly poured over her.

"I can't eat," she told Mirian. "Just let me drink in the sun."

Mirian almost picked up the spoon she'd brought with Lilia's porridge, but she thought better of it and tapped her fingers on the tray instead. She seated herself beside Lilia, looked toward the open window, and squinted in the sun.

"It's stronger outside," she said. "I went out early this morning—it's a good light the sun gives today."

"It would be lovely not to be confined," Lilia said.

Mirian turned and looked at her queen. She frowned. "Why are you?" she asked.

"What?" Lilia asked.

"Can you walk?" Mirian asked.

Lilia hesitated a moment. "If my stomach will stay still, yes," she said.

"Then let us go out," Mirian said.

Lilia smiled and looked away. "You tease me," she said. "Annar hasn't called." Her smile faded a moment. "I don't know whether to wish he would."

"I wasn't talking about Annar," Mirian said. "Walking from this room to his chambers is not 'out.'"

"What do you mean then?" Lilia asked.

"Out!" Mirian exclaimed. She pointed to the window. "Out there, out with the sun."

Lilia looked at her, a half-puzzled frown on her face. "I don't—" she said, "I don't go out."

Mirian cleared her throat. "In all your life—" she began.

"I've always lived in a tower," Lilia said.

Mirian stopped. The words sank in slowly. "When you were a child?" she asked.

"My father wouldn't let me out," Lilia said. "Perhaps he was afraid I would run away."

"Would you?" Mirian asked.

Lilia shook her head, smiling as she often did now, with her sweet, slow smile. "No," she said. "I would have been afraid to."

"Well," Mirian said, clearing her throat again, "you may not go out. But I do. Will you go with me?"

"If you'll show me the way," Lilia answered.

*   *   *

An hour later the two slipped out the gates. Mirian knew the servants on the wall better than they did; she knew exactly when their eyes would be turned away from any activity, so they left the castle without suspicion. Both women wore heavy cloaks; Lilia's hands were gloved and her feet well covered. Mirian wore the usual rags tied around her feet; her fingers were free and cold. Still, the air felt good—exhilarating—free. The fields greeted them, snow striping the old brown furrows under a brilliant blue sky. A few hardy ravens still picked at the cold ground, looking not for worms but for the last remaining chaff. Beyond the fields, the woods rose up dark and distant. The wind blew from them, carrying the scent of cedar and snow with it.

Lilia walked slowly forward. She turned and smiled at Mirian, a smile that touched her grey eyes and made a child of her. "It's beautiful," she said.

"It is no castle," Mirian agreed. "That is why I like it. In the spring and summer it is green and alive, and you can watch the hunters returning from the forest. In the fall there is harvest to be brought in. These fields are better to us than stone and towers could be."

They walked side by side a little while, into the fields. The air was cold enough to make their faces tingle, but the wind when it blew was not harsh, and the sky overhead was blue enough to make them forget the cold.

"I am surprised you have never run away," Lilia said, suddenly.

Mirian lowered her eyes. "You forget that slaves do not have rights no matter how far they run," she said. "They would hunt me down and make me regret it."

"Do you fear that?" Lilia asked. "I am surprised."

Mirian looked at her companion. "No," she said. "I don't fear it. I stay here because—this is home."

"But you have no family," Lilia said. "No ties to keep you here."

Mirian looked away. They stood in silence until Lilia began to grow worried; then Mirian turned back to her and said, "Come this way. I want to show you something."

*   *   *

The gnarled branches of the tree striped the ground with shadows. Lilia stepped gingerly over its roots, steadying herself with one hand on its great trunk. Mirian had already found her place; she leaned back into the tree's embrace and closed her eyes. The wind blew up again; spicing the air evergreen; chilling the shadows. Lilia waited.

When Mirian opened her eyes again, they were clear and

calm. "This is the tie that keeps me here," Mirian said. "My family is buried—here." She pointed to a spot under the branches of the tree, then to another. "And here—there—my father is there, and my brothers are here."

She stepped away from the ridges that had protected her, moving to a place some five feet from the tree. There was nothing to mark the ground; no stone or wooden stave, but Mirian was precisely sure of it. She looked down at the ground beneath her feet.

"My mother is here," she said. Something caught in her voice as she spoke. She cleared her throat, shaking her head, but did not raise her eyes.

"I'm sorry," Lilia said.

Mirian looked up. Her eyes had clouded over. She smiled and brushed a tear away with the back of her hand. "They are not good ties, perhaps," she said. "They are all dead. But I have no one living, not anywhere. So this tree is the best I can do."

Lilia moved forward, carefully navigating the tangle of roots, and laid her hand on Mirian's arm. They regarded each other a long time, eyes speaking understanding.

"I am glad you did not run away," Lilia said.

Mirian nodded: an awkward, hasty nod. Abruptly she raised her hand to cover Lilia's.

"I have not been glad," Mirian whispered. "I have never been glad of anything."

Lilia smiled. "I understand," she said.

*   *   *

There was blood on the wind. Taerith could smell it. It made the horses snort and shake their heads.

Kardas's eyes were narrowed. "The tribesmen are close," he said.

Taerith regarded his companion silently. He had wondered about Kardas—about the half-mistrust with which the others sometimes regarded him; about whatever it was that simmered under the surface of his face. He had wondered, until he had seen one of the raiders. They had caught the man at night while he raided a sheep cote, but his two companions got away.

He could have been Kardas's brother.

"Loyalty lies where there is debt, not only where blood is shared," Kardas had answered to Taerith's question. Taerith asked no more.

The road wound its way through scrub and open fields. The thick forest lay behind them. In the rise and fall of the rocky terrain there were many places for men to hide and many places for a horse to twist its leg and fall. The land made Taerith uneasy. He rode with a frown, listening. Nothing met his ears but the clop of hooves, yet the smell—sharp and cloying—was unmistakable.

He dismounted suddenly. He left the road, stepping slowly and lightly over the frostbitten ground. A line of boulders rose up to meet him. The first had a natural ledge in its side; he stepped up and peered over. His heart beat faster. What had looked from the road like shadows from the boulders was in fact a ravine, plunging some seven feet down. Directly below him he could make out the shape of an animal carcass—the source of the smell.

He turned his head west, eyes following the ravine as it paralleled the road. It only took him a minute to see them. At least six men, long dark hair bound in braids, huddled in a knot of bare skin and animal furs where the ravine widened. Borden had just reached the point in the row directly opposite them.

As Taerith watched, one of the men crawled above the others. The knife clenched between the man's teeth told Taerith all he needed to know. He ran forward, across the tops of the boulders, and shouted, "In the ravine!"

Borden's horse neighed as he jerked back on the reins, stopping the line. His sword was already in his hand as he pointed toward Taerith and shouted "There!" His men turned their heads, forgetting their confusion in shouts as the first of the tribesmen emerged from the ravine. Tridian notched an arrow and let it fly. It missed the barbarian but got another in the shoulder as he climbed out behind the first.

Taerith was nearly above the huddle of wild men when something hit him from behind. The force of it pushed him forward, and his heart beat wildly as he fought to keep his balance. He turned his head and looked back down the ravine: straight down through the gloom to the shaft of an arrow pointed directly at him. He threw himself away, hitting the ground as the arrow whizzed over his head. He scrambled up and ran toward Kardas and the other men, who were even now engaging the barbarians hand-to-hand. He had seen enough. There were others in the ravine, coming from behind, enough to even out the odds.

His arm came up, sword in hand, blocking a spear-thrust as one of the wild men turned to meet him in the field before he reached the road. The man roared and pulled out his sword. He swung it; Taerith ducked. The man was unbalanced by his swing. Taerith buffeted him on the side with the flat of his sword, and his adversary fell, gasping for breath. Taerith left him on the ground and sprinted to the road.

Kardas had finished off two men and was facing another. Taerith sheathed his sword as he ran and leaped onto the man's back, one arm over the barbarian's eyes and the other around his neck. Kardas dealt him a blow to the knees, and while he staggered, Taerith jumped off his back and shoved him off the road. He rolled down the rocky incline.

Borden's war cry broke over the sounds of the scuffle, and his soldiers joined him: whooping, calling, yelling, grunting, they drove the barbarians off the road and back toward the ravine. Taerith ran up through the ranks, fighting to reach Borden.

"There are others!" he yelled, pointing back in the direction where had seen them. Borden caught Taerith's eye from his perch atop his horse, and nodded. He spurred his horse forward, driving the barbarians backwards until they tripped over the boulders and toppled back into the ravine. With his horse's forelegs standing atop the boulders, Borden blew his battle horn and pointed energetically toward the hidden barbarians. His men caught his meaning. Arrows, rocks, knives rained down. The hidden tribesmen had waited too long to emerge. They were beaten before they could react.

Borden and his men returned to the road, laughing and wiping away dirt and blood. Borden spit from atop his horse and looked down at Taerith.

"Good man," he said. "You gave us the advantage."

He rode off. Taerith stayed in the road, watching his leader ride away. The others remounted and followed him. Taerith still stood, as the bodies of horses and men jogged away on either side of him.

Kardas approached, the reins of two horses in his hand. He looked at Taerith a long moment.

"How many men did you kill?" he asked.

Taerith looked away. His shoulder was bleeding. A minor cut; he hadn't noticed it before. He touched it and brought his fingertips away black and red with dirt and blood.

"How many?" Kardas asked.

"I don't know," Taerith answered.

"You can't fight a bloodless war," Kardas told him. He handed Taerith his reins. "Look at yourself. You kill or they'll kill you."

Taerith mounted. The others had drawn ahead of them. They'd have to catch up. The field was eerily quiet. The wet-rust smell of blood was stronger than ever. The ravine became visible as they rode farther on, the boulders clearing away and making the gash in the ground plain.

"Why didn't they come out?" Taerith asked suddenly. "They could have evened it out. Given their fellows a better chance at victory."

"The other tribesmen?" Kardas asked.

"Yes."

"They don't think like that," Kardas said. "It's every man for himself. They weren't ready to emerge, so they didn't."

Overhead, a hawk keened. Taerith watched it as it circled above the field, drawn by the smell. He wondered what it could see, down in the ravine.

He fingered his sword hilt. It was slick with sweat and blood. Whose, he didn't know. The answer to Kardas's question was plain enough to him: he had not, with own hands, killed a single man.

Shades of Braedoch tugged at his heart. Taerith the fisherman, tending his river nets in the green glade. Taerith the thinker, never one to act rashly. The hawk called out again.

Taerith raised his eyes and whispered, "Deus with wings, let me see what You see."

Chapter Fourteen

Snow.

Snow swirled down into his dreams.

A tower, tall and grey in a greyer sky. Doves flying all around it. And something else—dark red and sinuous, vining up the tower. No, not a vine—its scaled body moved. Taerith stood at the base and looked up, but the snow swirled down and marred his vision. Doves' wings, snowflakes, blinding him; he strained to see… the red thing moved. He drew his sword. The hilt was cold and covered with dried blood. Black in the world of white and grey. His fingers cleaved to it.

"Wake up."

The voice was Kardas's, low and spoken near his ear. Taerith was awake in an instant, blinking away the snowflakes. The snow-fall was gentle: big flakes, falling softly. They made a shining halo around the moon and mixed with the smoke of the campfire.

"What is it?" Taerith asked, reaching beneath his cloak for his sword. His arm was stiff. His whole shoulder and neck ached when he moved. He ignored the pain.

"Something is wrong," Kardas said. He had been only half-roused, propped up on his hands, when he called Taerith awake.

Now he rose slowly, eyes sweeping the camp. Taerith turned his head and searched the night likewise. Nothing. There was nothing. No smell, no sound. Only one of the soldiers, standing sentry near the fire, silently watching the snow fall.

A flicker of movement beyond the dying firelight. Both men saw it at once. Taerith scrambled to his feet. Something leaped out of the darkness: a flash of grey, and the sentry went down with a scream of pain and fear. Kardas was already running, Taerith on his heels. The thing snarled, snapped; the sentry cried out again. The soldiers awakened, swearing and reaching for their swords.

Another movement, another flash of grey—to the left this time, only feet away from Taerith. Another cry. This time the creature was met with a sword, and it jumped back. Into the firelight, where they could see it.

Wolf. The snow fell across its grey pelt and gleaming black eyes; the snow made it something unreal. It was huge, as big as a pony. Huge and hungry. The snow couldn't obscure the way the creature's ribs protruded.

Taerith stood half-crouched, circling, wary. The wolf watched him. It could smell the blood still in the men's clothes and on their weapons. The smell drove it, crazed it.

The wolf lunged. Taerith leaped aside, narrowly missing the animal's teeth as they snapped at his arm. It turned, growling deep within its throat. The fire behind it flared as the scuffle with the other wolf knocked kindling onto the flames. Taerith looked up for a split second. In the next the wolf was on him.

He could feel its teeth in his shoulder as its weight bore him to the ground. Pain stabbed through his arm. Teeth clenched, he jammed his hand beneath the wolf's jaw and pushed with all his strength, trying to keep it away from his throat. The wolf tightened its grip on his shoulder and he cried out. For a moment there was nothing in the world but shadows: moving, rushing all around him, through the snow and the flaring firelight.

The wolf let go and howled, jerking its head away. Blood ran into Taerith's face and spilled over his hand, warm and thick. The wolf twisted itself, trying to fight its new assailant. It was no good. A seizure of pain took it and it flipped its hindquarters away, howling again.

Taerith fought the black spots that obscured his vision. He gritted his teeth against the pain, placing a bloody hand over his shoulder. He could feel something in his hand. His fingers hurt. His whole fist ached. He looked down and the shape of the sword took form in his eyes. He was still clutching its hilt.

A hand clapped down on his good shoulder, and Kardas was before him, kneeling. "Are you all right?" he asked. He was spattered with blood. The snowflakes stuck to it before they began to melt. Taerith nodded, and groaned as pain flooded through his shoulder and arm again.

Beyond Kardas, a new form took shape in the darkness. A great mound of fur and bone—the wolf lay dead. Over it stood a man with his hand still on his sword hilt, its blade thrust fast through the creature's heart.

The man raised his head and looked at Taerith. Snow swirled around the dark hair and beard. It was Borden.

*   *   *

Lilia ran her finger along the gilt edges of the book before letting it fall open in her hand. The pages rustled down, revealing carefully drawn sketches of a pine forest and its fauna, two owls and a fox. Each creature was carefully labeled with delicate, sweeping strokes. Lilia smiled as she read the lines in the central columns. Already the words were familiar to her; like a scent that brought pleasant memories. She had read them every night before falling asleep. The author's matter-of-fact assertions had a poetry of their own; his descriptions of the woodlands were stirringly familiar. Lilia had only ever known the world through the pages of books, and so the only world she was comfortable in was one tinged ever so faintly with the smell of ink.

Her stomach lurched as she reached for a cup of water beside the bed. She gave up and laid back against her pillows, closing her eyes. Her hand sought out her belly and rested there, her fingers cold but gentle against the roiling discomfort within.

Her door opened and she looked up to speak to Mirian, but it was not Mirian.

Her husband stood in the door.

Lilia drew herself up, pulling the sheets closer with one hand and smoothing them down with the other. "Welcome," she said softly.

He looked around him as though he was in some foreign place, testing the air. The look on his face indicated that he didn't like what met his senses. He came closer, more awkward in his approach than Mirian had ever been, because he wanted to look like the master of his new surroundings and succeeded only in looking like a stranger in them.

Lilia relaxed a little when he came close enough to smell. There were only traces of ale in his scent; he wasn't drunk.

He looked down at her and cleared his throat, lifting his eyes again before saying anything. He looked up, around, at the bare stone walls and the window with its partially drawn purple curtains; the white bed and the wooden chest with dresses draped over it.

"It's not much of a room," he said.

"It suits me," Lilia answered.

He cleared his throat again and waved his hand at her. He didn't meet her eyes as he spoke. "You bearing up well?"

"Well enough," she answered. "Thank you." She looked away from him—he wasn't looking back anyway—at the empty seat beside her bed. "Will you sit down?" she asked.

He looked at the chair for a moment and then shook his head. "No," he muttered. "No. I came to see…" He cut himself off. "I won't be needing you for a while," he said. "Take care of yourself. That child is all I have."

He turned and left the room, slamming the door behind him.

Lilia looked back at the book in her hands. The sketches blurred. She blinked and they came back: fine lines, beautiful dark branches. She stared at them for a few minutes without comprehending and then closed the book, slowly.

She brought both her hands to her midsection and smiled down at them. "You see, little one? Papa loves you," she whispered. "You're all either of us has."

*   *   *

Borden watched, arms folded across his chest, as Emmet went to work on Taerith's shoulder with needle and thread. Taerith was ashen-faced. His cheek, shoulders, and torso were spattered with blood—the wolf's and his own. He held a stick in both hands and tightened his grip on it as Emmet worked.

"You're very strong," Borden commented.

Taerith looked up at him, his dark hair in sweaty curls across his face. His jaw was clenched, his eyes slightly glazed, but he focused on Borden. The crown prince looked on him with approval and sympathy. "I have seen worse," Borden said. "It will heal quickly. But that's not where your strength lies—in tolerating pain. It lies in tolerating fear."

Taerith opened his mouth with calculated effort. "I have no fear," he said.

"Why not?" Borden asked. "Every man is afraid of something."

Taerith shook his head and said nothing. He breathed in sharply through his nose, and Emmet grunted. "A few more minutes, lad," he said.

"To stare into a wolf's mouth and not be undone is an impressive feat," Borden said. He unfolded his arms and began to turn away. "I am glad to have you with us."

Taerith found Borden forty minutes later, sitting by the fire.

"To kill a wolf and save a man's life is also impressive," Taerith said. "I am in your debt."

Borden looked up and half-snorted. "Don't be indebted to me, boy," he said. "The wolf was a threat to all of us."

Taerith smiled. "But I am the only one who was in its teeth when you killed it."

"True enough," Borden said, standing. He regarded the shirt Taerith had donned. It wasn't much protection against the wind, but he imagined the weight of a cloak would tear uncomfortably at the newly-sewn wounds. "Even so," he said. "You owe me nothing. You do not want to owe me."

He turned away. The land lay stretched out before him, a light snow over it. The sun had risen on a cold day. The clouds were low and ominous like veins of ice in a still-water sky. It looked familiar—all of it. So familiar. He wondered how long it would be till they faced the wild men again. Somehow they needed to find them in greater numbers, great enough that to defeat them would send all the barbarians a message instead of just punishing a few renegades. If only they would gather together and fight like an army of men instead of roaming like carrion crows.

Familiar.

It had been so many years since the day Corran had first lost control of its northern border, yet as Borden looked out over the frozen plain it seemed that he could still see them—the small army his father had amassed to repel the barbarians, the contingent Hosten had sent to help them. He could see the slaughtered bodies lying in the frost the morning after their last fight. The sounds of the camp behind him became the echo of hoofbeats, the jingle of tack and the shouts of men—his own shouts—as they came upon their companions.

The wind was cold in Borden's face, but he did not turn away. Memory gripped him. There—a dark patch on the earth. Dark with the stain of blood. His father had lain there. He had taken him up in his own arms, pulled him close, trying to feel warmth—breath—something.

The wind had been even colder that day. It had whipped at his hair and stung his face and his eyes as he raised them to his brother, astride his horse, as Annar rode up and looked down on them.

Whatever he had shouted that day, the wind had carried it away. He couldn't remember the words. All he could remember was the raw pain in his throat as he ripped the words from his throat and flung them at Annar; as pain and grief rose up and choked him.

He could remember Annar's words, shouted down through the wind.

"This is not my fault."

"My lord?" Taerith's voice intruded into his memories, cutting them off. Borden jerked his gaze from the empty field and riveted his eyes on Taerith.

"Pardon me," Taerith asked. "But… are you injured in some way?"

Borden made no answer.

"You're shaking," Taerith said, his voice apologetic.

He was. Borden looked down at his own hands and saw the way he shook. He folded his arms, tucking his hands close to his body. It did not help. The shaking came from within. From the memories.

"It's nothing," Borden said. "It's the cold. Go… find Kardas. Prepare to go home."

Taerith bent his head, as though the wind had blocked his hearing and he did not trust the words that had come from Borden's mouth. "Sir?" he asked.

"You're not fit to fight until you've healed up," Borden said. "You can't do it riding with us. Kardas will see you home before he rejoins us."

His eyes wandered back to the field even as he spoke. Emotion was heaving within him; rising up to harshen his words and make his voice gruff. He stiffened himself, willing the shaking to cease. It was still there: the past, lying before him in the field where no other could see it.

It *had* been Annar's fault—the bloody result of Annar's strategic blunder. And that very night Borden and a coterie of priests had crowned him king. Nothing in life was so vile as the atmosphere in the battle tent the night they set the crown on Annar's head… the atmosphere that still poisoned the air three days later when the new king signed his kingdom into the bondage of tribute to Hosten, so that the neighbouring boar would protect Corran while Annar went home in his father's stead to drink and feast upon the throne, pretending that the threat in the north had been dealt with.

Borden turned and looked at the little camp his men had erected. A few tents, sleeping rolls spread on the ground, horses staked around the perimeter. The wind blew the dull green pennants of the camp wildly. The ground was blood-stained near the black remains of the night's fire. A wolf howled somewhere far off, and the wind carried the sound into the camp.

"Such an inheritance you left me, brother," Borden said. He bowed his head in his bitterness. It hurt to send Taerith away. There were so few men without him.

And the wild men would not stay hidden in the ravines forever.

*　*　*

His wine-coloured cloak billowed around him as the priest walked down the mid-street of the village. Early morning light cast a pallor on the dust of the road. Children and dogs scattered away from his coming, both eyeing him with distrust. He noted their retreat with approval. They were thin. Dogs and children both. Thin and haggard and begrimed with want.

He walked out of the town, up the sloping road toward the forest. A muscle in his face twitched as he passed beneath the evergreen branches. A wind blew in them, moving the branches behind him as though something walked on his heels. A sudden disturbance above jerked his eyes upward. A crow took to flight, a thin branch bobbing behind it, its sweeping black wings leaving the pine needles aquiver.

A half-hidden path led off the road and down a steep slope, toward the stink of standing water, leaves still rotting in its half-frozen depths. A shallow bog lay before him, but he skirted it and ducked into the opening of a cave.

He stepped into the darkness, ignoring the few torches that leaned against the cave wall just inside the entrance. The opening led sharply down, plunging into stillness and an utter lack of light. He walked down, not even steadying himself against the wall. The darkness soothed him. The wind did not disturb him here. Nothing dared follow Meronane into his den.

Without warning the floor leveled out and the close walls disappeared. The ground beneath his feet was hard-packed dirt. The cavern smelled: a wet, musty, rotting smell, not unmixed with the old drying smell of blood. Meronane followed a familiar rut to the center of the cavern. He did not have to bump into the chair to know it was there, though the darkness was too deep for any eye's adjustment, and he turned and sank into it, resting his elbows on its wooden arms while he folded his hands before him and waited.

Half an hour passed.

Above, a light was struck. A torch flared to life. Its sound reached the cavern. Meronane looked up.

Footsteps in the tunnel. Two men. They entered the cavern, their faces masked, a single torch between them. It flickered on the cavern ceiling and danced shadows on the walls, catching the red stripes that marked the surface with jagged lines. The men took their places against the wall without a word.

Again, they waited. Again, the sound of striking flint made its way into the depths of the cave. A light appeared, bobbing through the darkness. One, two, three men this time. Again, they took their places. Silence.

It went on for an hour. Meronane waited, his fingers laced, his eyes lifted to the tunnel exit. He did move or speak a word till every man had arrived. Eighteen in all.

At last Meronane stood. He was a tall man, powerfully built and broad. His cloak fell across his shoulders as he stood, encasing him. He lifted his hands. A long knife, encased in a wine-red leather sheath, was in them. He pulled the sheath away slowly, revealing its sharp edge and curving beauty. Twelve torches flickered in the hands of their carriers, reflecting in the blade.

"It is time," Meronane said.

The spy, who had lately spent much time in the castle and brought word to Meronane that Borden had taken himself and his men away, cleared his throat. He was a small dark man, nothing much to look at, but possessed of unusual favour with the priest.

"You have said that we should wait," he said. "The people hunger now, but soon they will hunger more. Will they willingly hail you as king while they still have corn in their cribs?"

"Yes," Meronane said. His eyes were fixed on the blade, held still before his face. "Deus has sent me dreams. We must move now, for the demon Borden will soon return."

"So quickly?" one of the men asked. "He has only just left."

Meronane turned slowly and regarded the man. "And what god has given you wisdom?" he asked. The man bowed his head and did not answer. Meronane turned back to face forward. He straightened the knife so that it pointed up, and he followed its point with his eyes and raised them to the stony ceiling.

"The devil is delivered into our hands," he said.

Chapter Fifteen

Taerith stood at the base of the tower. Its grey stones appeared nearly white, etched across a starless sky black as pitch. He was staring up, to the pinnacle where a single window opened a dark hole in the stone: lonely window, with a tattered bit of purple curtain blowing at the behest of an unfelt wind.

Lightning flashed, and Taerith saw a long, sinuous body, wine red against the stark white of the stones: a serpent, winding up the tower. As he looked up, the snake reached the window. It disturbed a tiny flock of doves. They left their roost in the windowsill with a blinding flash of wings, and suddenly from their feathers snow was falling again, into Taerith's eyes, white assailants that blinded him. He lurched forward, trying to pull out a sword that would not come, and reached out to lay hold of the red body that he could see like a gash through the snow. But as he touched it, it changed: no longer red scales, no more malevolent life; the red now was that of blood running down from the window, hot over the back of his hand.

Taerith woke with a gasp. His body was warm; far too warm for a winter's night; he felt as though some great pressure was bearing down on him. He could hardly breathe. He could see neither stars nor moon. Instead it seemed as though a great wing lay over him, feathers overlapping and powerful, life pulsing through them. The wine red colour of the snake flashed before him. His memory conjured an image to match: a cloak, worn by the evil priest Meronane.

In a trice it was gone, and he could see a clear moon in the cold sky overhead.

"Kardas!" He rolled over, searching the gloom for his companion. Both lay with their feet nearly in the ashes of the fire. Kardas was awake almost as soon as his name left Taerith's mouth, and just as quickly was on his feet, crouched in the last glow of the fire. Taerith also rose, grimacing as pain lanced through his stiff shoulder.

"Return to Borden," Taerith said. "Tell him Meronane is going to attack the castle. We need men."

Kardas cocked his head. "How do you know this?" he asked.

"I dreamed it," Taerith answered. His hand strayed to his bandaged shoulder. His fingers plucked for a moment at the bandages, as though he would tear them away and the wounds with them. He clenched his fingers into a fist and pulled his hand away. "Go quickly; find Borden and bring as many men as you can."

"And you?"

"I will ride on tonight," Taerith said. "I don't know how much time we have."

Kardas's eyes went to Taerith's torn shoulder and narrowed. He was silent. He nodded curtly. "I will rejoin you soon," he said. "Meronane's men are not children. Fight wisely."

"I will," Taerith answered. "Thank you."

Kardas rose without another word. Within minutes he had mounted his horse. He urged it to a gallop, and Taerith was left alone with the embers of the fire, staring into the darkness where his friend had disappeared.

His horse whinnied and stepped into the meager light. Taerith turned, gathered up his cloak from the ground, and laid his hand on the horse's warm neck. For a split second he was filled again with heat; a pressure in the air gathered around his heart and urged him forward. He mounted, drew a deep breath, and plunged into the night.

*　*　*

The sun had only begun to rise when the rear men called out that someone was coming. The dark shape of horse and rider rose up from the low roads in the south, riding furiously. Borden knew them, both from the hue of the horse and from the rider's skillful abandon. He didn't wait for them to approach, taking to the road on foot. His stride turned into a half-run. Some of the soldiers, seeing him go, drew their swords and followed.

The mouth and flanks of Kardas's horse were flecked with foam as he reined it to a stop only feet away from Borden.

"What is it?" Borden demanded. "Have you been ambushed?"

"No," Kardas answered. "Taerith has gone on. He sent me to bid you back to the castle; Meronane will attack."

Borden was speechless for a moment, and his face darkened with anger.

"And how do you pretend to know this?"

"Taerith dreamed it," Kardas answered.

"You have come to take me away from our real enemies on the strength of a dream?" Borden asked. "You are as superstitious as your people."

Kardas looked down on him, dark face impassive. "My ancestry does not make me wrong," he said. "Meronane will attack. I feel it."

"There are men to defend the castle," Borden said.

"Not enough," Kardas said. He swung down from his saddle, landing lightly in the road, and crossed his arms over his chest. "Return," he said. "The castle needs you."

Borden turned away. Emmet stood in the road just behind him, a look of discomfort on his bristled face.

"If you go, my lord," Emmet said in a low voice, "we will press the battle here."

"You think I should listen to this?" Borden snapped.

"It is Kardas," Emmet said.

Borden cast a glance over his shoulder. Kardas had not moved. He still stood in the road, his black horse panting beside him, looking as dark and dangerous as a whole tribe of barbarians in the body of one man.

"I am no believer in superstition," Emmet said. "But you know as well as I that Kardas can smell the future on the wind, and he knows Meronane better than any man alive."

"And Taerith?" Borden said. "How many prophets am I cursed with?"

Emmet looked down. "I will hold the battle here," he said, "if you choose to go. Take as many men as you need."

A cold wind had begun to blow. Borden thought he could hear battle cries in it. Kardas still waited.

"Curse it all," Borden said.

*   *   *

The dim light of the rising sun hardly reached through the thick branches and dead leaves of the swamp. Taerith gritted his teeth as his horse stepped carefully through the thin layer of ice over muck, jarring his shoulder every time the ground sank beneath its hooves. The urgency had not left him: it flocked at his heels, pushing him forward. Movement was too slow through the swamp. Where the road was he did not know; he had lost it in the dark. His shoulder burned and itched; the cold, poisonous air of the swamp filled his lungs with its inhospitality.

Twin thoughts pulled at his mind: foremost, an image of the tower with its serpentine attacker; an image that focused his mind on Lilia. He could see her as he rode, grey eyes fearful on the night he had rescued her from attackers by the side of the road, her face sweet and hopeful through her fears. He had stayed to protect Lilia, to be a friend to her, and against his better judgment left to ride north with Borden. The other image was that of Kardas, looking intently at him in the emberlight, accepting his word without question, and riding into the darkness.

The pain in his shoulder mocked him. If Kardas was not successful, he had little chance of defeating the serpent alone.

Spurred by his thoughts, he urged his horse to move more quickly. The animal obeyed, all but leaped forward. Taerith felt its feet slip; the horse's cry of pain split the air even as its hooves churned the icy water, and as its wrenched ankle gave way, Taerith was thrown to one side.

The shock of cold water hit him even as pain burned through his neck, shoulder, and side. He scrambled to get out of the stinking mire, water soaking his pants and part of his shirt, mud spattered everywhere, weighing down his cloak. Tears filled his eyes as he used a dead branch to pull himself out. His horse made no sound. It could not rise; he could see that clearly enough. Cursing himself for his carelessness, he waded back into the water and drew his sword. It was the work of a few moments to end the horse's life.

Blinking away stinging tears of frustration, he clambered back onto solid ground. He set his teeth to keep them from chattering, wrung water from his clothes as best he could, and set out on foot.

*　　*　　*

Mirian watched the sun set from atop the castle parapet, a shawl wrapped tightly around her shoulders. Her long hair blew behind her as she looked into the cold, dying light. The guards were playing dice to the left of her; their jests and comments went unheard.

She was uneasy.

Mistress Grey had relieved her of her duties for a few hours, but she could not get Lilia off of her mind. Despite cook's assurance that it was perfectly normal for a woman with child to be weak and sick, she had hoped to see Lilia gain some strength back by now. Yet, after their one visit to the tree in the field, Mirian had been afraid she would have to carry Lilia up the stairs again… and she'd grown worse in the last few days. Something had happened to sap the girl again. It had something to do with Annar, Mirian was almost certain. He had been in Lilia's room one day and had not called for her since.

A flock of carrion crows in the field below flew up suddenly, cawing and squabbling over something beneath them. They distracted Mirian for a moment, pulling her out of her worries. It was a waste of energy, worry. Of all the emotions she'd felt in her life, worry was a strange one to her. She disliked it.

Repressing a sigh, she turned away from the parapet and started down the stone steps to the courtyard.

*   *   *

Meronane signaled for two of his men to approach. They came, one on either side of him. His eyes remained fixed on the castle wall, where the slave girl had left an empty place. A man rose and moved along the ledge, his movement clearly visible from the place where Meronane watched.

The man on his left spoke. "Thirty minutes more, and both guards will abandon their post for a meal," he said. "They are worse than worthless."

"But of great worth to us," Meronane said with a smile. "The other servants, you feel, will be equally as easy."

"They will join us, some of them," the man said.

"But not that one," Meronane said, indicating the empty place on the wall.

"She is no friend to anyone," the man answered.

"I think we will not kill her, nonetheless," Meronane said. "The devil was right to keep her in his den. Last scions of old races can sometimes be useful with the people."

"And if not, they make handsome trophies," the man answered. The memory of Mirian's accosting him in the stairwell beneath the tower still rankled him.

"Thirty minutes more." Meronane raised his voice slightly so that the others, his small army of twelve men, could hear him. "In thirty minutes you will take your places, and then we wait for the full moon. The kingdom has very nearly come."

Rachel Starr Thomson   175

*   *   *

Mistress Grey still held sway over the tower and Lilia, and Mirian waited restlessly at the bottom of the steps for a quarter of an hour before wandering through the castle corridors again. To the kitchen, to the stairs, to the steward's quarter.

"You are usually glad for your freedom," Master Grey said with a slight twinkle in his eye. Mirian did not answer him, looking down at her feet instead.

"My wife does know how to care for the queen, probably better than you do," Master Grey said.

"I like freedom, not idleness," Mirian said.

Master Grey threw her a tablet with markings all over it.

"Then make yourself useful. Tally that."

Mirian looked down at it for a moment before laying it on a table and pulling her shawl closer to her. "I can't read," she said.

"That's right," Master Grey said. "We didn't teach you that. You're a slave, Mirian. When they want you idle, be idle, and be content."

She let out an impatient snort and turned on her heel. She followed her feet until they took her back outside. The moon, full and stark, was beginning its climb in the cold sky. She shivered. There was something in the air deeper than cold; something she hated but could not place.

A scuffling noise met her ears from the corner of the courtyard. She turned, trying to seek out the shadows for its source. She saw nothing—but there, a movement. Someone was there. Before she could call out to know who it was, the chill of the night sank deeper than her skin.

Something was wrong.

"Jerran?" she called out to one of the guards, searching the parapet for him.

There was no answer, nor did any familiar form meet her eyes.

Slowly, eyes searching on the courtyard shadows, she reached behind her till her fingers met the cold stone of the door frame, then backed up until she was safely inside. She turned, took her skirts in hand, and raced toward the tower stairs.

*   *   *

Lilia's eyes were closed, but she could still see the candle that burned beside her. Mistress Grey was just gone, finally, leaving exhaustion in the wake of her brusque manners and busy tending. Lilia had found the strength to speak voluntarily to her only once, and she smiled a little to remember it.

"The slave who tends you treats you well enough, I suppose?" Mistress Grey said, voice dripping with sarcasm.

"Like a queen," Lilia had answered.

Mistress Grey confined her questions to health after that, not daring to mention Mirian again.

The door of the tower room burst open. Lilia opened her eyes to see Mirian enter like a contained hurricane. She began to smile in welcome, but the storm in Mirian's eyes quelled the smile.

"What is it?" Lilia asked, straightening.

"I don't know," Mirian said. She went to the window and stuck her head half-out, searching the darkness. They were too high; she could see nothing.

She had just begun to turn away when a sound reached them from below. Lilia's heart leaped to her throat. Someone had screamed. The sound was followed by shouts, hardly legible at such a distance, but Mirian's throat tightened as she made out the words, "To the king!"

Slowly, noiseless as a panther, she crossed the floor to the chest where Lilia's dresses were still draped. Pushing them aside, she reached into the chest and drew out its last treasure.

A sword.

Chapter Sixteen

Mud sucked at Taerith's legs as he struggled through the swamp. The gloom had deepened with the setting sun until there was no light, not even a glimmer to light his way. He pulled against the mud, arms held out before him to brush away the low-hanging branches that tore at his clothing when he got too close. Reeking swamp; pounding heart; cold… it was so cold. His feet broke thin panes of ice with every step. The shards caught in his clothing. Fear beat where his heart should be: Lilia, the castle, Meronane…

An owl called, and Taerith pushed aside a branch. His fingers slipped. The branch snapped back and caught him in the shoulder, ripping away bandaging. He caught a cry between his teeth. The wound began to bleed.

"Deus!" he shouted. The swamp was too close, too thick even to bear his own voice back to him. "Where are you? Help me! Guide me!" His eyes were full of tears, pain and panic springing up to obscure his vision and sting the scratches on his face.

The last word had barely escaped his mouth when a sound met his ears, scattering around him like a broken echo. Hoofbeats. Voices… did he imagine them? The drum of horse's hooves sounded not in water or mud but on a hard, packed road.

"Here!" he shouted, stumbling forward. "Here, I'm here!" Another sound came: the swoop of wings, the ghostly call of an owl. The bird swept down from the trees above him. It was white. It seemed to bear moonlight on its wings, to shed light on the evil slough beneath it. Taerith lurched after it, fighting the mud and water and ice.

Before his eyes the ground rose: a hill; atop it, a road. Wooden staves and stones shored it up again the swamp's encroachment. Taerith laid hold of one of the staves and pulled himself out of the mire. Hands on his knees, he pushed himself up to his full height and looked toward the now-unmistakable sound of hoofbeats.

*　　*　　*

Meronane watched as his men shoved the guard to his knees and jerked his head back. The young man's eyes were wild with fright.

"Please," he begged, "please, don't hurt me."

"How many are there guarding the castle?" Meronane asked.

"Few," the young man choked. "Six… six and the servants, not enough to stand in your way."

The men of the Path watched their leader's face for direction. Crackling torchlight glared in the whites of the prisoner's eyes.

"Let us bring down the odds even further," he said. He turned his back. As his wine-coloured robes settled about him, he heard the knife plunge. His breath came a little faster as his fingers closed over the hilt of his sword. A smile pulled at his lips, twitching, convulsing. He stood on the wall, facing the courtyard, and his eyes swept up to the tower where the queen slept.

"There are only five soldiers left," Meronane said. "Unless he was lying, which is likely. Deal with them; then take the servants' quarters. Let those join you who will; kill the rest. Secure the king's chambers and wait for my arrival. Curdoc, come with me."

The small, dark man who had scouted out the castle appeared at Meronane's side. The priest had not taken his eyes from the tower.

"We deal first with the devil's spawn," Meronane said. He raised his hand and beckoned two more men to his side.

*　　*　　*

Master Grey could see them on the wall, moving in the torchlight. He watched as ten of them descended the stone steps in a silent flurry of cloaks and drawn swords. Three of the guards rushed out to meet them, howling, swinging their swords.

He turned from the window. His hands shook, but his voice was steady. He pushed a heavy iron keyring into his wife's hands. "Take all of the women below," he commanded. "To the dungeon. Lock yourselves in. There are weapons in a cache; you know where. Avail yourselves of them."

"They cannot fight," Mistress Grey said, taking the keys and glancing behind her to the steward's quarters where the servants had huddled together.

"They may have to," Master Grey answered.

"The king—" his wife began.

"There are some men with him. Send the servant boys. They will have to be enough," Master Grey said. He looked down the long corridor. "I go to the queen."

Mistress Grey raised a thin, strong hand to the steward's hollow cheek.

"My husband," she said. He took her fingers with his hand, and his own ceased to shake. He removed her hand. His old eyes watered just a little. She saw the glimmer and turned away at once, clutching the iron keyring close to her wiry frame.

Master Grey crossed the hall and pushed a threadbare tapestry away from the hole it concealed. Within was a sword: old, long unused, but sharp. He took it out and looked at it for a moment, then pulled the blade free of its cover, dropped the sheath on the floor, and jogged in the direction of the tower.

*　*　*

"Taerith!" Kardas reined in abruptly, putting up his sword as his horse turned a circle on the swamp road. His dark eyes took in the filthy, bloody form of his friend.

"You did not reach the castle," Borden said. "Then they are unwarned."

"Take me up," Taerith said. "We have no time to waste. Meronane is already there." His voice was tight with pain, with conviction.

Kardas held his horse still while Taerith mounted behind him, ignoring the searing pain in his shoulder. Kardas could smell the night's struggle in his friend. The reek of swamp and blood was sharp.

"Ha!" Borden kicked his horse. Kardas soundlessly followed. They thundered down the road toward the castle.

*　*　*

"Down, down!" Mistress Grey whispered, her voice dry and barking over the stone dungeon steps. The servant women cringed as they descended into the stinking darkness. They stumbled down the stairs and cried as the shadows folded over them.

Mistress Grey's hand found a torch. She lit it and hefted it high. The dungeon doors had closed behind her; she did not fear discovery now. A sword hung at her waist; a knife was tucked into her belt. She herded the castle women ahead of her without mercy, denying even to herself the acrid bite of fear that drove her.

"Keep going!" she commanded, as the women bunched together at the bottom of the stairs. "Deeper in, or they'll find you." She all but pushed them forward.

A male voice suddenly boomed out from the darkness before them.

"What's going on?"

One of the servant girls shrieked and nearly fainted. Mistress Grey pinched her arm. "Hold yourself together," she commanded. She held the torch higher, but its light didn't reach to the end of the tight corridor.

"Who are you?" she asked.

"Joachim, the priest," answered the voice. "What's going on?"

"We are attacked by the Narrow Path," Mistress Grey said. "Can you fight?"

"Yes," Joachim said. "Give me a sword."

Mistress Grey snatched a blade from the swooning servant girl. She marched forward in the darkness, thrusting the torch ahead of her until it illuminated the dripping bars of a cell, and beyond it, the bearded, filthy form of the priest. He sat in a mess of straw against a wall of clay and rock. Etchings marked every inch of the wall around him: words, tally marks, numbers, pictures. He seemed to be at the center of a strange illumination, inked onto the vellum of some old book.

"We can trust you?" Mistress Grey asked.

"To help you? Yes," said the priest.

Mistress Grey pulled a heavy key from her belt and fit it into the door. With a twist and a clank, it opened. She grasped one of the bars and pulled the heavy door open wide enough to let a man through.

"In here, please," Joachim said. "My ankle is also chained or I would be at your side by now."

Mistress Grey heard the gasps and cries of the girls behind her as she marched through the door, into the cold, damp air of the cell. She pushed mouldy straw aside as she searched for the priest's ankle. In moments she had unshackled him. He stood, one hand against the wall to support him, too slowly for her liking. He stretched and tested his weight with a groan. He looked up at her, and his eyes twinkled. "I will be well enough in a minute," he said. "Give me that sword."

*　　*　　*

Ten men of the Path swept through the corridors of the castle like a dark-hued wind. The doors of the servant's quarters were locked against them.

The biggest of the men, a leader and favourite with Meronane, beat the hilt of his sword against the wood. "Cowards," he said. He grinned, lifted his foot to the doors, pushing with all his might. The doors cracked and groaned before his weight.

He stepped back and waved the others forward. Three of them charged at the doors, shoulders first, swords in hand. The locks gave way before them. The doors burst open and the men of the Path stepped into the room, deliberately, unhurried.

The servant men stood against the wall on the other side of the room, huddled together.

"Women," the big man spat. "Who among you wretches is man enough to join us?"

No one moved. The big man smiled.

"Come now," he said. "We are only going to kill Annar. What loyalty has the devil earned from any of you?"

A man stumbled forward from the servants' ranks. His face was flushed. "I'll join you," he said. Two others followed. "And I."

"The rest of you?" the big man asked. He raised his sword. "The rest of you die."

A knife whistled through the air and lodged itself in the big man's shoulder. He bellowed with rage and pain and whirled around. A brown-robed figure stood in the doorway, bearded face hot, bare feet spread in battle-stance. He held a naked sword in his hand. He looked past the Path to the servants.

"Where is your courage?" Joachim shouted. "In the name of God, get up and fight like men!"

Two men of the Path closed in on the young priest. He met them with confidence, but he was weak: he met their blows, but staggered beneath them. One of the servants, galvanized by the sight, unsheathed his own sword and ran into the fray with a yell. His fellows followed after him. Three servants fell in minutes, prey to the practiced skill of the Path. The others fought their way through so that they stood between the Path and the doors, blocking their way to the king.

"Deus, lend us aid!" Joachim called.

*   *   *

Master Grey hurried through the corridor, shuddering as the shouts and clashes of battle reached him. The servants had been found. For a moment he wondered how many would stay loyal, but he pushed the thought aside. What did it matter? His only hope was that some of them would live.

"God help them," he whispered.

He reached the base of the tower and started up the steps. His heart pounded in his old chest as he rounded one corner. He stopped, his eyes widening. Two men stood in his way. Their swords were sheathed beneath long cloaks; their arms folded across their chests.

"Where are you going, old man?" one of them asked.

Master Grey forced his courage to speak. "I am going to my queen," he said.

The man shook his head. "On the contrary," he said, "you are turning around, and going back to your quarters. Lock yourself in. I won't kill a grey head."

"My business is up there," Master Grey said.

"I am sorry," the man said. "But you'll have to wait until Meronane has finished with his."

*   *   *

Mirian's hand trembled slightly. Her eyes were fixed on the door. She held the sword with one hand, the blade extended, tip pointed at the door. She tensed with every footstep from beyond its wooden face.

Behind her, Lilia tried to speak. Mirian silenced her with a raise of her hand.

"Stay where you are," she said. Her voice was low, even in her own ears. The footsteps were louder to her than her own words.

Lilia, on her knees behind the bed in the farthest corner of the room, could only nod. The tears in her eyes were frozen: suspended in pain as her heart twisted within her. Her hand rested over her womb.

A hand tried the door. The lock stopped the intruder from entering.

Mirian forced her hand to stop trembling.

Something heavy came down on the door. The wood shuddered and cracked, but the door held. Mirian's throat tightened as she steeled herself.

The door splintered as the lock gave way beneath the force of a second blow. Sword hilt and hand came through the wood, and the door was kicked open.

Malevolent eyes met Mirian from beneath a wine-coloured hood. Meronane cocked an eyebrow as the dark man beside him all but rubbed his hands together. The priest's eyes dismissed Mirian in an instant and roved the room.

"You are looking in the wrong place," Mirian said. "I am here."

Meronane's eyes came back to Mirian. "You are not the one I wish to deal with," he said.

"And what does that matter?" Mirian asked. "It is me you will deal with, whether you wish to or not."

"I seek only the queen of this place," Meronane said.

"To that title, I have the prior right," Mirian answered.

"Yes," Meronane said. "So you do. Yet here you are, defending the one who has taken your place. Defending the family that slew your fathers. You defend the devil himself."

"No," Mirian said quietly. "Only the devil's wife."

Meronane's sword lashed out so quickly Mirian barely had time to respond, but she caught the blow and deflected it. Meronane held his sword at the ready. The dark man, Curdoc, stepped up to his side. Mirian looked between them, tense, waiting for the first strike.

"You cannot win this," Meronane said. He struck again. The blow was powerful. Pain shot up Mirian's arm, and she breathed hard as she drew back. "A wise woman would lay down her arms now. God himself has sent me here."

"Then God himself will kill me," Mirian said. "I will not let you pass."

"Hmm," Meronane said. For a moment he relaxed and lowered his sword. "What if I offered to restore you? Your queen is cowering in the corner while you stand and fight. How much more do you deserve her throne?"

Involuntarily, Mirian's eyes went to Lilia. She had put one hand against the stone wall and was standing slowly. The flood of emotion in her grey eyes caught Mirian off guard. "Mirian," Lilia said.

Meronane moved too fast to block. He struck Mirian's head and neck with the flat of his blade. The strength of the blow knocked her to the ground. The edge of the blade sliced into her clothing and drew blood in a thin line across her neck and collarbone. Pain split her head. Involuntarily, her fingers convulsed and she dropped her sword with a clatter on the flagstones. Black and purple blinded her as she groped for the sword, but someone kicked her hand away. In an instant she was propelled to her feet and shoved against the wall. The tip of Meronane's blade rested in the hollow of her throat. Her vision returned, streaked with red. "Bring the creature here," Meronane snarled. Curdoc grabbed Lilia by the arm. Lilia saw the look in Mirian's eyes and pulled away. She stumbled back and grabbed the candlestick from the table beside the bed. He had nearly reached her. She threw the candlestick at him, but he knocked it away and reached for her again. She bit him. He backhanded her. Her head snapped to one side and she seemed about to fall. Curdoc moved behind her and grabbed both her arms, pushing her forward.

Meronane turned his head and drank in the sight of her, pale face flushed where Curdoc had slapped her, grey eyes glaring. His sword stayed where it was: perfectly balanced at Mirian's throat. Meronane motioned with his head, and Curdoc pushed Lilia to the wall beside Mirian. Her back was to the attackers, her cheek against the cool stone, and she turned her head so she faced Mirian.

"I'm sorry," she said.

"You will not speak," Meronane thundered. Lilia closed her eyes. Meronane continued. "You stand in the presence of a man of God. You will keep silent."

Lilia opened her eyes again and glanced at Meronane with disdain. She turned her eyes back to Mirian. "Thank you for everything," she said. She reached out with trembling fingers and touched Mirian's arm. Blood had run down from Mirian's neck, and it stained Lilia's fingers now.

Meronane's jaw twitched. Slowly, he lowered his sword. "Curdoc." The dark man appeared at his side. Meronane handed him his sword. Curdoc took it and held it at the ready, watching Mirian.

Meronane stepped forward and closed his fingers over the back of Lilia's neck. He spoke nearly in her ear. "Are you not afraid?"

The vice grip on her neck nearly stopped her, but Lilia shook her head to the extent that she could. A smile appeared on her face, ghostly and frightening. "Of a worm?" she asked.

Meronane let go of her as if she had burned him. He took her shoulder and spun her around. She pressed herself against the wall, breathing hard as Meronane reached into his cloak and drew out a hideously carved knife. She could barely stop herself from trembling. A wild light danced in her eyes, courage and fear in terrible display.

"Die," Meronane said.

Mirian saw her moment. Curdoc had looked away, drawn by the confrontation between his master and Lilia. She hurled herself forward, catching Curdoc and shoving him between Meronane and Lilia. The knife plunged deep into Curdoc's body.

Meronane turned on Mirian. The wrath in his eyes took her aback. She snatched up her sword from the floor where it had fallen, just in time to counter his first blow. He was even stronger than before: seething with rage.

"You!" A blow toward the head; she just managed to stop it. Her sword rang; she wondered that it did not shatter.

"For you I have broken my vow," Meronane snarled. He swung at her again; she jumped up onto the bed. He pulled at the blankets and wrenched them away. Mirian lost her footing. Meronane's sword ploughed straight down. She rolled away. His blow sliced into the bed, filling the air with a cloud of feathers. She raised her sword as she scrambled to her feet, taking another blow. Red and black streaked her vision again; her head ached; her feet wanted to give way.

"Lilia!" she cried, her voice breaking as she deflected another blow. This time, the tip of Meronane's sword caught her in the elbow and ripped part of her arm open. "Lilia, run!"

If Lilia answered, her voice was drowned out by the rushing in Mirian's ears. Her knees gave way as her sword caught one final blow, and she fell to her hands and knees. She tightened her fingers around the sword hilt and tried desperately to raise the weapon again.

Red and black frayed her vision until she did recognize her own hand. Her fingers loosened of their own accord. Head bowed, she waited.

A shout came through the roar. Blades clashing. Not her own.

She raised her head slowly, hand shielding her eyes. Gentle arms were around her suddenly, helping her to raise her head, keeping her from falling. She recognized Lilia's long black hair and the blood stains on her fingers.

Still someone was fighting. Sight came back in snatches. Meronane's wine-red robe, his back turned to them. He fought a dark apparition, a filthy, stinking thing, yet a man.

Three blows and it was over. Meronane lay dead at the feet of the man.

Lilia had buried her face in Mirian's shoulder. Mirian reached up and laid her fingers over Lilia's hand, comforting her. She struggled to make her eyes work. To recognize the form that stood before her.

Piercing blue eyes. Careworn eyes, compassionate. She knew him.

Taerith. She tried to speak his name, but could only smile.

Chapter Seventeen

"Grip my hand."

Kardas's voice was steady as he rested his palm over Mirian's. For all that he pressed her hand lightly, she could feel the strength waiting in his arm. She didn't answer him; didn't respond except to set her teeth.

She couldn't look in his direction without seeing her arm again. Last time she'd thought she glimpsed bone and nearly fainted again. What amazed her was how much it didn't hurt. She didn't have time to feel pain: breathing took all her attention. One breath after another.

She drew a sharp one when the needle went in. Now it hurt. Her arm tried to jerk away even as her fingers clenched Kardas's hand. He held her down.

Her eyes blurred with tears and she looked—at the arm laid open from her elbow halfway to her wrist, at the dark soldier with his vice grip, at Taerith as he carefully stitched the wound closed. The mingled smells of blood and herbs were astringent in the air.

Oh, but it hurt. She closed her eyes and let the blur seep out and wet her face.

Every muscle in her body was tense. Eyes still closed, she focused herself to find the rhythm again. Concentrate. One breath, then another.

Taerith glanced up at her. Strands of red hair stood out like curling tongues of fire across her white face. Pain glanced over her features, quickly mastered by greater determination. The same determination, Taerith thought with an admiration that was quickly growing to affection, that had held its own against the serpent Meronane.

The last stitch in place, he took a rag and dipped it in a shallow bowl of water and herbs. He cleaned the blood away from the stitching carefully. Her eyes remained closed; her breathing steady and laboured with pain. For a few moments, on the floor of the tower room, she had not breathed. She seemed determined not to make that mistake again.

They were sitting at a low table in the servants' quarters, an empty room, surrounded by cold stone. Mirian had insisted on sitting. A tall window across from them let in one strong beam of moonlight, while around them torches crackled and made the grey of the room seem blue.

Taerith heard movement across the room, so light it was hardly perceptible—heard it with more than his ears. He looked up and saw the pale shadow dressed in grey, who stood silently in the door. Kardas turned and saw her too, and he started to rise before realizing that Mirian still held tightly to his hand.

Lilia entered the room, hesitantly, like a bird about to take flight. She kept her eyes down, but not with fear. She slid into a chair beside Kardas and pried Mirian's fingers loose, replacing the soldier's hand with her own small one.

Mirian's eyes opened, and she smiled slightly. Lilia smiled back.

"I'm glad you're alive," Lilia said.

"It isn't easy," Mirian answered.

"Don't do that again," Lilia returned. She covered Mirian's fingers with her other hand and looked away for a moment. "I thought you were dead."

Taerith dropped the cloth back into the cool water. He motioned for Lilia to let go while he wrapped Mirian's arm in bandages. Kardas had retreated to the door and stood watching them all.

As he finished his work, Taerith felt her eyes on him. He looked up, forcing himself to meet the queen's gaze.

"Thank you," she said.

He nodded. He wanted to say it—to vent all the wild relief he'd felt when Meronane fell and he realized that he had come in time. "I thought you were dead." Yes. And how much fear, how much near failure were in those words.

Instead he kept his mouth closed, smiled a little, and gathered the remaining bandages. He piled them neatly near the bowl of water, stained red like rust.

"Taerith."

Her voice forced him to look at her again. To let emotion threaten him again.

"You can't stay," she said.

He nodded. He knew that. Now more than ever.

Mirian had laid her head on the table, but she turned a little and looked up at him. She couldn't say it—pain and pride kept her equally silent—but he saw the gratitude in her green eyes also, as deep and raw as the thanks in Lilia's hurtful words.

Compulsively Taerith reached out and brushed a strand of hair from Mirian's eyes. He smiled down on her, and there were tears in his blue eyes. The moonlight shone in, steady upon the three, as each thanked the other for the saving of lives most precious to them.

Kardas spoke. "Someone's coming."

Mirian closed her eyes again, resting, as Lilia released her hand and Taerith moved to greet the newcomers. There was talk; things being moved; voices in the moonlight. She could still feel their touch, both of them—Lilia's strong grip on her hand; Taerith's gentle motion across her face. She smiled to herself.

Was her mother there?

She opened her eyes. No, of course not.

Darkness was there, though, rising like a cool mist before her eyes. She let it come but first made sure she was still breathing.

One breath, then another.

*   *   *

Annar greeted Borden from the chair in his quarters, without smile or courtesy. Borden, who had hardly bothered to wash the blood from his beard and hands, answered in kind.

"It is too much to ask, I know," he said. "Gratitude."

"To you?" Annar asked. "I am pleased to be alive, but a priest from my dungeon and a handful of servants fought while you arrived just when it suited you." He looked away and muttered, "A marvelous coincidence."

"Your meaning," Borden demanded.

"I think your timing must have been off," Annar said, leaning back in his chair. "You miscalculated when Meronane would attack? Or perhaps you thought no one would defend me, and so you would of course arrive too late."

"I had no foreknowledge of Meronane's attack," Borden said.

"You knew there was a threat," Annar said. "Why else would you come back?"

"I've asked myself that question," Borden said through gritted teeth. "Several times."

"You're sorry they didn't kill me," Annar said.

"No, I'm not," Borden said. "If they'd killed you while I was in the north, they might as well have handed the kingdom to Hosten."

Annar smiled. "How does it go in the north, brother?"

"There are many of them, and they've pushed a long way south—they're hungry. It is a bad winter for all. The wolves also fight us. They nearly killed a good man."

"Shall I tell Hosten that the wolves are trying you?" Annar asked. "All these years he kept the border, and you can hardly even stay there."

Borden's eyes flashed. His voice was low. "I am going back. Keep your kingdom while you can. It will not belong to you much longer."

He turned on his heel and left the room in a quiet fury. Beyond it, a huddle of armed servants waited. Some were wounded and still bloody. At their head, the bearded priest Joachim stood, a sword still in his hand. He met Borden's eyes.

"You have done well," Borden said. "You've proved yourselves more than servants. You're soldiers, all of you." He grimaced, and straightened his back slightly. "When I took my men away I thought I left the castle without a garrison to guard it. I was wrong. You have all done well."

The men flushed and looked at one another. Borden smiled inwardly. He knew Annar had not thanked them—had hardly even recognized the courage with which his untrained servants had fought.

"As for you," Borden said, reaching a hand to Joachim. "Your loyalties are as unpredictable as your tongue. Why guard the king you publicly cursed?"

"I only spoke the judgment of Deus on him," Joachim said. "My words remain true. This time next year Annar will no longer have a throne. But Meronane was not the one who will bring judgment."

Joachim's eyes seemed to look into Borden's soul. Priest and prince still held to each other's hand with a vice grip. Unreasonable apprehension washed over Borden, and he kept his eyes fixed on the priest. "How much of the future do you see?" he asked.

Joachim nearly smiled. He relaxed his grip and drew his hand away slowly. "No more than you do," he said.

"Will you stay with us?" Borden asked. "I will see to it that no one throws you in the dungeon again."

The priest shook his sandy head. "No. I have done—and spoken—all that I came for."

Borden nodded. He acknowledged the other servants once more with a nod, and stalked back toward the courtyard. Joachim's words whirled through his head, mingling with the acid aftertaste of his conversation with Annar. The north was calling to him: calling him to come back, to wipe out the threat that had so long kept them bound to Hosten, and then to return and take the throne.

The throne that was rightfully his, and always had been.

Lilia was in the courtyard, walking toward Annar's chambers followed by two servants. Borden nearly spat at the sight of the queen. Her pregnancy was beginning to show. Bitterly he realized that Meronane had nearly destroyed both queen and heir.

But Taerith had saved her. With sharp clarity, he remembered the look on Taerith's face when he had reported back, covered in blood.

"Meronane is dead," he said. "He was in the queen's chambers."

"And the queen?" Borden demanded.

"Safe," Taerith had answered, his voice nearly breaking. "She is safe."

Borden smiled. He had seen a great deal in Taerith's eyes. Perhaps, after all, the king would lose his queen because of this night.

*　*　*

They were laughing, because children always laugh. Beautiful little girls. He sat and watched them from the edge of the trees. They made his blue eyes smile. His little sisters.

"You can't stay."

"Taerith…"

He looked across the fire at the man in black. The one who spoke the words. He shook his head in confusion. I thought I was beginning to understand you. Why now?

"You can't stay."

He wasn't sure what woke him, but he looked up to see Borden standing over him with his arms crossed over his chest. He scrambled to his feet.

Borden cleared his throat. "You did well to kill Meronane. I expect his craven pack is scattered without him. Still… some of them have escaped; they may gather others. I want you to stay here when I go north."

Taerith heard the words tumbling out of his own mouth. "I can't stay," he said.

Borden stepped back. "I should think you'd like the chance. Lilia may need you again."

Taerith looked at Borden steadily. "You hate your brother a great deal," he said.

Borden looked away and cursed under his breath slightly. A smile reached his face despite him. "I do," he said. "You don't hate him enough, I see. Or else you don't love enough."

"That's the trouble with hate," Taerith said. "You can't even see love for what it is."

"What will you do if I order you to stay here?" Borden asked.

"Respectfully refuse," Taerith answered.

"If I won't take you north again?"

"Leave."

Borden looked up at him with the twisted smile again. "Haven't you done enough leaving?" he asked. "All right, then. Come north. You may be of use this time… now that you've finally killed a man."

Taerith bowed his head and did not answer.

*   *   *

Mirian opened her eyes and tried to push herself up. Pain stopped her immediately; sharp pain in her arm and head, a dull ache everywhere else.

"Lie down," Mistress Grey commanded. "Rest."

Obediently, Mirian relaxed and lowered her head to the pillow. She wanted to turn and look at the woman beside her, but her head and neck seemed at once aflame and stiff.

Master Grey came into view, standing benevolently over her with a look of mingled consternation and pride.

"Your grandfather would have been proud," he said. In the background, Mistress Grey slapped her work too loudly. Mirian formed her words carefully.

"Don't tell them," she said.

Master Grey frowned. "Tell who?"

"The king," Mirian said. "Or… Borden. Tell them Taerith saved her. Nothing else."

"Did you think we would tell them anything else?" Mistress Grey snapped. "You presume too much. What does your part matter now?"

Mirian tried to shake her head, but the pain flared and she kept still. The wound on her neck where Meronane's sword had caught her was irritated by her slave collar, and it made her more aware of its weight than she'd been in years—and yet, somehow, it mattered less than it ever had. She understood Mistress Grey well enough. Of course it didn't matter. She knew it didn't. The glory would go to Borden, who had arrived in time.

She almost smiled to herself. The true glory was a secret, drenched in moonlight, belonging to her and held as tightly as the memory of Taerith's gentle touch. She liked having such a secret. It was a part of her entirely free of bondage.

And Borden, she thought, Borden should never know that so much of the victory had been hers, or how close she had come to dying for Lilia. Lilia, who was also a part of her moonlit secret.

A part of her freedom.

Chapter Eighteen

Joachim made a point of returning his sword to Mistress Grey. He knelt and lifted it on the ends of his fingers, like a warrior paying homage to his lady.

"I thank you," he said, "for allowing me a part in this."

Bereft of his sword or any other weapon, he took up a staff, tied a small pouch with a few coins and a bit of dried meat—all the reward he would accept from Master Grey, and far more than Annar had offered—to his belt, and set off on the road going east.

Borden, astride his horse outside the castle walls, watched him go. Kardas stood beside him, armed and dressed for the ride north. The rest of the soldiers had already gone ahead. Borden reached down and touched Kardas's shoulder lightly.

"Follow him," Borden said, his eyes still on Joachim's hooded form.

"My lord?" Kardas asked.

Borden looked down and met Kardas's eyes without flinching. "Kill him," he said. "Do it quickly and come back to us. We will need you in the north."

Kardas looked up and regarded Borden, his dark face questioning but silent. Borden gave him no answer.

Kardas turned his eyes on the priest and began to follow him.

*   *   *

Taerith carefully unwrapped the bandages from his shoulder, opening the ravaged flesh to the sting of cold air. He twisted his head to see and ran his fingers lightly over the tooth marks. The skin around the wounds was bruised purple and green, but there was no sign of infection and he was glad of it.

Borden watched him from across the small fire as Taerith dipped the tips of his fingers into an ointment made of dry herbs and water and spread it across the wounds. The stuff stank, but neither man reacted to it.

"You have some wisdom in healing," Borden said.

"My youngest brother taught me," Taerith said. He paused for a moment, then finished spreading the ointment across his shoulder. He wiped his fingers clean on his trousers and started to rewrap his shoulder.

"And some power in killing," Borden continued. "I would not have believed a wounded man could have killed Meronane."

Again, Taerith paused. He thought, but did not say, *My oldest brother taught me that.*

"Where did you come from?" Borden asked. The anger that had laced his voice since leaving the castle had ebbed.

"A long way from here," Taerith replied. "A place called Brae-doch Forest."

"You left it because—"

"I couldn't stay," Taerith said. He stood and walked to the horse he'd taken from the castle, replacing the herbs and bandages in the saddle bag.

"I know a thing or two about healing myself," Borden said.

"Learned on the battlefield. I could not make you stay with my brother, but I will not take you back into battle yet. There is a village not far from here. Alanse. You will stay there a few more days, until your shoulder has closed up properly."

Taerith turned and frowned. "I would rather go with you," he said.

"Nevertheless," Borden answered. "I want you to heal before you try your sword hand again. Let Meronane's death be victory enough for now."

Taerith began to protest, but stopped himself. Meronane's death was death enough. His hands still shook when he thought of it. He wasn't eager to kill again.

Behind him, Borden mounted his horse. A wind was blowing down from the north. The two men set their heels to the horses' sides and rode into it.

*　*　*

Lilia sat by her window, her hand resting, as it so often did, on her womb. She could feel the slight swelling through the folds of her clothing, and she smiled a little without realizing it. Her eyes were lifted to the skies, tracing pictures in the clouds. Birds soaring. Sailing ships festooned with ribbon. A tower: stretching higher than her own tower had ever reached, carrying its occupants into the very stars—away into a universe she could not see except at night when the clouds cleared away and all the wonder of the worlds beyond was opened to her soul.

Wonder. The skies, the clouds and their stories, they told her of wonder. Of miracles. The child Lilia had loved to think of miracles, of stories that took place somewhere in the stars. As a woman she had forgotten how, or at least had forgotten how to delight in them. But now… now with a child growing in her womb and the very recent memory of love coming to her rescue in Taerith, in Mirian, now she was beginning to remember.

She smiled, and the tears running down her face caught in the corners of her mouth. There had always been something very like hurt in wonder. She felt it more keenly now.

She stood and turned away from the window. Without Mirian the room was very empty: empty and grey and cold. She wrapped her shawl around her shoulders and descended the twisting tower steps, aware with every step she took of life—of living—of how much that meant.

Death was waiting for her in the kitchen. One of the servant boys was carrying out an old dog. Its ribs showed through its skin in sharp relief. The boy was crying.

Tears sprang to her eyes anew at the sight. She reached out her hand and touched the creature's head. It was still warm.

"It starved to death." The voice was Mistress Grey's. There was little emotion in it. "We hadn't enough to feed the old creature."

"I'm sorry," Lilia said. The kitchen smelled like food: her husband's dinner, and her own, stewing over the fire. Master Grey stood at the sound of her voice. He had been sitting near the cooking fire, his old head bent, hair whiter than ever.

"Why are you here, my lady?" he asked.

Lilia looked down. "I wondered how Mirian was doing," she said. She cast her grey eyes on the mistress. "You know?"

"She's fine," Mistress Grey said. "There's enough strength in that girl to heal a dozen wounds."

Lilia nodded. "Good."

"Can I do anything for you?" Master Grey asked. "Something to eat… to drink?" His voice was mildly reproachful. "You shouldn't be in the kitchen."

Lilia smiled. "Why not?" she asked. "It's my kitchen. The tower is lonely."

Master and Mistress Grey exchanged a glance. Master Grey cleared his throat. "We could send…"

"No," Lilia said, smiling at him. "Don't worry yourself about it."

She turned, her long skirt brushing along the stone floor. "Where is Mirian?"

Halfway up to her own tower room, Lilia stopped on the landing and pushed open the wooden door to the servants' room. A bedroll lay across the floor on the far side of the small room. Mirian was stretched out on it, sleeping with her injured arm held close. A bowl of water and herbs sat on a small table near her head.

Lilia crossed the floor quietly and looked down on the sleeping slave. She lowered herself to the floor, dipping her hand in the bowl first and wringing out a small cloth. Gently she washed Mirian's brow. Her face was bruised, her head turned so that the crusted line along her neck and collarbone were clearly visible. Lilia washed them too, and touched the slave collar with something like abhorrence.

"Taerith?" Mirian murmured.

"I sent him away," Lilia whispered. She dabbed at Mirian's brow, then leaned over and kissed her forehead. "Thank you."

Mirian opened her eyes. A sound escaped her that was much like a sigh.

"Why did you make Meronane angry?" Mirian asked. Her voice sounded as though it came out of sleep. "He could have killed you."

"I thought it might help you," Lilia said, dropping the cloth back into the bowl. She laid her damp hand in her lap and stretched her legs out on the cold stone, leaning on one hand and looking down at Mirian.

Mirian shook her head. "He might have killed you," she said again. "And the baby."

Lilia lowered her head a little so her voice could be heard though she dropped it, smiling like a child with a secret. "It would have been an honour to die helping you fight," she said.

Something came into Mirian's eyes that Lilia had never seen there before. She reached out and took Lilia's hand.

"You're sitting on the floor like a slave," Mirian said.

Lilia shook her head. A lock of dark hair fell over her shoulder. "Both of us," she said. "Like free women."

* * *

Evening was beginning to fold in over the woods. Joachim had made himself a fire. Its light flickered through the branches and announced his presence, along with the faint sound of iron striking flint. He sat cross-legged beside the fire, sharpening a hunting knife with a rhythmic stroke.

Kardas crept forward and looked through the branches at the bearded priest. Joachim was humming to himself. Kardas almost smiled.

He drew his sword and stepped out of the trees.

Joachim hardly seemed surprised to see him. He looked up with a wry expression in his eyes. "Do you always melt out of the darkness like that?" he said.

Kardas said nothing. Joachim laid down his knife and flint and set his hands on his knees.

"Loyalty is a strange thing, isn't it?" he asked. "It means so much, and yet people can so easily use it against you. I know," he said, smiling a little now at the barely-visible expression on Kardas's face. "I've guessed why you follow Borden. I lived with the northern tribes for a little while. They taught me how to sharpen a knife."

"Do you know why I'm here?" Kardas asked.

"If I had to guess," Joachim said, "I'd say that I frightened Borden by knowing his heart too well. I won't betray him, though he thinks I will. The heart that is preparing to betray cannot imagine that anyone else would not." Joachim stood, stretching as he did. "He should have paid more attention to you all these years."

Kardas still held his sword in his hand. The fire behind Joachim was small and had already begun to die. The priest spread his arms out.

"Well?" he asked. "What are you waiting for? I cannot defend myself."

Kardas threw his sword down. The movement surprised even him. "What do you know of my future?" he asked. "Deus has shown you a great deal."

Joachim smiled. "I have seen you," he said. "In some of my better dreams."

"Your killer?" Kardas asked.

"The loyal one," Joachim replied. "It takes a very loyal heart to sit a throne without claiming it."

Kardas cocked his head. "I don't understand you."

"You will," Joachim answered.

The last tongue of fire sank into the kindling and burned itself out. A few glowing embers were all that still lit the gloom of the fading day. The men seemed to wane in the shadows even as they faced one another.

"I don't know what to do now," Kardas said. "I do not wish to carry out my orders."

"Perhaps," Joachim said, smiling again, "I should spare you the agony of decision."

He lifted his hands. In an instant the beat of wings like a thunderclap filled the twilight, and a shadow fell before Kardas's eyes, blinding him. It lifted a moment later.

Joachim was gone. All that remained to mark his passage were the scattered ashes of the fire.

*   *   *

The smell of charring wood was their first warning, the noise of battle their second.

Alanse was over the next hill. The fields that surrounded it looked more bare than ever winter field ought; the harvesters had not merely cleared them, but laid them waste. It was illusion, Taerith knew, but it spoke of the hunger that had gripped Annar's kingdom, and worse, it spoke of the marauding force that swept over it since Hosten's abandonment.

Taerith and Borden looked at one another for a second before Borden shouted and galloped ahead. His sword was already in his hand. Taerith urged his horse forward, flying to Borden's side. He reached for his own sword as he did, his fingers gripping the hilt but leaving the steel sheathed.

They crested the hill. The village was in flames. The wild men were everywhere. Back to back in the center of the village, facing out at the barbarians who outnumbered them, were Emmet and the rest of Borden's men.

Taerith drew his sword and charged down the hill.

Chapter Nineteen

They rode in screaming like wild men themselves, Borden's sword brandished high. Taerith leaned forward in the saddle, head low, bracing himself for impact as he charged into the scattering tribesmen. Clash. Surging forward, breaking over the men like a battering wave. They flung themselves at him and he beat them back, clubbing, slashing, riding them down. Borden, beside and then ahead of him, killed.

The attack gave Emmet the moment he needed. He led the others forward with a shout. The weariness in their eyes and limbs dissolved in renewed hope. Battle rejoined, they drove outward from their huddle and pushed the wild men back.

It was over sooner than Taerith expected. He dismounted in a muddy street awash with blood and melted snow. Jonas, one of Borden's soldiers, laid a bruised hand on Taerith's shoulder as their leader dismounted and looked around him, his face dark.

"Why are they so far south?" Borden asked.

"They are everywhere," Emmet said. "When you left they came out of hiding. They struck everywhere at once; we could not fight them all."

Borden looked at him, understanding lighting his eyes like a dark moon. "What have we lost?" he asked.

"Three villages," Emmet said. "A few others were attacked, but not destroyed."

Borden breathed out. "We have only been gone a few days."

"There are hundreds of them," Emmet said. "But they fight as they always have—in scattered groups, without a single purpose. They see no shame in retreat or glory in complete victory. They are bloody thieves."

"Thieves who are plundering the little we have left," Borden replied.

Emmet nodded. "We have done our best to protect the villages, but…"

"We will continue to do our best," Borden said. "We will do better than our best. We will push them north again."

"To do that we'd have to face them in a real battle," Jonas said. "We can push them nowhere as long as they are content to dodge us like sparrows pecking at a crow."

Borden nodded. His fist tightened around the reins of the horse that stamped its black legs behind him in the mud.

"When we found you, you were huddled in the center of the village," Borden said. "Never again. From now on we drive them inward. We are herders, my friends, and we must bring the sheep to slaughter. We will surround and destroy them."

"Hundreds of them?" Emmet asked.

"One small group at a time," Borden answered. "Until the others realize the threat and retreat, as they will. As they always do."

He looked at Taerith as he strode past. "There is no place for mercy any longer," he said. "Next time they do not come out of the ravines. Next time we go in. We cannot defend the kingdom unless we become aggressors ourselves."

No one contradicted him. The men were silent, breathing hard in the aftermath of the fight, stinking of blood, sweat, and mud. Each let the implications of Borden's words sink in. They had come to act as border guards. Instead, they were starting a war.

And yet, there was nothing else they could do.

Borden led his black horse through the street and back up the hill. The others followed. If any of the villagers had survived the attack of the wild men, they were still in hiding. There was nothing to be done in the town, so Borden and his men made camp atop the hill, where they could see the outlying country and watch for signs of life in the streets below.

Hours later, a lone figure rode into the camp: Kardas. He dismounted and began to care for his horse, removing saddle and bridle and brushing the creature down. Borden looked up at him from his place near a fire.

"Did you find him?" he asked.

Kardas turned from his work, his dark face as implacable as ever. "I found him," he said.

Borden nodded and looked down. He said nothing more.

Taerith approached Kardas and held out a dry piece of bread. "Are you hungry?" he asked.

Kardas took the bread and tore a piece off with his teeth. He went back to work on his horse without another glance at Taerith or Borden or any other man in the camp. A moment later he drew his sword and whirled around. Someone was coming through the underbrush.

A young man stepped out of the bush, thin hands held out beseechingly. He nearly fell to his knees in the snow.

"My lord Borden," he said.

Borden touched the young man's shoulder. "Rise," he said.

The newcomer looked up. There were tears in his eyes, haunted tears, of hunger or of loss Taerith could not tell. "That was my village," he said, pointing down the hill. "There is nothing left. Let me join you."

Borden looked over the emaciated form and shaking hands. He nodded gruffly and beckoned to Emmet.

"Feed him," he said. "However you can. And find him a sword."

* * *

Annar unrolled the message carefully, reading it for the third time. He clenched his fist suddenly, making the parchment warp and crumple in his hand. He raised his eyes to Master Grey, who stood waiting in the corner.

"My brother calls for food," Annar said.

Master Grey licked his lips. "My lord, we have a little…"

"No," Annar said. "We have nothing to give him. Let the men hunt their own food."

"In the north?" Master Grey asked. "What is there left to hunt?"

"We have nothing to give him," Annar repeated. He brought a cup of ale to his lips, leaning his forehead on his other hand. "I am hungry in my own house and my brother dares ask me to aid him in his little war. He has not been back in a month. If he will leave, then he will suffer the consequences for leaving."

Master Grey left the throne room in a silent paroxysm of anger. He had seen the wild men before—had lived long enough to remember the days before Hosten kept the northern borders. Annar could complain of his empty stomach all he liked, but if not for Borden, the king would likely be past caring whether his stomach was full or empty.

Mirian stood in the hall. She had listened at the door, a growing habit with her. She met Master Gray's eyes. He shook his head slightly.

A cold wind found its way into the castle corridors. Mirian pulled her shawl closer as she followed Master Gray's stooped form to the kitchen. A pot of oats, thin and grey, was boiling. She spooned some into a bowl, cupping it in her hands to soak up the warmth, and made the long climb to Lilia's room.

The queen lay in her bed, as she usually did now. She opened her eyes and smiled a little at Mirian's approach. Her hand rested on her swollen womb, but she moved it and started to push herself up.

"How do you feel?" Mirian asked.

"Weak," Lilia answered. "But well. Very well."

*　　*　　*

Winter let its force loose as the ranks grew. Villagers, farmers, and vagabonds joined themselves to Borden's men. What little game was left in Corran disappeared in white. Even the wolves were cowed by the bitter cold as Borden and his men pushed the wild men north.

Two months had passed. Jonas and a handful of men entered the camp in the early morning light, under the cover of a soft snowfall. Neither the cold nor the snow could mask the smell.

"Where did you get it?" Emmet asked Jonas, his voice rough even as he set to work dismembering the pig.

"Someone left it in the road," Jonas answered.

Taerith had been on watch. He rose and joined the men, pulling his hunting knife from his belt. His stomach churned as he worked. Butchering meant food, and the very idea of it was already torturing him.

Borden joined the group and laid a hand on Jonas's shoulder. "Distribute it fairly," he said. "No one eats more than anyone else. See to it that the newcomers aren't overlooked."

A pair of hungry eyes belonging to former villagers fixed on Borden's face, thanks etched painfully in their features. Taerith stood with a piece of meat and handed it to them. "Go," he said. "Start the fires. There is no reason to waste time."

He turned back to the butchering, but something stopped him. He raised his eyes to see Kardas leaning against a tree, watching with his arms folded across his chest. The dark man had grown leaner and more taciturn in the last month. Something in the north called to him: he seemed feral here, almost more than human. It was well that every man among Borden's soldiers knew Kardas, or they might have mistaken him for a tribesman in battle.

Taerith handed his hunting knife to someone else and approached Kardas. "What is it?" he asked.

Kardas looked down on the slaughter. "You know they stole it," he said.

"I don't want to know," Taerith said. A sharp note heightened his voice.

"We won't beat the enemy by becoming them," Kardas said.

"We won't beat them by starving to death either," Taerith said. "Borden is nearly content. We need only drive the wild men past our northern border, and then things will change. We can send out more hunting parties—find ways to pay the people for food. We will do it, Kardas. I will see to it myself if Borden will let me."

Kardas did not answer. He had lifted his eyes and was look-ing north, into the increasing snowfall. The look on his face was not comforting.

*   *   *

The oatmeal had weakened till it was little more than gruel. Mirian cupped the bowl in her hands even so, holding it like a sacred thing, and carried it up the long stairs. She had lost count of how many times a day she made this trek.

"I don't want to eat," Lilia said.

"You don't have a choice," Mirian answered. She set the bowl down and let it steam away beside Lilia's bed. The queen's small form was tucked up in white sheets, her knees pulled up, her abdomen large. Her book lay on the bed beside her. She picked it up.

"I am not hungry," she insisted.

"That hardly seems possible," Mirian said. "Everyone is hun-gry. How can you read when you've not eaten?"

"There's a food in books," Lilia said. "I lived on it as a child. Food for the heart."

Mirian smiled. "I wish I understood you," she said.

Lilia looked up as though she was seeing Mirian for the first time. "Why shouldn't you?" she asked. "Of course you should un-derstand me. Sit."

Mirian did, awkward but curious. Lilia pulled a bit of the sheet up beside her and began to trace letters in its folds. "Do you know what these mean?" Lilia asked.

"They mean you are being stubborn," Mirian said. "Your gruel is calling."

"Hush. Look. Try and read this."

"I can't."

"You can if you'll try. Listen to me."

Outside the window, the wind howled its hardest as the pair bent over the sheets. Mirian struggled while Lilia explained each letter and its sound.

"M is for Mirian," she said. "For mortal and for miracle."

"What do you know about miracles?" Mirian asked. For the first time she noticed how the wind shrieked at them, as though it wished to bring the tower down and them with it. Its vocal emptiness exacerbated the ache in her stomach.

"Much," Lilia said. "As a child I always wanted to see a miracle, but I think I missed the miracles already before me."

Mirian stood. "Are there miracles before you now?" she asked.

"Yes," Lilia said. She smoothed away the letters in the sheets and reached for the bowl of gruel. It was cold; no steam warmed her face as she sniffed it. She wrinkled her nose but dipped her spoon into it anyway.

"I am alive and I think that is a miracle," she said. "This child is a miracle. And you—you are a miracle."

"Why?" Mirian asked.

"Because, despite everything, you have loved me in this place," Lilia said. Her clear grey eyes seemed stronger than they ever had; her voice was sure in its audacity. Mirian's eyes filled with tears. The wind howled and beat against the stones.

"I am not the only one," she said. She looked at the curtains drawn tightly across the window, willing herself to see through the cloth and the storm to those who fought somewhere beyond it. She looked back at Lilia. Earnest eyes looked back, child-like eyes. The bowl of gruel lay unnoticed in her hands, an inconsequential thing for the moment.

"Eat," Mirian whispered.

*　　*　　*

Tridian brought word to the camp early in the day. The men were mounted in moments, their recent acquisition of several days' worth of beef making them strong.

"They are attacking Engnor," he said. "On the border."

"Drive them north," Borden said. "Show no quarter."

"My lord," Tridian said, stopping Borden as he strode toward his horse. "There are many."

"Then many will fall," Borden said. "This is our chance."

Engnor sat in a shallow valley. As the men crested the rocky ridge above it, Emmet let out an involuntary exclamation.

"Deus help us."

There had to be two hundred of them. The largest group of tribesmen Taerith had ever seen in one place. This was no single band. They had done what wild men never did: they had joined together.

Borden rode to the front of his men and prepared to signal the charge. Taerith leaned forward in anticipation, but Kardas's low voice next to him made him pause.

"This is no time to herd sheep," he said. "We have to scatter them. Divide their loyalties."

"How?" Taerith asked.

In answer, Kardas reached to his own shoulder and pulled

the edge of his shirt away. A blue tattoo, the outline of a serpent, was coiled there.

"Look for the tattooed men and attack them," he said. "Be careful. Don't kill them… try to draw them away from the others. Their bands will follow."

Kardas touched his heels to his horse's side and rode up to Borden, where he spoke in the same low, urgent tones.

Taerith drew his sword.

Behind him, Kardas screamed a battle cry into the still air. The wild men in the valley turned, saw them, answered the cry.

They rode into the valley like falling thunder. Plunge into destruction. Every muscle strained, every nerve steeled, every chance taken, Taerith fought through the crowd in search of the tattooed men. The confused mass of battle raged like darkness on every side. He saw him: a big man, young, with his chest bared and a blue serpent stretched across his collarbone.

He started toward him, but the wild men seemed determined that he should never reach the man. With every step there was another to meet him. They slowed his advance till he seemed to fight through a swamp of human effort that sucked him down and pushed him back.

Still he kept his eyes on the prize and fought on.

Two men engaged him at once. He fought now for his life; sharp and quick he was, and well-trained in swordplay, but these men had the advantage of long years of experience. One fell as Kardas appeared at his side. Their eyes met. Kardas looked toward the tattooed man and then crossed swords with the second of Taerith's assailants.

Taerith lunged forward. The man was so close he could nearly touch him. The tattooed man spun around a second before Taerith reached him. His sword came up. Steel met steel with a force that sent shock traveling into Taerith's shoulder. Taerith grabbed his hilt with both hands and dealt the tattooed man another blow. It glanced off the wild man's sword.

Behind him, Kardas screamed out his war cry again. There was triumph in his voice. He fought with the abandon and passion of the tribesmen, yet with greater force, greater skill. He saw what Taerith did not: that in pressing the battle to the tattooed man, they had driven a band of the wild men away from the others, and that small groups of Borden's soldiers had done the same, and together they were splintering the coalition of tribesmen and turning them into bands again—bands lacking cohesion, small groups who would act in their own interests only.

Taerith jumped away from the swing of the tattooed man's sword, seeing as he did so that others were closing in around him. Kardas's cry split the air, but he too was hard pressed.

Around them still, the darkness raged.

*　　*　　*

Annar stared at the boy before him. Rail thin, the boy yet possessed anger enough to swell with it. There were tears in his eyes.

"Please," he said. "If there is anything in your cellars, share it! Your men took the last of what we had. I will lose my mother if this goes on another day."

Annar stared at him, feeling his fist clench involuntarily. He felt his mouth open; heard his own voice speak. "There is nothing."

"But—" the boy said.

"Nothing!" Annar repeated. He stood. "Be gone, boy. Tell those who conspire with you to plague me that there is nothing."

The boy's tears, water of anger and hunger and grief, fell down his cheeks without shame. "You are our king," he said. "Can you not find a way to feed us?"

*　　*　　*

Smoke drifted through the valley. The dead lay where they had fallen. Too many to count. Wild men and Borden's vagabonds lay together in peace now, while the remaining of Borden's captains gathered around him.

He stood with his sword drawn and dripping still. His voice was eerily calm.

"We have done it," he said. "They will not recover from this. Not this winter."

His eyes focused and he began to look around him, sword still unsheathed. "Emmet," he said. "My soldiers. Where is Taerith? Kardas?"

Emmet and Jonas exchanged a look.

"Where?" Borden demanded.

In answer, smoke drifted through the valley.

*　　*　　*

The dining hall stood vast and empty, full of well-fed ghosts. At the king's board, Annar sat alone.

Master Grey entered the room. He cleared his throat, his eyes troubled. He did not look directly at the king.

"I have sent word as you ordered, my lord," he said. "To Hosten of Moralia."

Rachel Starr Thomson 221

Chapter Twenty

Borden had been right. Two weeks more proved it. Their victory against the wild men had been enough. The border, once left in the hands of Emmet and a few small troops, would stay secure for the winter.

Moreover, they were eating again.

Tridian returned from a raiding party with corn stores wrested from a barbarian band he had chased over the moors. His men bore it in sacks on their backs and in wagons. Borden divided out enough for his men and sent the rest to the stock he was building. Enough to take home. Enough to tide the people over—to give the kingdom some hope, as only he could do.

Tridian gave his report as usual. "We killed most of them," he said. "They'd stored up what you see—not much."

"But enough," Borden said. He looked up from his place by the fire. Tridian's young face was weary. His clothes stank of blood and horses. Behind him, the pale winter sky was streaked with purple clouds.

"Was there any sign?" Borden asked.

Tridian shook his head. "Nothing, my lord."

"They cannot be dead," Borden said, half to himself. "I would know." He stood. "There is another band encamped to the west. Ride on them tomorrow night. Keep looking for Kardas and Tae-rith. They are still out there somewhere."

"Forgive me, my lord," Tridian said, "but—supposing we do not find them—how much longer will it be before we end these raids and return home? We have as much food as we can possibly take back with us."

"Not quite," Borden said. "We can take a little more. Deus knows it will be needed."

His eyes looked past Tridian and scanned the hilly ground of the borderlands. Searching in vain.

They had to be out there somewhere.

*　　*　　*

You are our king. Can you not feed us?

Annar felt the emptiness in his own stomach constrict. His body felt weak; almost indifferent; yet deep inside somewhere he was ravenous, and the words kept playing themselves through his mind.

Can you not feed us?

As ravenous as appetite, such words. They demanded an answer.

The king of Corran stood and crossed the throne room. He paused before the window. In the yard, two of Grey's lackeys led the new arrivals' horses to the stables. Mistress Grey spoke with Hosten's men and led them away to their rooms. They would prepare themselves and come into Annar's presence soon, and perhaps for the last time he would be a king in their eyes. They came with the air of conquerors, but he was not ready to release his pride quite yet.

He thought of Borden on the border. Borden would never, never allow this: not if the people had to starve to prevent it. Annar's lip curled. Ever the hero, his warrior brother; ever the ambitious son. But Annar's was the hunger and thus the compassion. Borden was not human enough to give in to his own lusts. He sneered at Annar—he always had—for allowing himself to live as he wanted to live.

He thought of his wife. Small, once-beautiful Lilia, waning now in the throes of need, carrying his child.

Can you not? Can you not feed us?

Footsteps in the hall. Annar turned away from the window and returned to his throne. He placed a hand on the arm and stood waiting, stern as he could be. Master Grey ushered in the visitors.

"How much is Hosten willing to give us?" Annar demanded.

"He has stored up much for the winter," the chief messenger answered. "He can feed your people bread enough for the winter—and there is wine and meat for you."

Annar smiled to himself.

For wine and meat in the midst of hunger—was a kingdom truly such a price to pay?

*   *   *

He was stiff and and he was sore. These, along with the cold, were Taerith's chief complaints. He kept them at bay, buried in his mind so they couldn't come out his mouth and tint the days darker. Kardas had not complained; had hardly opened his mouth since they were taken captive. Instead he watched and listened.

His uncomplaining attitude suited Taerith even if his silence did not entirely. It was good not to be alone.

His arms were bound behind him most of the time, tightly pinioned with several thin cords. Each evening the barbarians cut loose the cords and watched him with a curiosity that was almost friendly, five or six standing guard at a time, while he swung his arms and rubbed them and set his teeth against the pain, allowing circulation to come back, making sure his arms stayed strong. He dropped to the ground and pushed himself up a few times, even as his bare hands slipped and ached in the cold snow and the colder mud. Aiden's lessons, on survival and fighting the wilderness when it refused to be any longer the companion Taerith loved, thundered in the newly released blood flow through his arms and fingers. It hurt, but it was good. There were white and blue patches on his hands and feet where frostbite was setting in, and his face stung, but he was alive and still grateful for it.

Kardas was also cut loose every night, but the guards stood away from him, averting their eyes, as though he deserved some respect that Taerith did not. He also kept himself strong, in his own ways, and in his silence watched the wild men who had taken them captive with eyes that saw everything.

Their fifteenth night with the wild men was lit by a full white moon, beaming ghostly down so unlike sunshine, cold and beautiful and utterly without warmth. Kardas waited until their guards had moved away a little and said, "Tomorrow is the first day of the waning moon. It's an ill omen for them. They may kill you."

Taerith mulled the words over a moment. There was a sad uselessness in them; the emotional echo of the words that had banished him from Braedoch. "Why?" he asked. "When?"

"There is always a gathering of tribes in the waning moon.

They band together to beseech their spirit enemies for mercy. Borden has bested them and they are afraid; they think the north itself has turned against them. In fear they sometimes kill outsiders because they think the spirits will be appeased."

Taerith bowed his head, resting his forehead on his knees. "And you?"

Something in Kardas's eyes glimmered darkly. "Let them try me. My mother was one of them. They will give me the chance to fight my way free."

"Your mother?" Taerith asked. His eyes drifted to the tattoo just visible above Kardas's shirt. The dark man dropped his own eyes.

"I was also one of them for a time."

"Why did you leave?" Taerith asked.

"Borden," Kardas answered.

The moonlight over them made the moorish shadows shift. Kardas was silent again, looking away over the hillocks under patches of snow. The wild men lay around them like dead men; sleeping as they always did, deeply and yet alert, as though it was their last night under a haunted sky.

"The wild men know little of honour, so Borden has always told me," Kardas said. "In some ways he is right. They do not know that a full victory is to be sought, or that retreat is cowardice. They do not know that they ought to make a way of life for themselves without thievery. They are little better than crows. Yet there are codes among them… things that bind us. Blood debt is the strongest. The one saved owes his loyalty as long as both men live."

"Borden saved your life, then," Taerith said.

"Long ago," Kardas answered.

"You have acquitted your debt well," Taerith said.

Something flickered in Kardas's face. It suddenly occured to Taerith to wonder how old he was: surely not much older than Taerith himself. Aiden's age—young, really. And yet somehow possessed of a spirit old as the hills and the wolves and winter itself. A spirit that manifested itself in faithfulness.

A faithfulness that bound him. Kardas's words still hung in the air: *"The chance to fight my way free."* Comprehension settled in. Kardas planned to take up a sword and fight until he had released himself from the longest bondage of his life.

Kardas's head was bent. With the moonlight in his dark hair and illuminating the blue tattoo, he looked like the prince of barbarians—less like a man than a wolf, a thing of the night. Taerith wondered, and stopped himself from asking, what Kardas had been meant to be—what he was before Borden claimed his loyalty. A memory stirred: attacking the tattooed men in the battle, and somehow splitting the entire army of barbarians by doing so because the small bands followed their tattooed leaders above all else.

Things that bind us, Kardas had said. Blood debt—and something else.

"And who will you fight?" Taerith asked. "If they give you this chance?"

Kardas's eyes glinted in the night like an animal's. "Whoever I can," he said.

An idea was weaving itself into the memory of battle, taking shape like the snake tattooed across Kardas's collarbone. Taerith bit it back; refused to let the words form on his tongue. Yet his mind still raced, and he argued with it: *I have no right. I cannot ask him to live if he wants to die. To be a barbarian again—to go home when he does not wish to… go home…*

The sting of his face worsened as bile rose in his throat. He swallowed hard. Words escaped him, rasping out. "I want to go home again," he said. He looked up and met Kardas's eyes hard. "I was banished, sent away for reasons I don't understand, but I know now—I want to go home again. Someday. If I die here that will never happen."

Kardas regarded him a long time. "You believe I can help you?" he asked.

"Yes," Taerith said. His racing mind was calling up pictures before him, and they all tangled together: the battle, his sisters, birds in flight. Lilia and the castle and defeating Meronane. Mirian whose arm he had mended. And Kardas—Kardas in battle, Kardas who fought like a wolf in winter.

"Tell me how," Kardas said.

"Fight the tattooed men," Taerith said. The words came out of the past, from the battle where Kardas had first said them. What else had he said?

"To kill one is to win the enmity of the whole band," Kardas said. "Their loyalties belong to the leaders."

"I said fight them," Taerith said. "Don't kill them."

"That would only—" Kardas began. He bit the words off. "I see."

From the look on his face, Taerith knew that he did.

*   *   *

Emmet said it first.

"You can take no more back with you." His voice was low.

"We have searched everywhere, my lord. We have killed every barbarian within riding distance. They are beyond our reach."

Borden did not answer. He stared into the sunrise, his jaw set.

"The people of Corran are hungry," Emmet said. "If you wait much longer they will begin to die, and then they will resent you when you return because you did not return sooner." His voice dropped even lower. "That, my lord, would not serve your purposes well."

Borden turned his head and regarded Emmet without a change of expression. "What do you know of my purposes?" he asked.

Emmet looked down. "Enough," he said. "I will hold the border for you, but you alone can do what must be done in Corran."

Borden's fingers had been tightly coiled around his sword hilt. He let go. "You are right," he said. "Tell the men. We will leave now."

He cast a last glance over the moors. "I'm sorry," he said into the air. "You're on your own now."

*   *   *

They walked long and hard the next day under a clear sky. A bitter wind blew in their faces, whistling over the open moor. There was something tense in the march; the sense of something building. In the middle of the day they cut Taerith loose as they always did, and watched as he stretched fingers and wrists and elbows, rolled his shoulders and tried to push his own weight off the ground.

Evening came early, and the sky, instead of closing in as it did on cloudy days, seemed instead to grow, making the world immeasurably larger above them. The stars came out with a sharp clarity Taerith had never seen before. He had read somewhere, long ago in another life, that stars were clearest in the north. The dark sky and its stars, more of them appearing every minute, dancing above them in vast circles, found an answer in Kardas's eyes and in Taerith's soul. In the wild men around them, it only inspired fear.

The unmarked road took them up a ridge of small hills. When they crested it, a vast circular plateau lay before them, patches of snow alternating with black ground, gleaming in the starlight with a silver fire they did not possess under the light of the moon only.

At the center of the plateau were six great stones, standing upright. Gathered around them was a host of wild men that nearly matched those Borden had fought at Engnor. A dozen small bands, each led by a tattooed leader—some old, some young. Their own band passed through the crowd and approached nearly to the stones, where a grizzled giant as old as the standing stones stood waiting.

The band spread out a little. Each man seemed to know his place in the crowd, though not a word was said. Four arranged themselves around Taerith and Kardas. Fear seemed to pulse through the crowd, a stifling fear that stopped the breath in their very lungs. Taerith lifted his eyes to the stars and felt himself swept up into the sky's peace and wild beauty. The constricting bands of fear fell away from him.

In the center of the standing stones, a fire pit lay beneath four pillars of stone crested with crossing bars of iron. The old giant of a man lifted a torch and began to intone something in words Taerith did not understand. He kept his eyes fixed on the stars as the wild men around him picked up the chant. Their voices were low and rumbling, the sound like that of an animal when it is cornered. For a moment Taerith let himself slip back into the atmosphere of fear, and he felt it: the strong sense of something surrounding them, nipping at their heels, threating them with bared teeth and lowered head. He raised his eyes again and the sky set him free.

He blinked. Something moved across the sky, dimming the stars for a moment—something like the motion of a great wing across the star-circles.

The old giant threw his torch into the fire pit, and it blazed to life, flames licking up around the iron bars and blackening the stone—not for the first time, nor for the last, under the waning moon. The light of the ancient altar drew Taerith's eyes away from the sky, and suddenly he found himself cut loose. He stretched his arms and fingers in wonderment as the crowd around him began to pick up a new strain in their chant—a high, keening song, frightening and frightened.

He knew—he felt—that he was about to die. It was a death song they sang. He had no weapon, nothing with which to face it, and so he turned to meet death wherever it would come.

But something else came instead.

A wind swept over the plateau, cutting through the crowd and throwing back those who stood nearest to Taerith. At the same time, the ear-splitting cry of an eagle rang through the starry air. It pierced the death-song and shattered it. The wild men fell to their knees, some crying in terror, others struggling to hold their own against the wind.

As quickly as it had come, it left. But as the barbarians fell, Kardas did not. He grabbed a sword from a man near him, and in a few short steps he had mounted the rise to the standing stones, and with a leap he stood atop the ancient altar, the flames cowed by the strange wind beneath his feet. He lifted the sword and cried out a challenge in the guttural speech of his people. His eyes searched the crowd until they rested on a tattooed man. He pointed the tip of his sword at the man and once again called out his challenge.

The man had fallen beneath the wind, but now he staggered to his feet and drew his sword. He was an older man, greying in his long hair and beard, but still strong. He wore a necklace of wolves' teeth about his neck. He stood, sword drawn, facing Kardas, and then charged up the hill with a bloodcurdling scream.

Kardas met him and their swords rang out in the clear air, flashing through the drifting smoke of the fire. Around the altar they danced, the wild man driving Kardas before him but unable to catch him, unable to finish the hunt. Then suddenly the tables turned: Kardas drove his adversary with blow after blow until the man lost his footing on the slope and fell back. Kardas's sword was at his throat, nicked it, drew blood.

But he did not kill him. He pulled the tip of his sword away and kicked the man down the hill. In the same motion he turned and leaped once again onto the altar: again he pointed his sword at a tattooed man, again he called the challenge.

This man was young and inexperienced, and Kardas dealt with him in minutes. He drove him up against the pillar stones of the altar, and the young man faltered and dropped his sword. It fell into the fire pit, blackened in an instant by the heat of the flames.

Kardas held his sword against the young man's heart. His eyes narrowed, and he pulled the sword back. He shoved the young man away.

232 Taerith

And again, atop the altar. And again, the challenge called.

Taerith watched with his heart beating in strange rhythm with Kardas's battle-dance. He had never seen before—never understood how truly gifted Kardas was, how easily he defeated his enemies. One after the other, he defeated the tattooed leaders of the wild men.

When he had beaten the last, there was silence. Kardas stood below the altar, his chest heaving with exertion. Silent. His eyes swept the crowd, waiting for any to challenge him. No one did.

The grizzled giant approached him. He spoke a few guttural words. Kardas did not look at him, but the words lit a strange fire in his face.

He lifted his sword once again and cried out. His words swept over the crowd like a wind in themselves. His voice died away and then he repeated himself, more quietly, in the language that Taerith knew.

"I have defeated you and have not killed you," he said. "The Blood Debt is mine. I claim your loyalty."

One by one, the men Kardas had defeated came forward and bowed at his feet. He laid his hand upon each head, black-haired and grey, and said three words. One by one, they withdrew back into their bands, and then as one the crowd knelt. The fire behind Kardas flared up. The stars still danced.

Kardas threw back his head and howled like a wolf in the light of the waning moon.

Chapter Twenty-One

The stars still shone out clearly over the plateau. As the wild men knelt, Taerith felt something growing within him, alive and primal like the earth springing forth in response to the sun. The awareness of a Presence drew his heart and made it beat faster.

Lightning flashed in the dark winter sky. In its split-second aura Taerith saw the image of a great bird, large as the moon, perched atop the standing stones with its wings spread over them. His heart leaped at the sight. Thunder rolled as his heart threatened to burst. The image was gone but the Presence was not; it grew greater, grew stronger, and Taerith found himself baptized in awareness keener than any he had experienced in all his life.

Deus with wings.

It was a great bird he had seen, and yet as he tried to hold onto its image it changed, and he was no longer sure that the lightning had not illuminated the form of a man: a man whose shoulders were in the sky, in whose eyes the stars found their source.

With the presence of Deus pounding in his heart and ears and throat, he hardly heard the voice that spoke out over the stillness of the plateau. Yet he saw every barbarian head as it turned— saw the shock in Kardas's face.

"It is no evil that has come to you this night," the voice said. "The spirits of winter which you feared are cowering in the presence of a greater. One has come to seek you out and has bound you to that man"—a finger pointed at Kardas—"that you may be found."

Taerith turned his head also. The voice belonged to Joachim. He stood behind the crowd, his voice clear to all, though it was calm. The edges of his cloak seemed to Taerith both feathered and shining. And there was, Taerith realized, another miracle— the wild men understood Joachim. It was evident in their faces; in their murmured responses. What language did the priest speak?

"Mercy has bound you," Joachim said, his eyes taking in the wild men in their bands. "Do not be afraid."

He lifted his eyes to Kardas. Taerith turned and looked at his friend. The sense of Presence was dying down—not that the winged spirit had gone, but that Taerith's senses dulled with the minutes. Kardas's dark face was inscrutable, but his eyes were awash with anguish. He seemed unwilling to move. He shook his head slightly as he regarded Joachim, almost as though he was warning him away.

Joachim began to move forward despite the warning. The wild men parted for him until he had reached the base of the rise where the standing stones stood out in the clear light of the moon and stars. Kardas still stood before the altar.

Joachim stopped. Taerith knew, somehow, that his words were no longer intelligible to the wild men all around. "Do not fear me, Lord of the Twelve Bands," Joachim said. "I will not come so close that your sword can reach me—whatever you have promised to do, you cannot do it while there is distance between us." He smiled. "I did not truly think our roads would bring us here…

but Deus always works beyond imagination."

"I do not understand," Kardas answered. His voice was quiet. The anguish had not abated from his eyes. "Why has all this happened?"

Joachim leaned on his staff, and for an instant the young priest with light in the edges of his cloak seemed an ancient patriarch come lately down from the stars. "Your people are thieves and murderers, but Deus has sought them out. Tonight you are the hand of mercy."

Kardas lifted his eyes to the wild men as he spoke. "What mercy is there in binding men?" he asked.

Joachim ignored the question. "Give me your protection. There is a message in me; let me teach it to your people without fear of being driven away or killed."

Kardas bowed his head. "It is done," he said.

Taerith approached the men. He stood beside Joachim and looked up to Kardas—to Kardas who had saved his life, who had shown so much mercy, and paid so much for it. There should be freedom in this: in conquering, in becoming a king. And yet Kardas had not set himself free, for he had not died, and so he was bound just as he had been before. Taerith knew the answer to his question before he asked it.

"And you?"

"I return to Corran," Kardas answered, his voice little more than a rasp.

Taerith nodded. Even though he had expected it, the words still hurt.

Joachim turned and regarded Taerith. "And you, brother?" he asked.

Taerith looked at him with stars in his own eyes. The memory of impending death was too strong: he felt alive now, and knew why he was alive. "I have ties of my own to honour," he said. "I will go back and honour them."

Back to Lilia. To Borden. And then… somewhere in the shadows of the future, home lurked.

He would go back to Braedoch Forest.

*   *   *

Long ago, in another winter, Borden had come home from the north both as victor and bereaved son, still clutching the pain of his father's death to his bitter heart, riding behind his newly crowned brother. In that return there had been no celebration. Even Annar had choked back the pride of kingship and allowed those in his train to mourn.

But now, as they passed through the villages and fields of Corran, grim, deliberate celebration passed through with them. Borden allowed his men, especially the new recruits who had joined him for the final fight and then the glorious weeks of chasing barbarians further beyond the border, to tell stories and exaggerate them, to make of it all something filled with power and light. They gave out food. In the northern villages they had to pretend it was enough to replace what they had taken to feed the army, but as they went south, pretense fell away and every morsel was received with gladness.

And they adored him. They all adored him. Everywhere he went the people came into the streets and watched him pass with their hats doffed and their heads bowed, women with tears in their eyes, men proud. Even the children watched him ride.

They had once regarded Annar this way, when first he was

king. Before he hired Hosten with tribute money and proved himself a coward and drunkard.

They rode down the wide street of Esktown. So close to home, now, and the people were gaunt—even worse than they had been in the north, for Annar's taxes had struck harder here. They watched the returning warriors with hunger in their eyes.

Five men stood in the road, arms folded. Borden reigned in his horse and regarded them, frowning.

Jonas rode to his side and drew his sword.

"Will you bow before your prince?" he asked.

"No," said the biggest of the men. Borden reached for his sword without a word. Before his fingers could tighten on the hilt, the man dropped to one knee in the snow-packed earth.

"But I will bow before my king." The man raised his eyes and his hands together. "Yours, Lord Borden, as far as you will take us."

Wordlessly, the other four dropped to the earth beside their leader. They waited.

Guilt, a tiny snatch of it, tugged at Borden's mind as he looked at them. This was treason. It ought to be punished.

Instead, he met the man's eyes and nodded. Without another word spoken, the five rose and moved back into the crowd. Into the waiting town, among people who had seen and heard it all and knew, now, that those who owned Borden king would go unpunished.

Who knew, now, the heart of their prince.

*   *   *

Mirian sat with her forehead against one palm, fingers playing with her tangled hair as she frowned down at the page. She held the book open in her other hand, resting it on her knee, and struggled to sound the words out in her head.

"It's easier if you do it out loud at first," Lilia said from across the room.

Mirian tightened her fingers, half-pulling her own hair. "I don't want to," she said.

Lilia smiled and said nothing. Mirian looked up and saw the expression. "I'll sound like a fool," she said.

"Only a little like a child," Lilia answered. "It is not the same thing."

"Yes, it is," Mirian muttered. People had said that her mother was like a child in her imbecility, and from the moment she understood what that meant, Mirian had sworn never to be one.

"I wish you would read it out loud," Lilia said. Her voice was faint, as it always was, strained by hunger. "My eyes don't want to fix on the page anymore. I can't read it to myself."

Mirian snorted, but after a minute she began to try—shaping the sounds in her mouth, letting them out with awkward grace. Lilia closed her eyes and smiled.

Mirian read for a few minutes. After a while Lilia's breathing showed that she'd fallen asleep. Mirian's tongue relented before the gnawing in her stomach and she fell silent. She nearly stood to pace the room, but her head felt light and her stomach queasy. She stayed where she was.

Outside, freezing rain tapped against the stone walls and wet the heavy curtains. Winter was beginning to thaw. A single candle, glowing in a nook beside Mirian, was the only light in the room. The sun had long since gone down.

Mirian closed her eyes and let the atmosphere of the night sink in. It sank a long way: deep into a soul that was calmer than it had been in years. Hungry she was, worried to some degree about the future, and yet there was peace in her.

Freedom in her.

"Taerith!" The name was just perceptible as Lilia cried out, tossing beneath her coverlet. Mirian rose, ignoring the rush in her head and the shakiness of her legs, and crossed the room quickly. She laid a hand on Lilia's head. She was hot—it was nothing new. Her cheeks were flushed and the rest of her pale.

"Taerith," she said again.

"Hush," Mirian murmured. She pulled the blankets closer around Lilia's shoulders and stroked her head a little.

"I need…" Lilia said. Her breathing was faster than it had been, and she turned over again. "I need you," she said. "Take the baby."

Silence. Mirian sat on the side of the bed and watched as Lilia's breathing grew even again. Deeper sleep was claiming her now. Before she succumbed to it, Lilia whispered, "I need you."

*　　*　　*

Mirian awoke. She wondered a moment why she was so stiff, and then knew… she had fallen asleep sitting beside Lilia, bent almost double so that she could rest her head on her arms. The tapping of icy rain had ceased. Mirian stood and stretched, groaning a little, and crossed to the window. She moved the curtain just enough to see that the sun was rising over the dark blot of the fens.

She was about to turn away when she saw the riders.

She recognized the horse in the lead almost instantly. Borden had returned.

Hope leapt inside. They were home—Taerith, Borden. They drew wagons behind them, and was it? Was there food in the wagons?

She whirled away from the window, pausing only to make sure Lilia was still asleep, and flew down the stairs as fast as her slight dizziness would let her.

She ran into the courtyard and out through the small door in the side of the wall. The rising sun filled her eyes as she slipped over the icy fields toward the riders. On the horizon, her tree stretched its bare branches out toward her. She lifted a hand to it and turned back to face the coming riders.

She was the first thing Borden saw as he approached the castle. A tall figure with her hair streaming in the cold wind, hands and feet bare and impervious to the cold. The sun illuminated her face and the hope in it. Borden smiled at the sight.

He stopped his horse for her. She bowed her head a moment, then began to search the train with her eyes.

"We've brought provisions," Borden said. "A little help until spring comes again."

She nodded, hardly able to speak. Some of the men were grumbling behind Borden; they had stopped for a slave, and didn't like it. Borden raised his hand and waved them ahead. He stayed mounted where he was, with Mirian standing below him.

"The wild men?" she asked.

"They are vanquished," Borden answered.

She closed her eyes. He realized suddenly how weak she

looked, even in her strength. She wasn't steady on her feet. He nearly dismounted to help her, but managed to restrain himself in time.

She opened her eyes again and looked to the horsemen who rode by her on both sides. "Where is Taerith?" she asked.

Borden looked away. She read his face before he answered, and her own face fell.

"We lost him," Borden said. "He and Kardas. They played a brave part."

Mirian nodded. She turned away. Borden urged his horse forward a step and offered his hand.

"Ride behind me," he said. "Back to the castle; you're not well."

Mirian looked up at him. For a moment she stared, a small frown wrinkling her brow. Then she shook her head. "No," she said. "It wouldn't be right." And with that declaration she began to walk back to the castle, slipping on patches of ice in the furrows, stumbling with every step.

Borden watched her for a moment, then put his heels to his horse and galloped the rest of the way to the castle gate.

*　　*　　*

It was the work of an hour to unload all of the food into Master Grey's kitchen. Borden stood by the ovens with his arms folded, watching the servants as they worked.

The door opened. Mirian came in with a cold wind on her heels. Borden sank back into the shadows. He watched her move through the room, speaking with servants here and there, collecting food from various places and piling it all into a wooden bowl. No one stopped her.

She finished and pushed through a back door into a corridor. Borden followed.

Mirian had not gone far down the corridor when she heard his footsteps behind her. She whirled around. "Who's there?"

Borden stepped out of the shadows. "It's only me," he said. "You've made a fine collection."

Mirian looked down at the bowl in her hands. "For Lilia," she said.

"So you have managed to keep that job in my absence," Borden said. He was half-smiling. "Good. Are you nearly finished feeding the queen?"

"I don't know what you mean," Mirian said.

"You'll not be a lady's maid forever," Borden said. He reached out suddenly as though he would touch her, but she moved out of his range. He stopped.

His voice when he spoke again was low, almost a whisper. His heart was pounding as he spoke. The image of her waiting in the field to greet him seemed imposed on the image of her now, and he wanted, longed for, a glimpse of the fire that was in her and the strength that could increase his own.

"Things are going to change here," he said. "Truly change. They can. Our victory in the north has opened the way."

Mirian shook her head and drew back, farther into the shadows. "I don't know what you mean," she said.

"Long ago I asked what you thought of my brother," Borden said.

Mirian looked down and flushed slightly. "I said he was a fool."

"Fools should not sit thrones forever," Borden said.

Mirian looked at him a long minute. Then, slowly, "But who will depose them?"

"I will," Borden whispered. "We will."

"That's treason." The words were out of her mouth before she could stop them.

"Not treason," he said. He was almost pleading. He wanted her fire, but not against him, not this time. He wanted it behind him. He wanted it to burn for his own plans. "Not treason. I have taken a position of greater influence in this kingdom and I mean to make my brother listen to me. We will rule together, he and I."

She cocked an eyebrow. "And you don't want to be king?"

"I want to rule," Borden answered. "Whether they call me king or not doesn't matter."

"It does matter," Mirian started to say. He cut her off.

"I am being honest with you," he said. "I'm telling you my heart. I want your help, Mirian."

She shook her head. He was speaking to her as an equal, and it wasn't—she wasn't—something wasn't right. He saw her confusion and reached out again, catching her hand up and holding it tightly.

"Tell me you'll help me," he said.

She looked at him a long moment, cradling Lilia's bowl to her as though it was something precious. Finally she said, "Look to your brother. We have all been hungry, and he wants to solve it, but he is not—he is not wise."

Borden let go of her. "What do you mean?"

She shook her head again. "I don't know… I shouldn't speak of it. Talk to him. Try to help him do what's right."

Borden's mouth curled in a smile. "I knew you would help me."

In answer, Mirian looked down at the bowl in her hand. "Excuse me, my lord," she said. "The queen is hungry."

She turned and began to hurry down the corridor, putting out a hand to steady herself. He did not follow her, but his mind did: he watched her go to the tower, into slavery, into subjection to a queen so much less than herself. He told himself it would not be much longer.

Things, indeed, were going to change.

Chapter Twenty-Two

Confusion chased Mirian up the steps to the tower. When she reached the top she was flushed and her head was spinning, and it wasn't only hunger and effort that did it. She took a deep breath and pushed her way into Lilia's chambers.

Lilia had pushed herself up against the pillows. She was pale as ever. There was a look in her eyes that would have alarmed Mirian had she seen it—but she didn't look Lilia in the face.

"Borden is home," Mirian said. "They've won; they brought food."

"Where is Taerith?" Lilia asked.

Mirian glanced up, but not long enough to communicate with the look in Lilia's eyes. "Gone," she said. "Lost in battle."

They were silent. Neither would speak of her sorrow. Grief and regret welled up in Lilia, but that which inspired the look in her eyes kept it at bay.

"I need something from you," Lilia said.

"What is it?" Mirian asked. She set the bowl of food next to the bed and waited.

"Before Taerith left, he came to me with a request," Lilia said. "There is a boy in the village who lives with his widowed mother.

Taerith made me promise that if food came to us, I would feed him. I wanted to go myself."

"Very well then," Mirian said. The thought of getting outside the castle was like a promise of clear air in the midst of her manifold confusion, and she seized it. "You shall go. It will do you good to get out again."

"No," Lilia said.

"The air is not so cold as it has been," Mirian charged on. "We'll take a coach, and I'll help you walk where you must."

"No, Mirian."

Mirian looked Lilia in the eyes at last, but the look was masked now, carefully veiled. Mirian saw only the affection of her friend and a slight smile.

"I am tired today," Lilia said. "I want to rest. I can tell you where to go—Taerith's directions were clear. Go without me. Stay awhile if you like."

"Why would I like to do that?" Mirian asked. Memories of her encounter with Borden burst back into her consciousness and she felt a sudden strong desire to tell Lilia all about it, but Lilia held up a finger to motion her to silence. The young queen shook her head slightly.

"Don't argue with me," Lilia said. "You've been a caged thing all winter. Go." Something in her eyes flickered; for a bare moment a shadow passed over her face and sorrow was there in the room. Her voice was even softer than before. "I'll be here when you come back."

*   *   *

Borden left his meeting with Mirian in a state of frustration. He felt both affirmed and denied. She hadn't promised to help him—hadn't really told him that she would support him, and yet she would, she must. Like the men in the road who had owned him king, she must know that his was the true kingship, no matter how he denied that he wanted a throne. She hated Annar as he did. The king had enslaved her, and Mirian's greatest desire was to be free.

And she had, after all, warned him. Whatever Annar was trying to do, whatever unwisdom afflicted the kingdom this time, Mirian knew of it and had warned him.

He strode through the corridors of the castle until he reached Annar's throne room. He did not bother to announce himself, pushing past the nervous guards, who barely stammered out a word against him, and thrusting open the doors.

Annar looked up. There were two men with him. They wore the livery of Hosten's men.

Borden frowned. Hosten's servants turned to face him, and one of them blanched at the sight of the warrior prince newly returned from battle.

"Get out," Borden said.

The men looked at Annar. The king, obviously displeased, waved his fingers. "Go," he said. "Return in an hour."

The men turned and left in haste, the iron in Borden's eyes accosting them as they went.

Borden's eyes narrowed as he faced his brother in the newly emptied room. "What were they doing here?" he asked.

Annar had not risen from his throne. Insolence in his eyes met the iron in Borden's. Perverse triumph shone in them. Something in the corners of Annar's mouth crowed over his brother, like it had the day Annar was crowned.

Borden crossed the room in three strides and grabbed his brother by the collar, hauling him half-off the throne.

"What were they doing here?" he shouted. Any control he had over his voice was quickly slipping away.

Annar looked away, but he sneered as he did so. "You protect the kingdom your way," he said. "I'll protect it mine."

Borden dropped him. A cloud was growing inside him, a black, turbulent cloud, roiling with hatred and fear. The image of Hosten's servants was stark before him. He could almost hear the words Annar had spoken. Red rushed before his eyes.

A thousand scenes… a thousand slights, a thousand betrayals. Annar as a child, sulking and mean. Annar as a man, always drunk, always a fool. Annar on the battlefield, looking down at brother and dead father without remorse, with only excuses.

This is not my fault.

Borden could feel his father's weight in his arms. The red in his eyes was changing to black. Through it he saw Lilia's arrival. Annar's stubborn determination to produce an heir who would replace his brother.

Annar's voice reached him through the black scenes, at once far away and horridly close, as close as a demon's whisper in the ear.

"We were starving," Annar said. "You took too long. Playing your games in the north. Making a hero out of yourself. I know what you were trying to do. Hosten can feed us."

There was a taste like blood in Borden's mouth. He spit the words out. "At what price?"

Annar sat back. The old light was in his eyes. The mean child, the drunken fool, the one who did everything only to hurt his brother, was peering out of those eyes like a weasel cornered by a wolf.

"I may lose my rule," Annar said. "But you won't have it either."

And the red, the black, covered Borden's eyes and swallowed up his soul in a cauldron of seething hatred.

"I've signed it away," Annar said. "It's Hosten's now. There is no throne for you anymore."

*   *   *

Mirian knew from the moment she stepped back into the courtyard that something was wrong. The sense of it propelled her forward, faster until she was nearly running as she crossed the courtyard and passed through the door.

Two servants stood at the base of the stairs. Their faces told her everything. She started forward but one of the men stepped into her way. "You can't," he said. "No one else is to pass. They said to keep you out…"

She charged forward and the men grabbed onto her arms. She pushed against them, frustrated by her own weakness.

"Please, Mirian," one of the servants said. "Mistress Grey's orders…"

"Let go of me!" Mirian insisted. She tore herself away from them. She rushed up the stairs, knees nearly buckling, tripping herself. Terror drove her, grew with every breath she took. She nearly collided with one of the serving women, who was carrying an armload of rags from the landing to Lilia's room. The door stood slightly ajar.

A baby was crying.

The force that had driven her gave way just outside the door.

She was trembling now. She pushed the door open as she had done a thousand times, knowing dread as she had never known it. She smelled blood and something else.

Mistress Grey stood near the window with a baby in her arms. She looked up just as Mirian entered. Her eyes quickened; there were, as ever, sharp words on her tongue, but she did not speak them.

"Mirian."

Lilia's voice was quieter than it had ever been, and yet it was the only thing Mirian heard. She ran to the bed and fell on her knees beside it.

Lilia reached out with monumental effort and laid her pale hand on Mirian's wild head. Her gentle grey eyes hid nothing now. They spoke of pain and sorrow both, but overlying them— almost drowning them as it had never done before—was wonder.

"My miracle," she whispered. Her voice was ragged with pain, but she tried to smile through it. The baby's crying sounded far away. Mirian looked up at Mistress Grey and her bundle again, and then back to Lilia.

"Thank you," Lilia said. "For everything. And tell Taerith…"

Mirian reached over the sheets and grasped Lilia's hands. Tears sprang to her eyes but no words to her mouth.

Lilia's voice was hardly a whisper. "I always knew he loved me," she said. "Like an angel. Deus was good… to give me two of you."

The child-queen closed her eyes and sank more deeply into her pillows. One convulsive sob gripped Mirian. She lifted Lilia's hands and kissed them.

Eyes still closed, Lilia smiled.

Time passed. A hand touched Mirian's shoulder. She didn't react.

"Mirian," a voice said. Master Grey stood beyond her, almost pulling at her shoulder.

"Mirian," he said again. "Mirian, she's dead. Leave her."

Mirian turned her head. Tears were pouring down her face. She tried to speak, but words refused her their mastery. Master Grey was still pulling at her, insistent. She dropped Lilia's hands. Stood, unwilling, shaking her head.

Someone else took her other arm. They led her away, halfway down the stairs, before she pulled away from them and ran, out of the castle, into the cold day and the wind that was howling now, into the pain that swallowed her in sobbing. She reached the base of her tree and threw herself down among the roots and mud where the snow was melting and forming rivulets in the earth. All the ghosts of yesterday wept along with her.

*   *   *

Borden found her at the base of the tree. Tears and dirt streaked her face; her head ached, her eyes were blurred with weeping. It was a moment before she saw that his hands were covered with blood.

She stared up at him, propped herself up on her hands, and began shaking her head. She dragged her voice up from the pit that was her pain.

"What have you done?" she asked.

He held out his hands almost beseechingly, but there was something in his eyes that terrified her. "He sold us to Hosten," Borden said. "I stopped him. I kept us free. Mirian…"

She couldn't look at him. She looked down at her hands, covered in dirt and snow and tears. "No."

Desperation welled up in him as he looked down at her, sitting among the roots, devastated and yet still proud, and resisting him—resisting him when he needed her so much.

"There was nothing else I could do!" he said.

She looked up at him. The force of her green eyes caught him off balance, and he nearly staggered back. "You killed him."

Borden licked his lips and tasted blood. "He sold us."

Slowly, Mirian began to rise. The raw pain in her face struck him.

"What happened?" he asked. "Why are you crying?"

"Lilia…" she said, and her voice choked itself out.

His hands were shaking. His face contorted with emotion he didn't know how to handle. "It had to be," he said. "It's ours now, don't you see that? There is no one left to challenge us."

Mirian's tear-streaked face turned to stone at the words.

"I challenge you," she said.

He stood as if struck. Mirian's eyes went from his face to his hands—bloody hands, red and reeking with what he had done.

"Long ago you asked me what I thought of you," Mirian said. "I told you that I did not admire you. That changed—but not now, not anymore. The throne can't be yours. Not now."

Her face looked hollow, spent with grief, even as her voice quavered with fire trying to break loose. "It can't belong to a murderer."

And it was there again, red and black before his eyes, desperation raging. He snatched the riding whip from his waist and struck her across the face with it. A dark line of blood rose across her cheekbone, but she did not respond.

"I have made you free!" Borden shouted. There were tears in his own eyes, running into his dark beard. "They kept us enslaved; denied us what we are. Free, Mirian. The blood on my hands makes you free."

Mirian turned her head and looked at him. She had stopped crying. Blood mingled with dirt and dried tears on her cheek. There was pain in her eyes, and defiance.

"Speak to me!" Borden cried.

Her green eyes flashed a challenge. Slowly, deliberately, Mirian turned her other cheek.

He struck her again. Once more the blood stood out, beginning to trickle down her face as she closed her eyes and shut him out.

Shut him out forever.

The wind was sobbing through the branches of the tree. Suddenly every twig was in motion, waving and wailing like a creature come to life. Mirian's hair blew with the wind as she stood, ragged clothes blowing, standing against him.

He turned and staggered back to the castle.

*   *   *

The blood had nearly dried on his hands when he found Hosten's men, beat them, and sent them away with every contract of Annar's forever closed.

He could not walk in a straight line, and so he lurched to a small room on the castle wall where he stayed three days. Mourning. Raging. Exulting in the kingdom he had saved and trembling.

And then he remembered the child.

Borden came back into the light of day and sought out Master Grey like a hound flushing out a pheasant. Yes, Lilia had given birth to a child.

A child, Master Grey told him, who had disappeared.

Borden cursed. Mirian.

He had his challenge.

Chapter Twenty-Three

Steady, grey rain drizzled down as Taerith and Kardas made their way home. It melted off the snow and turned the roads to mud. The fens, still brown and dead and cold, swelled even as winter winds blew their last laments over them.

They journeyed on foot. Their horses had not survived capture by the wild men, and so they trudged over mud and swamp road, an exiled brother and a barbarian king going back to the place each had called "home" for his own reasons. They spoke little.

Through the trickle of rain and melting snow, the birds and beasts began to come back. Kardas made himself a spear and a bow so they could feed themselves. More than once they stopped by flowing waters where Taerith rigged up fishing lines. In its own way, the journey called up an old part of him: the Romany brother, the philosophical fisherman who watched the seasons change in the forest and helped feed his family as best he could. It was home to Corran he went, and yet he knew that the journey would not end there—that this road must take him all the way to Braedoch again.

But not now. There were promises to play out first, spoken and unspoken. Lilia to protect and love as he could. Kardas to stand by, Borden to report back to. And Mirian.

He smiled as he thought of Mirian. The day he had stitched the gash in her arm was vivid in his memory, and mingling with it was the scent of a night full of torchsmoke and horses when he had rebuked her for bullying Lilia, when he told the slave to lend her strength to a queen. She had done it… done more. She had nearly given her life for Lilia, and in that, Taerith knew, he was somehow bound to her, too.

The days did not run together. Taerith counted each one, counted every step back.

Kardas was first to hear the cries in the village ahead. Taerith heard them a moment later and reached for his sword, but Kardas put out a hand to stop him.

"There is no danger," he said. "It's the town crier."

They walked into the village side by side, sodden but steady, with a strength shining in their faces that spoke more loudly than the filth of the road ever could.

Both heard the words at once. They looked at one another.

"The king is dead!"

The crier stood in the village square, ringing a bell as he repeated his call. Kardas and Taerith came up behind him, one on either side, and Taerith laid a hand on his shoulder. The little man hadn't seen them coming. He jumped.

"Peace," Taerith said. "What happened?"

"The king is dead," the crier told them.

"We know that," Kardas said. "But how?"

The little man tried to stand straighter. He looked for a moment like a child defensive over some pleasure, and yet beneath that expression fear lurked. Taerith felt his heart sink.

"They say…" the crier said. "They say the prince killed him. But he's king now! Borden is king, and long may he reign!"

Taerith did not look at Kardas. He feared what he might see in the other's face. Besides, another fear had gripped him. He took hold of the little man with both hands and asked, "But what of the queen and her child?"

The town crier shook his head. "Borden is king," he said. "That's all I know."

*   *   *

Lookouts on the castle wall saw them coming up the long brown road. Kardas raised his hand in greeting. Even from so far below Taerith knew they'd been recognized. The gates were opened to them. Kardas at once disappeared into the shadows of the castle wall, and Taerith hurried through the thick morning mist to find shelter within—shelter, and the faces of those he had come back for.

It was Master Grey's face he saw, bent over a table in the kitchen. The steward looked up at him with firelight angling off his aged cheek.

"I want to see Lilia," Taerith said.

Master Grey turned his face back to the numbers he'd been adding on the table. He closed his eyes a moment and then straightened himself, standing tall as if the effort hurt. He sighed. "Oh, lad," he said.

*   *   *

They stood at the base of Mirian's tree. A wind had begun to blow, carrying cold drops of rain with it even as it dispersed the mist. The smells of roots and still newly-turned earth imprinted themselves on Taerith's heart.

"Mirian buried the girl herself," Master Grey said. He cleared his throat. "Here with her family. God knows what Borden would have done if he'd known."

Taerith swallowed. Overhanging branches—sod and rain—these couldn't be all that was left of Lilia.

And they weren't. He knelt by the unmarked grave and saw, darkened by the water and mud, three dove feathers that had been tied together with a bit of twine. He reached out and touched them, and something harder met his fingers. He dug for it a little, and pulled the dull, tarnished edge of a slave collar from the ground.

He looked up at Master Grey, blue eyes keen with questions. "Where is the child?" he asked.

"Dead," Master Grey answered. He lowered his voice. "Didn't survive childbirth, or so they say."

Taerith stood slowly, letting his fingers linger a moment on the slave collar first. "What do you mean?"

"Borden wants no opposition," Master Grey said. "He says the child died shortly after he was born. But then—he claims Hosten's men killed Annar."

"No one believes him," Taerith said. He knew the rumours that were in the villages, that inspired fear and uncertainty even as they proclaimed a new dawn and some sort of freedom.

"Yes, well," Master Grey answered. "My wife says the babe was healthy. All I know is that Annar had a son, and now he's gone… and so is Mirian."

Light sprang into Taerith's eyes. "And what does Borden say happened to her?"

"Why should he say anything?" Master Grey asked. "She's a slave; for all he's concerned she never existed." There was something in his eyes, in his face—pride perhaps. He lowered his voice still more. "He's hunting for her. He's found men—hired men, not his own soldiers—and sent them out everywhere with orders to find her."

"But he hasn't," Taerith said. "Not yet."

The old steward met Taerith's eyes and smiled. "Not yet," he agreed.

Taerith looked down at the grave and the rain that ran over it, and then lifted his eyes to the spreading branches. Birds were circling in the air above, caught between the clouds and the water that fell lightly from the sky. Tears formed in his eyes and ran down with the rain. The world seemed all a river, and he one with it—a river that rushed through a dark night, so long ago, when a beautiful girl told him about dreams with real things in it, about longing for freedom from tower heights and hearing songs in the water that made the moon cry.

He swallowed again. When he looked back at Master Grey his eyes were impossibly bright. Loss was written across his face, and yet it ennobled him somehow, made an angel of him. Master Grey had thought himself finished with crying, but tears sprang to his old eyes at the sight of the young man who faced him so earnestly.

"I'll find them," Taerith said.

But it wasn't to Master Grey he spoke, not really. It was not a new promise but the continuation of an old one. If the spirit of the girl to whom it had been made lingered still over the wet earth, both men were sure that she was glad to hear it.

*　　*　　*

Mirian's hand shook as she ran the fingers of one hand over the letters on the page, in a little hand-bound book propped up on her knee. The writing was large and black, the lines a little blurred where Lilia had used too much ink. The pages were smudged with dirt and fingerprints, ink and memories.

Letters drawn in the sheets on the bed, paper begged off a peddlar without Annar's knowledge, lessons in the tower while the wind outside tried to blow them down.

M is for Miracle.

For Mirian.

For Mortal.

Under the dark brown shawl that covered her from head to waist, Mirian held the baby tightly to her. He was sleeping, but fitfully. A flask of goat's milk, gift of mercy from a tavernkeeper's wife, contained just enough for one or two more feedings. When it was gone she would have to beg again.

Stiff, she shifted position against the barn wall. Straw and dust shifted with her in the faint light that came through cracks in the wall. The barn was old and ill-kept. She sat in one of the only dry patches. Just beyond her feet, raindrops still dripped from a hole in the roof.

The little book nearly fell as she moved, but she caught it. In the hours she'd spent hiding and holding the little one, the book had been her only recourse from reality. Not that it said much— Lilia had written the alphabet in it, and a few verses of old poetry. She had sketched a pair of conifers and a dove in the windowsill on the last two pages.

The fingerprints that marked the pages from the past few days left coppery stains. On her first flight through the fens, Mirian had managed to catch her cheek on a branch and rip open one of the gashes Borden had dealt her. Stopping the bloodflow had meant the use of her hands and her skirts, and since then there had not been a moment to stop and clean herself—not till this barn and its dripping roof. The cold raindrops stung and streaked her with dirt, but she wet her fingers with them and cleaned off some of the blood, all the while clutching the baby close to her with her other arm.

Something moved in the barnyard. Mirian froze. Her breath caught. Almost at the same time, she relaxed. The sound was too slight; it had only been the diseased old goat she'd seen in the yard when she climbed over a fence and let herself in through a hole in the barn wall the night before.

It was hard to catch her breath. In times like these, even the meanderings of a diseased goat were enough to make her heart pound.

The baby moved. Carefully, Mirian drew back her shawl, revealing the tiny face. She'd wrapped the baby up tightly in a grey blanket, tucking in his arms and bundling him securely as Mistress Grey had taught her to do, quickly and by candelight minutes before she fled.

A wry smile reached her face at the memory. Mistress Grey had no children and had always refused to take Mirian as her own—or else Mirian had refused to be taken, who could tell after so many years?—but in the end she'd told Mirian everything she knew about mothering and sent her out into the night.

And Mirian, terrifyingly aware that she knew nothing about caring for a child and was taking her life into her hands by abducting the king's heir, was grateful for it.

Mirian ran one finger along the baby's velvet cheek. She was tired—dreadfully tired, soul and body, and aching—and yet the sight of the little one revived her somehow. It seemed absurd that such a small one, to whom even sleep was new and tomorrow was free of burdens, should be the center of such a storm.

A clatter in the barnyard sent Mirian to her feet. She swept the shawl around the baby and pressed herself into the shadows where the water dripped slowly and pooled in dark spots on the floor. Heart in her throat, she pressed the baby to her until she feared she held him too tight. He stayed quiet. Miracle baby, truly.

In the barnyard, the splash of hooves in puddles and the shouts of men proclaimed the presence of trouble. Panic rushed in her ears so loudly that she could not make out what the men were saying.

A boy's voice shouted bravely in answer, and Mirian managed to sort out what he said.

"Not here," the boy said. "There's no one here but but my old mother and I."

Mirian sank deeper into the shadows, moving toward an old cow stall as quietly as she could. The mud and old manure within was ankle-deep, but a piece of the wall on the other side was completely gone, and she would flee through it if she had to. Dim light shone through the jagged hole.

One of the men had shouted an answer. The boy answered, his voice holding amazingly steady.

"Come in and see for yourselves, then. There's no one here."

Mirian set her jaw as she stepped into the muck, moving as quietly as she could and hoping the mud wouldn't audibly suck at her feet. The baby made a sound. She jostled him a little. "Shhhh."

The man's voice came through the rotting walls. "We'll have a look in there as well."

The boy's voice cracked a little, but from age, not nerves. "As you please. I warn you, it's a sinkhole. Mud and dung is all."

The men laughed. One of them threw out something about there being no man in the house to keep the barn up. Mirian reached out to steady herself against the wet boards of the wall. The mud was dragging at her skirts. Dim light lay over the mud just beyond her feet. She was nearly there.

"My father died," the boy said. His voice cracked again; he was angry. But the men didn't hear it. They laughed and made another comment.

A moment later, they pushed open the front doors of the barn. The doors groaned on their hinges, scraping across the muddy floor. One of the men dismounted and thrust his way in, torch blazing through the gloom.

The barn was empty.

Outside, Mirian raced behind a line of bare trees, eyes toward the shadows of the village. She didn't dare look back. The boy, man of his house, followed her with his eyes. Voices came from the barn, swearing loudly at the mud, and the boy smiled.

"Run, Mirian," he murmured. "God go with you."

*   *   *

Adrenaline carried her as far as the village and abruptly failed to hold her up. Mirian stumbled and nearly fell in the doorway of an inn. The streets were busy and no one paid her much mind, but she could hear hoofbeats—riders coming—Borden's men tracking her down. She pulled her shawl over her head, low so that she sat almost cowled as her eyes searched the street for danger.

They were there. Riders, three of them. Whether they were mercenaries or no, she couldn't tell, but she forced her eyes down until their shadows fell across her. They stopped.

Mirian held her breath. Her lungs cried out for air after her flight; every ounce of her needed air, needed food, needed something to give her strength. Her heart beat so hard she thought the men must be able to hear it. She needed sustenance; she had only fear.

The leader of the men kicked his horse and they moved on. She let her breath out. It came out shaking. She was shaking. The baby cried out.

"Hush." She looked down, moved the shawl aside so she could see the tiny face. Fine eyebrows, pink face. It struck her suddenly that he looked like Lilia.

The little one screwed up his face and started to cry in earnest. Mirian leaned against the doorpost as she stood, needing its support. She jiggled the baby as she did so, looking around as though someone might offer her help at any moment. The flask of goat's milk was gone; torn from her waist by a tree branch as she ran.

She looked up the street and saw that the men had stopped and were turning around.

She ducked through the inn door, into a smoky room full of men. The baby was still crying, more loudly now, and a table of patrons looked up at her with obvious annoyance and distaste. Well they might; she was a filthy, bloody beggar woman carrying a baby into a man's world. She made for the kitchen at the back of the inn, tripping over her own feet. Despite lamps and torches, the inn only grew darker as she went. The darkness wasn't in the room now; it was in her. Her grasp on the child was loosening.

She tried to step forward and somehow missed the floor. Darkness rushed at her.

And then there were arms around her from behind. She made one feeble attempt to free herself. But these were good arms, gentle arms. They held her up and kept the baby close to her. Half-standing, half-leaning against whoever was behind her, she turned her head so she could see him.

"Easy, Mirian," Taerith said. "Can you stand?"

She nodded. She could now. She forced her knees to straighten and stood on her own. Taerith's arms were still there. He guided her toward the kitchen.

"Keep going," he said, his voice low. "Don't look back. They're right behind you."

Chapter Twenty-Four

Taerith watched the men as they entered the tavern. Two of them, well-armed but roughly dressed. They pushed their way through the crowded dining room, skirting tables where men had huddled to drink or smoke their pipes. Taerith glanced behind him at Mirian, hidden in the shadows with Lilia's child in her arms. His stomach tightened.

Oh, Lilia.

Hand near his sword hilt, eyes still on the men, Taerith moved back into the shadows.

"Go through the kitchen," he said in a low voice. "Take the door into the street. Head for shelter and try not to be seen. I'll find you later."

Mirian nodded. She laid her hand on Taerith's arm, and he looked back at her. The bright strength in her green eyes nearly glowed in the darkness. She took her hand away and turned toward the kitchen.

The mercenaries had nearly reached the shadowy back of the room and were picking up their pace. Taerith folded his arms and stepped forward. The first of the men, a tall half-shaven brute, checked himself so as not to trip over him.

"Welcome," Taerith said. He wore a half-smile on his face and stood relaxed, as though the tavern was his and all the time in the world along with it.

The tall man declined to answer, trying instead to go past. Taerith moved into his way and smiled again.

"Is there something I can help you with?" he asked. The confrontation was beginning to draw the attention of the inn's regular patrons. A few men turned and watched from their close-drawn huddles.

The tall man grunted. He looked past Taerith once more and suddenly relaxed. "Girl come through here?" he asked.

"This is the way to the kitchen," Taerith answered. "Our guests don't make a habit of passing through." He stepped forward, and both men fell back a few feet. Taerith released his arms, resting the heel of one hand on his sword hilt.

"You look as though you've traveled far," he said. "Ale on the house?"

Inwardly, he tensed and waited for the tavernkeeper or someone else to protest. No one did. The tall man looked torn. His shorter companion burst into the conversation.

"We followed a girl in here," he said. "We want to know where she went. Out of our way, would you?"

A dangerous glint in Taerith's blue eyes warned the men that trouble had found them. "I think not," he said. He motioned toward a half-empty table. "Please… a drink?"

He swallowed as he waited for them to respond. He couldn't take his eyes away from them—couldn't let his challenge waver even for a moment. But without gauging the reactions of the other men in the tavern, he had no certainty that this would work.

The smaller man was obviously close to losing his temper. "You know where she went," he said. "Tell us, or we'll whip you through the streets, boy."

Taerith smiled again, sincerely this time. They had crossed the line and he knew it. He drew himself up a little straighter.

"Tell me, man," he said, raising his voice. "Where you come from, do men often give up women to hounds who hunt them?"

The smaller man flushed. "You know nothing about it," he said.

"True," Taerith said. "And by that token, if you're honest men, you'll have a drink with me and tell me your business. And if you're not, you'll not get past us."

He waited for the response. It came. More than one of the men in the tavern was on his feet, voicing assent. Some of the tension that had held Taerith in place released, and he folded his arms again. He could all but see Mirian hurrying down the rainy street—getting away. He kept his voice level but loud.

"She had a baby with her." He knew he was giving away too much—spreading information that Borden could use. Yet the victory here couldn't be his alone. He needed the help of the others. "Do you expect us to give up our children as well? You're mercenaries. Who's paid you to hunt us?"

The answering fury in the shorter man's eyes told Taerith all he needed to know. He moved first, stepping aside even as the mercenary lunged. With a quick motion, he tripped the man and shoved him. He sprawled into the forming crowd, hitting his head on the back of a wooden chair. The tall man stepped forward as though he would do something, but three of the tavern men moved menacingly into his way.

The mercenary on the floor glared up at the men around

him. Through gritted teeth he spat out, "Get out of my way. We'll be going."

A big, grizzled man, one who had been in the tavern drinking slowly most of the day, shook his bearded head. "Not yet," he said. "The lad asked you some good questions. I've a mind you should answer them."

Taerith stepped back and let the men of the tavern move in front of him. They were blocking the paths of both mercenaries now, prodded both by the beer in their blood and the challenge to their honour in Taerith's words. As heated words began to rise on both sides, he slipped through the kitchen and out the back door.

*   *   *

Taerith jogged into the street, looking north and south as he did. The night's sporadic drizzle had turned into a steady rain, falling straight and steady, with wide swaths of sunlight where the clouds opened up. The sun's rays made the wet dirt of the street golden and warm, full of living promise despite the deep puddles riddled with raindrops in every pothole and rut.

The men in the tavern would likely throw the mercenaries out on their ears any moment. Taerith spied a laneway between two buildings and ducked into it. He paused for a moment, looking at the deceptively calm face of the tavern. Sadness called a smile to his face. The men of the town might have been tricked into it, but now at last they defended Lilia.

He turned away. "All right, Mirian," he muttered. "Where are you?"

A shadow fell behind him, blocking the light of the sun and making the laneway suddenly colder. He turned to see the silhouette of a tall man with a long knife in his hand.

"Well met," the man said, and threw the knife.

*   *   *

The baby wouldn't stop crying. For the first time Mirian was glad that his cry was so weak. She muffled it as best she could without smothering the little one in her shawl. She jostled him as she half-walked, half-ran in search of shelter. She had no time or inclination to watch the mud puddles, and by the time she was on the outskirts of the town her skirts were soaked with cold brown water.

The baby's whole body heaved with his cries. She clutched him closer as she scrambled over a ditch toward a low dairy barn. A window on one side was open and she climbed through, dropping to the low dirt floor. Stone walls kept the place cold. The barn was nearly empty. Empty stalls spoke of better years, when livestock and their produce were plentiful, and of the receding winter that had destroyed so much. One cow remained. It turned to regard her with doleful brown eyes. The baby's cries seemed louder.

Mirian approached the cow and circled it gingerly. The swollen udder told her all she needed to know. A quick glance around the barn revealed a heap of hay in one corner. She took her shawl off, shivering in the damp cold, and wrapped the crying baby well. She laid him down, shushing him as she did so. He kept on crying with all the strength in his lungs.

With the baby down, she shook out her skirts, looking with little hope for some usable bit of cloth. What wasn't torn and ragged was filthy. For a moment she considered giving up, but the baby's cries grew louder and more frantic. The sound was nearly enough to send her nerves screaming, but she kept control. She knew well enough how hunger felt.

"I'm coming!" she said. The cries didn't abate.

Ropes, sacks, and other equipment hung from hooks on one wall. Mirian ran her hands over them in the gloom. Her fingers fell on tightly woven cloth behind a sack. She grabbed it and pulled it out. It would have to do. Quickly, she rubbed a small section on the stone wall, fraying the cloth and wearing it as thin as she could in such a concerted attack. She gathered the edges around the thin part and tied them together with threads torn from her sleeve, cutting it off from the rest of the cloth. Then she shook it out, bunched the ends to make a bag, and approached the cow.

"Just hold still," she said, putting out a hand against the cow's hot side. It shifted slightly, but stayed close enough. She crouched down, manuevering her bag awkwardly so she could milk into it. She propped it open on one arm and reached for the udder with her free hand. It was full. She squeezed and smiled with relief as a stream of milk shot into the bag.

The baby was still crying. She ignored the pain as her hand started to cramp and kept working until she had a fair amount of milk in the bottom of the bag. It might start to leak at any minute. She stood, gave the cow one good pat, and half-ran to the hay bales where Lilia's son proclaimed his hunger.

"Here, here," she said. She picked the baby up and rested him in the crook of her arm. With the other hand she tore away the threads binding the worn part of the cloth and squeezed her fingers around it to form a place for the baby to suck. As quickly as she could, she moved the bag till the end was in the little one's mouth. He sucked at it, stifling his own cries.

The bag felt damp under her arm. Her hand was still cramping. She cursed the thought of how much milk was soaking into the cloth. As the baby quieted, so did her heart. She'd hardly realized how hard it was beating.

The baby turned his head and milk smeared his cheek. "Here now," she said. She guided his face back, trying to make him latch on and keep feeding. He did for another moment and then turned away again.

"I'm sorry," she whispered. "I wish I could feed you like a mother would. I don't know how long you can keep this up."

Outside the barn, hoofbeats sounded. Mirian nearly dropped the bag as she tightened her grip on the baby. The hoofbeats passed, and she let out her breath.

"Taerith will come soon," she whispered. The baby looked up at her with glassy eyes. Doubt struck her and she forced it down again.

Taerith would make things right.

He had to.

*   *   *

Borden's men stood in ranks along the length of the hall. The stone walls and floor were cold and immovable as Borden paced up and down the line. Inspecting. Waiting. The men could see that his mind wasn't with them, but was roaming, searching, out somewhere they couldn't go. It was in his eyes.

He spoke as he paced. Matters of business. The men answered in low tones. They reported on patrols, on the game that was beginning to return, on the state of the farms. Borden nodded. Suddenly he stopped.

Borden looked at Kardas as though he was seeing him for the first time. He cocked his head as he regarded the dark man. Kardas looked back, his face a mask.

"You came back alone," Borden said. "Taerith was lost in the north?"

Kardas turned his eyes down. "No, my lord. He lives."

Borden roared his answer, every muscle in his face straining. "Then why didn't he come back to me?"

Borden's voice echoed in the room. He covered his eyes with his hand and groaned. When he lowered his hand, it was wearily. His voice was back to normal. He looked sidelong at Kardas as he spoke.

"He was my soldier. Why didn't he come back to me?"

Kardas made no answer. Borden waited. His dark eyes roiled with pain and anger together.

"Stay silent, then," he said. "You, at least, came back where I can look your disloyalty in the face."

He paced forward and turned so that he stood directly in front of Kardas. "Harsh word? What else is this silence if it isn't disloyalty? But don't fear—I won't force the matter. We will pretend this conversation didn't happen. I am glad, Kardas—glad that he lives."

At the other end of the hall, a new arrival drew Borden's attention. He turned from Kardas and waited, arms folded.

The man who entered was cloaked and small. He walked almost nervously, eyeing the soldiers who lined the hall, yet without balking. He stopped a few feet away from Borden and bowed shortly.

"We found her," he said.

Borden looked up at his men. "Out, all of you. Not you, Kardas."

The soldiers turned and filed out of the hall, some casting curious glances behind them. The newcomer waited until the door had closed behind the last of them.

"She has the child. All this time you've been sending us out, she's been right under your nose. In the nearest village."

Borden's jaw twitched. "Where is she?" he growled.

"We lost her," the man said. He didn't even flinch at the look on Borden's face. "The others followed her into a tavern, where they were delayed. A man stopped them. Started a fight and then disappeared. I started to follow him but was… discouraged. I think he went after her."

"And you didn't?" Borden said. He looked as though he would cuff the man.

"No," the man answered. "Sometimes I am slow on my feet. But she cannot have gone far."

Borden looked down, his tangled black hair shading his face. "You say a man stopped them. A young man?"

"Yes," the mercenary answered. "About the height of this man." He pointed to Kardas. "Dark hair. Quiet, but smart."

Borden looked at Kardas. His eyes nearly burned a hole through him. "So now we know," he said, "why he didn't come back. Kardas, saddle your horse and mine. We are going to finish this ourselves."

Chapter Twenty-Five

The knife whistled past Taerith's head. He let out a sharp breath as the blade thunked in a piece of wood. He turned. The knife had embedded itself in a hitching post in the street, fastening a piece of a small man's cloak along with it. The man in question looked up and quickly back down again, tugging at his cloak.

"He meant to follow you," the tall man in the alley said. "I apologize if I startled you."

Taerith smiled in wonderment as he turned. "Randal," he said.

The tall sword-swallower bowed. "At your service. That fellow will work his way free in a moment. Shall we remove?"

Taerith broke into a grin and grabbed Randal's hand and elbow with fierce joy even as he moved toward the back of the alley. "Let's."

They ducked behind the row of buildings and made for a low ditch screened by winter-dead bushes. "It's good to see you," Taerith said. "So good to see you. Where are the others?"

"Not far," Randal said. He stopped and looked at Taerith with concern in his eyes. "Tell me. How go things for you?"

Taerith shook his head. "Not as well as I could have hoped.

But I have work to do—that at least I have."

"Are you still in the queen's service?" Randal asked.

With a pang Taerith remembered that it had been Randal who first warned him that there was danger to Lilia in Corran—who had first urged him to stay and protect her. Randal had been there the night they rescued her from marauders on the road. Memories rushed at him and he pushed them back. He called up his first line of defense: Mirian's face, and the babe in her arms. He had work to do.

"She's dead," he said. They had reached the ditch. He pushed dead branches aside and dropped into it. Randal followed close behind. The bottom was water-logged, but their boots kept their feet dry as they slogged along.

"I'm sorry," Randal answered.

"Do you remember the slave girl?" Taerith asked. "The one who defended the unicorn?"

Randal smiled. "She's not easy to forget."

"I have to find her," Taerith said. "She's hiding here in the village somewhere with… with a child. Not her own child—an orphan she's caring for. Trouble is after her. I sent her away and told her I'd find her."

"You want our help," Randal said.

Taerith stopped. A cold breeze blew with the scent of wet, dead leaves and stagnant water. "If you'll give it."

"There is no if," Randal said. "How old is this child?"

"Less than three weeks," Taerith said.

Pain passed over Randal's face like a light. "So young," he said. "Too young to be motherless."

Taerith saw the hurt in Randal's eyes, but the image he'd called up of Mirian and the baby was pressing on him now. He had no time to ask questions. "Mirian will have headed for the edges of town, but not likely left it completely," Taerith said. "I need to find her quickly."

"Then search," Randal said. He was already turning away. "I am going for more help. We'll find her."

*   *   *

The baby fussed and squirmed until Mirian's nerves were raw. The milk bag grew damper. The fourth time she tried to milk into it, she watched every drop soak through and streak the flagstones with white. The baby's wails were growing frantic.

With a frustrated half-cry of her own, Mirian snatched the bag up, stood, and threw the sopping cloth on the floor. A wave of nausea hit her as she stood, and black spots appeared before her eyes. She leaned against the cow and glared across the room at the baby, hot tears in her eyes threatening to spill over.

The dizziness passed. She closed her eyes and sighed.

The baby kept crying.

She pushed herself off the side of the cow and wearily crossed the room. She picked the baby up off his heap of straw, held him in front of her, turned, and sank to the floor with her back to the hay. She jiggled him a little and his cries quieted slightly.

"Listen to me," she said. "I know you're hungry. I know it's cold in here. But this isn't going to last forever. You and I will be leaving soon, and I will keep you warm, and find you food, and you will grow and… and live." She swallowed. "I need you to stop crying. Someone might hear you and then I don't know what I'll do. Your mother never complained enough. Can't you take after her? Just for now?"

For a moment he stopped crying and met her eyes, his dark eyes peering back at her with seeming understanding. Then he screwed up his face and began to wail again.

"Oh, hush!" Mirian burst out. She drew the baby close, nestling him into her breast, and leaned against the hay. Tears were still coming to her eyes, stinging, and making the barn walls blur. She stroked the back of the child's head and started to hum—awkwardly, softly.

She was never sure which of them fell asleep first.

*   *   *

The small mercenary led Borden and Kardas through the street to the tavern. He walked with his back slightly hunched. The edge of his cloak was ragged where Randal's knife had pegged it.

He stopped before the tavern door and motioned inside.

"In there," he said.

Borden dismounted and walked into the smoky dining room. Furniture was still strewn around the floor, tables and chairs overturned, some pieces smashed. In the middle of it all his mercenaries sat, back to back. The tall one was asleep. The shorter one was singing. There were a few other men still in the room. They stood against the back wall, arms folded, taciturnly watching the drunks.

Borden walked slowly across the room, eyes on the men who lined the back wall. He reached the drunks and stopped inches from the singer. He looked down at them and raised an eyebrow.

The man kept singing. Behind him, his tall companion snored once.

Borden drew his foot back and kicked the singer in the leg. The man yelped and jumped up. He pointed a shaky finger.

"You shouldn't…" he started.

"Enough!" Borden roared. The man cowered at the strength of Borden's voice. Beneath the drunken sheen of his face, he paled.

"My lord Borden," he said.

The men in the back of the room stirred and muttered to themselves. Borden looked up at them.

"No fear," he said. "Help me get these wretches off your floor."

The smaller of the men was turning colours. "We tried, my lord," he said. "We chased her in here, but—"

He couldn't finish. Borden drew his sword and killed him where he stood.

The silence in the tavern resounded. The men on the back wall shifted uneasily as Borden stood over the bleeding body. He looked up at them. The dark fire in his eyes was the singular force in the room. He nodded at the taller mercenary. The man was awake now, his eyes wide.

"Come with me," Borden said. "The rest of you—go on with your day. And clean up in here."

He turned and left the tavern. Kardas, lurking in the shadows near the door, followed him. The tall mercenary came last of all, tripping over his own feet.

In the street, Borden wheeled on the man.

"Not a word in front of anyone," he said. "These people aren't to know."

The mercenary nodded. Borden grabbed him by the throat.

"Where did he go? The man who stopped you in the tavern?"

"I don't—don't know," the mercenary stammered.

Borden dropped him. He scrambled to stay on his feet.

"Ride behind Kardas," Borden said. He put his foot in the stirrup and looked down the street with his eyes narrowed. His words were faint. He was only half-listening to himself. "We may need you."

*   *   *

What drew him to the barn he wasn't sure, but as Taerith searched the lanes at the edge of the village, it commanded his attention. It was a low, stone building, a dairy barn built out of the ground. A flock of crows was perched atop it, looking sagely down at him. He looked back up at them. The sky overhead was clearing of rain, and through the clouds above the crows the sun was paling down.

The barn doors were barred. He circled the whitewashed stone walls until he found a window closed by a piece of wood. He pushed it and it nearly fell in. Carefully, he lifted it out of the way and climbed in.

The interior was gloomy, but the open window behind him let in a beam of light that illuminated a haystack and Mirian. She was asleep. The baby was in her arms, with his little head nestled at the base of her throat.

Taerith's own throat constricted as he looked at them. It had been dark in the tavern, and hurried; he hadn't had a good look at Mirian. She was filthy, ragged, and obviously exhausted. Gashes along both her cheekbones had scabbed over, but one had recently ripped open. Her face was streaked with dirt and traces of blood. Rough red callouses around her neck showed the place where the slave collar had rested most of her life. He wondered how young she'd been when she wore it for the first time.

Movement behind him startled him. He whirled around. Randal was letting himself in through the window.

That was quick, Taerith thought. *How did you find me so fast?* But he couldn't make words come out his mouth.

Randal looked soberly at Mirian and the baby. Then he turned and reached outside the window. A hand took his, and he helped Marta climb in. Little musclebound Orlin came in after her.

It was Marta who broke the silence.

"Oh, the poor dear child," she said. In an instant she crossed to the haymound and gathered Mirian in her arms. Mirian stirred and opened her eyes, laying her tangled red-brown head on Marta's shoulder. She looked up.

"Who are you?" she asked.

"Help," Marta answered.

Taerith stepped forward. Mirian saw him and relaxed still more deeply into Marta's embrace.

"You found me," she said.

Marta was looking over Mirian's shoulder at the baby. He was still asleep, lying close to Mirian's heart with his tiny mouth puckered up.

"What is his name?" Marta asked.

Taerith found suddenly that all eyes were on him. He looked down at Mirian. She smiled a little.

"We didn't name him," she said.

Marta clicked her tongue. "That won't do," she said.

Mirian was still looking at Taerith. She cocked her head. Through the exhaustion that lined her face, her green eyes were more vivid than ever.

"You tell us," she said.

Taerith stepped forward and knelt down beside Mirian and the baby. He reached out and touched the soft head, running his fingers down the little one's cheek. Little, fatherless, motherless. An outcast. Lilia's child.

"Isaak," he said. His voice was husky. "His name is Isaak."

"A good name," Randal said. His voice sounded far away. Taerith was absorbed in the baby. He reached out, and Mirian gently laid the baby in his arms. Carefully, Taerith drew his Isaak close. He stood, his eyes only on the child.

"It was my father's name," he said.

*   *   *

Kardas rode watchfully. The town stretched before them like a dark maze full of doors, full of secrets. The tall mercenary behind him, Doublin by name, held on with his knees and said not a word. Borden led them in fits and starts, a living storm, banging at doors, searching homes and outbuildings.

The people of the village watched him with fear in their eyes and made no move to prevent him. Once a man looked as though he would protest the invasion. Kardas and Doublin drew their swords and warned him away with their eyes. He listened.

They rode down the main street, doubled back, and took a side road. The clouds overhead had cleared away by the time they came upon the whitewashed barn. It shone in the sun. But the storm that rode with them darkened it with a shadow as they approached.

A flock of crows picked around the barnyard. They squawked

and flew up, alighting on the barn roof as Borden approached. He dismounted and drew his sword.

Kardas stayed mounted. Every muscle in his body was tense. He could see the footprints in the muddy ground, the signs of activity around the open window with a board lying in the bushes near it. Someone had been here.

Borden moved forward quietly. With a single motion he swung down through the window. Kardas waited. His horse stamped its foot.

A moment passed. Another.

Borden appeared in the window. He held a damp piece of cloth, full of holes, on the end of his sword. He threw it on the ground.

"They were here," he said.

Chapter Twenty-Six

The circus tents, faded and patched, were pitched on a level bit of ground on a hillside, above a pond still laced over with vestiges of ice. One striped flap was stirring in the cold breeze as they approached. Taerith, with a well-bundled Isaak in his arms and Mirian at his side, smiled at the sight. Fugitives they were, on the run, and yet somehow the tent's flimsy shelter could not have felt more secure. The wagons lay beyond the tents, and magnificent red Sol was hitched to a spindly tree near the pond.

Mirian walked with her shawl wound tightly around her, staggering a little as she went. Marta and Randal walked just behind her, keeping an anxious arm ready to catch or support her if she failed to keep her feet.

Findal appeared in the door of the tent, rising on his toes to see them approaching. His wispy hair blew in the breeze, around a solemn face shining with a quiet power—the power of help, of welcome. Taerith strode up the hill, holding Isaak to his chest, and stopped in front of the circus master.

"Thank you for your help," he said.

Findal nodded. "Come in, come in," he said. He stepped aside and ushered them all into the colourful confines of the tent. They stepped past stacks of crates and cushions, finding a makeshift seat wherever they could. Marta took Mirian's hand as the slave girl lowered herself onto a bed of woolen blankets and hay. A wiry brown dog jumped to its feet beside her and started licking her leg. Mirian smiled at it and rested her hand on its head.

Taerith started to sit on a crate, but as he did baby Isaak awoke. He rubbed his nose twice against Taerith's chest, and then began to whimper.

Marta was there instantly. She took Isaak carefully into her own arms, and with a teary-eyed smile at her husband, ducked behind a flap to another part of the tent.

"She'll feed him," Randal explained. Taerith looked at him, his question in his eyes.

"We lost one," Randal said. He didn't meet Taerith's eyes. "Only a week ago."

There was silence. Mirian broke it. "I'm sorry," she said. "But grateful."

Randal looked at her and smiled. "We serve as we can, my lady."

Mirian flushed and looked away. Taerith saw a stab of pain in her eyes, mingled with pleasure, and wondered what she was thinking. She had changed so much. The dog whined and pushed at her hand, begging for more active attention.

Taerith picked up a piece of straw and twisted it as he looked around the tent. They were all gathered: Orlin and Randal, Morris Syve twisted in knots in the far corner, Findal on a crate looking like an old gnome king. A goat pushed its way under the edge of the tent and meandered through, hardly drawing any attention.

"Where is Zhenya?" Taerith asked. The crippled boy's absence struck him for the first time.

An odd light came into Findal's eyes. "Oh, not far, not far," Findal said. "He's a good boy, Zhenya. Draws crowds for us when he wants to. Doesn't when he doesn't want to. Or when the unicorn doesn't want to. They're the reason, really, that we don't pitch in town anymore. Lonelier out here on hillsides, but sometimes it's better we keep our distance."

He was quiet for a moment, and then snorted. "It's a strange circus we are these days."

Randal interjected. "We're only passing through Corran. If word had reached us of the trouble here, we might not have come."

"Yes," Findal said. He furrowed his brow. "So tell us, lad. The child—it's the heir, isn't it?"

Taerith nodded. The straw in his hands was full of creases, and he smoothed it out. "He's in danger."

"You all are," Findal said. "Abducting the king's heir!"

Taerith looked up and met Findal's eyes. The blue in his own was intense. "We're only saving his life. Nothing more."

"We know that," Randal said. "There's no guile in you." He smiled crookedly. "You're one of us."

"But a circus is a good place to hide," Findal said. "Natural that we should be on the road, and people pay so much attention to us that they'll never actually notice anything. You'll stay with us."

Taerith opened his mouth, but Findal carried on. "We are going south. The famine was not quite so bad there; people still have money to pay. We've been treading hungry lands all winter and I'll tell you—it's enough to give a man a lifelong bellyache. No place so bad as Corran, though."

"Why did you stay in the north so long?" Taerith asked.

"People needed cheering up," Findal said. His eyes twinkled despite himself, but he saddened quickly. "It'll be none too cheery here now, with Borden king."

"Findal," Taerith said, "long ago you told me that Borden was a villain through and through."

The little man's eyes flashed. "I did, that. I know them when I see them. Greedy and inhuman…"

"No," Taerith interrupted. "You were wrong about him."

Findal looked up at the young man. His wizened face was puzzled, but he said nothing. Taerith looked down at his hands, stripping off a bit of straw.

"He's in too deep now," Taerith said. "But—but he could have been a good king, once. As he was a good captain." He stood abruptly. "I want some air. I'm going to scout the area. I'll be back."

He stopped at the tent flap. "We will go south with you," he said. "Only for a time. I don't know about Mirian, but I must go east."

"What's in the east, boy?" Findal asked.

"Home," Taerith answered.

*   *   *

The footprints were everywhere in the mud. Farther on, as they reached higher ground, they faded—but even there the passage of feet was obvious. The numbers were puzzling: there were more here than just Taerith and Mirian. Yet it was clear from the way Borden tracked them that he was convinced of who he followed. And Kardas, coming behind, was just as certain.

He prayed as he rode, to the great winged God. Prayed that the madman before him would fail. Prayed that there would be speed in Taerith's steps.

The king of the wild men rode with a mercenary behind him on his horse and wished with all his heart he was somewhere else.

*   *   *

Taerith breathed deeply of the spring air. The rain had stopped. Everything felt new—despite the cold, despite the ice and snow that stubbornly clung in places, despite the brown earth and dead branches and grasses on every side. Life was here—dormant perhaps, but waking.

He turned and looked down the hill at the tent, nestled by the pond, purple and yellow and red, Sol worrying the branches of the tree. Mirian and Marta were outside, conferring over a goat. Taerith smiled at the sight of them.

He was aware, suddenly, of a presence behind him.

He turned and looked into the black eyes of a unicorn. The creature stood with its head low, long mane and tail blowing shaggily in the breeze, silver horn gleaming in the sunlight that peered through the last rainclouds. Zhenya stood beside the unicorn with his hand on its back. His crutch was gone.

"Welcome back," Zhenya said.

Taerith held out his hand. "It is good to see you, little brother."

"Did you take care of her?" Zhenya asked.

It took Taerith a moment to figure out what he meant. Then, "Yes," he said. "As best as I could. But it wasn't enough—not in the end."

"Yes, it was," Zhenya said.

Silence a moment. "You sound very sure," Taerith said.

"You did all you could?" Zhenya said.

Taerith nodded.

"Then it was enough." The boy, older and taller now but still childlike—and deep, so deep Taerith could hardly look him in the eye—looked down at Mirian and Marta.

"I remember her."

"She fought for your unicorn once." Taerith half-chuckled. "Or perhaps my words are wrong. How can a creature like that belong to anyone?"

Zhenya looked up at him with his strange, dark eyes. "He does," he said. "He belongs to me. By choice. By love. That's the only real kind of belonging."

Taerith's throat tightened. He nodded.

* * *

Below them, Mirian finished her concerted goat-milking and looked up at Marta. Her face was serious, her green eyes strangely hungry, still marked as she spoke with the remnant of fear.

"Thank you," she said. "I was so afraid…"

Marta smiled and touched Mirian's chin. "I know, child."

"He was starving, and I couldn't feed him."

"He'll not starve now," Marta said. "He's none the worse for wear. You kept him warm and fed him enough." She smiled again. "You're both going to be fine."

Mirian looked down. She was smiling despite herself. She picked up the milk bucket and stood, patting the goat.

"She's a mighty fine nanny goat," Marta said. "Gives lots of good milk. She's been a boon to us."

Mirian nodded. Marta laid a hand on her arm. "Still," she said. "We don't need her."

Mirian cocked her head. "I think we're staying with you," she said.

"So do I!" Marta said. "I'm just saying. Eventualities. You never know what will happen. But yes, stay."

They turned together to go back to the tent. The view from the hillside swept away down the fens, thawing under the pale spring sun. The town sprawled at the border of them, and beyond that, the castle. Mirian thought she could see her tree.

Her whole world lay before her, visible from halfway up a hill. She had never really thought she'd leave. And for a little while, when Lilia was with her, she hadn't really wanted to.

Sorrow tugged at her heart as she looked at the castle towers. They were lonely. Achingly lonely. Only a moment passed before she couldn't bear to look anymore, and she ducked inside the tent without a word.

*   *   *

They sat at the base of the hill, hidden in a copse of trees, looking up. Kardas and Doublin dismounted after an hour. Doublin started to gather wood for a fire but Kardas put out a hand and stopped him. Borden would not want smoke. No sign of their presence.

Borden stayed mounted. He sat in the trees like a spirit of some darker spring, astride his horse, unmoving as the wind blew in the branches over him and crows cawed their forebodings. In old days Kardas had known his prince to lose himself in thought, but never so deeply—never so darkly.

On the hill, the circus tents sat, painted like the gaudy promise of terror.

Kardas swallowed as he looked up, past Borden to the tents. Terror, yes, but who felt it but him?

Borden's back was turned. He sat as still as stone. Kardas found his hand on his sword hilt, found himself tightening his fingers, found himself ready to stand, to move as silently as a moth in the night, to pierce the terror at its heart and let it ebb away where it could do no harm.

He loosened his fingers. Closed his eyes. Tears, loyal tears, struggled to slip by his eyelids.

They didn't.

Evening was coming.

*　*　*

Findal watched Taerith as he crossed the tent for the twelfth time and opened the flap to peer into the waning light. He chuckled wheezily.

"In the morning, lad," he said. "We'll go in the morning. Time enough."

Taerith said nothing. A sound came from without: a high, confused, rushing sound. Taerith disappeared through the flap. Hardly knowing why, Findal hurried to join him.

Taerith was standing near the edge of the pond. Overhead, a huge flock of birds raced toward the fens. This was no smooth migration: it was a roiling, terrified bid for life and liberty. They looked and sounded like creatures with winged wolves on their heels.

Taerith turned and faced Findal as the circus master approached. His blue eyes were sharp. "Tonight," he said.

Findal started to protest. He turned in the direction the birds had flown, looking down the hill to a copse of trees.

It seemed to him that something was there. Something not human—a shadow waiting.

He blinked and looked again, but could see nothing.

He nodded. "Tonight."

*　　*　　*

Doublin stared into the pile of branches he had collected and been unallowed to light. Kardas sat across from him, facing the hill. Borden had sunk farther back in the shadows and dismounted, but still he looked up.

There was movement on the hill. Kardas stood in surprise.

They were taking down the tents.

*　　*　　*

The long shadows of evening had reached the hillside as they worked. Findal talked, his usually breathless voice aggravated by the work of loading poles into the wagon.

"We'll go south for a week or so. Good towns down there, especially with spring coming. You can work with us… fix wagons or something. Can that Mirian do anything?"

"I'm sorry, Findal," Taerith said. He loaded a piece of tenting into the wagon and made sure it was secured by rope. "We're not going with you."

Findal blinked at him. "For a little while, though," he said. "I know you want to go home eventually, but…"

Taerith shook his head. "Did you see into that copse?"

Findal stopped and sighed. "I saw… something."

"It was Borden," Taerith said. "He's found us."

Findal paled. "We'll arm ourselves, then?"

Pain flickered across Taerith's face. "It's wise. But I don't plan to be here when he attacks. Findal, are you willing to act as a decoy?"

Findal smiled. "We're always willing to help a friend."

Taerith smiled in response, aware as he did that to smile in a situation like this was the ultimate declaration of abandon. "Then we'll go with you a ways. At some point we'll leave the caravan— covering our tracks as best we can. It will be dark. If all is well, he won't know we've left. I don't know how far he'll follow you before he realizes we're gone—or attacks."

"He may not follow us at all," Findal said. "Perhaps he'll see you leaving."

"We'll simply have to pray he doesn't," Taerith said.

Findal reached out and laid his hand on Taerith's shoulder. "Well then," he said. "We have a plan. Uphill?"

"No." Taerith shook his head. "Down into the fens. It's easier to become lost there."

"We'll have to go past the copse. And whoever's waiting there."

Taerith looked over his shoulder in the direction of the dark stand of trees. "He'll be too close on our heels that way. But if we go over the hill, he can look down and see us."

"Then he'll see us looping back around the base of the hills, straight for the fens. He'll have to catch up, and you can lose yourself however you like. Taerith—" Findal slapped his hands together, ridding them of sawdust and dirt. "Take care of yourself and the little one. And Mirian—she doesn't look like anyone has looked after her for a good while."

Taerith nodded. "Thank you, my friend. I will."

Chapter Twenty-Seven

Wind had dried the hillside out. The wagon wheels creaked over dry roads. Findal held the reins and brakes with an expert hand, careful not to let the horses go too fast even as he kept the wagon from riding on their heels. Before them, the sun slipped below the horizon.

Taerith and Mirian rode inside, Mirian with Isaak in her arms. He was sleeping soundly despite the bumps and jars, contented by Marta's milk and Mirian's arms. Marta and Randal sat at the back of the wagon, hand in hand, with friendship written in their eyes as they watched the others. To both Taerith and Mirian the silent couple gave strength and encouragement by their presence.

They left the hill behind them. The roads now were muddy and full of potholes. It grew darker and darker outside the wagon. All noise but the sounds of the wagon—creaking wheels, jangling tack, horses' hooves—faded into nothing. No birds called or insects sang.

On the driver's seat, Findal cleared his throat. "Entering the fens," he said quietly. They all heard him.

Taerith felt sleep creeping over him, trying to drag at his head and limbs, making his chest heavy. He hadn't really slept—

sheltered and free of worry—for so long. Mirian was wide awake. She watched him with her green eyes like a cat's in the dark.

What felt like hours suspended in limbo passed.

"It's time," Taerith said. Mirian was still awake, still watching him. She nodded.

On an impulse, he held out his hand. She took it. They got to their feet, careful to keep their balance in the swaying wagon. Taerith leaned forward and touched Findal's arm. A slight signal, but understood. Findal pulled up on the reins just enough to slow the wagon.

Taerith led the way, crouching on the seat next to Findal for an instant before releasing Mirian's hand and jumping down. His boots hit the ground and he moved off the road into the cover of dormant bushes. The ground sloped away beneath his feet, down to water and shards of ice. Mirian was right behind him. He turned to make sure she was all right, when she shoved Isaak into his arms and whispered, "Wait for me."

He bit back a curse as she dashed from cover and jumped into one of the other wagons in the caravan. The moonlight was slight, but enough to allow him to see her. He hated to think of who else might be watching. If they were attacked now he couldn't defend them—not with a baby in his arms. He held Isaak close and sank into a crouch beneath the cover of the bushes.

Clouds drifted over the moon, plunging the fens into darkness. He heard the sound of her feet on the road, barely perceptible beneath the quiet rumbling of the wagons. Dead branches moved and rustled. He started to stand.

Something bleated.

The clouds cleared a little. He saw her eyes first, shining.

She had a tiny smile on her face, curiously exultant at her own strength and speed and nerve. The goat in her arms bleated again.

"Mirian…" he whispered.

"You can't feed him," she answered.

Taerith nodded. "Make her be quiet. Has she got a tether?" Isaak stiffened in his arms. Taerith bounced him a little, willing him to stay asleep.

Mirian nodded. Moonlight was streaking her face with shadows. She set the goat down carefully, searching out the tether in the dark.

"Take Isaak," Taerith said. "I'll lead the goat."

Mirian reached out and gathered the little one into her arms. Taerith watched as Isaak relaxed in her tight embrace. He took the tether in one hand and drew his sword with the other. His eyes met Mirian's. Not a word passed between them—not a word needed to. They both understood the dangers.

Somewhere in the fens, water was trickling in the dark.

*   *   *

They had left their horses behind. Warriors could move as fast on foot as a wagon caravan could roll, and horses would make too much noise.

Kardas led the way. Like a dog hunting down his own kind, he loathed every step. Yet he could not free himself from the hunt, and so he let it thrill him in its own way—let it make his blood pump harder and his senses work at their edge.

There was not a chance of Borden's losing the trail, so it did no good to allow him to lead. This way, perhaps, Kardas might see something Borden wouldn't—might even block him from seeing.

The path was muddy. The wagon wheels were imprinted clearly and deeply enough to be obvious even in the dark. It was a trail to make a hunter lazy, if he didn't know that the real quarry was something lighter, faster, more clever than a wagon. Borden knew it as well as Kardas did.

The shadows deepened more and more as they descended lower into the fens. Kardas kept up his pace, jogging lightly, just enough to stay out of sight of the wagons. His eyes scanned the road. For a moment his heart skipped a beat. They were there. New tracks, headed off the road into the wild. Just as he had expected.

A hand on his shoulder stopped him.

"Here," Borden said.

Kardas's heart sank. Borden knelt and examined the tracks. When he stood, the frightening fire had returned to his eyes.

*   *   *

They followed them through the night. Deep into the dark heart of the fens. Silently, Kardas marveled at the stamina that kept Taerith and Mirian going. Men, guided by nothing but skill, would have lost their trail in the night. But Borden was somehow more than a man, and obsession guided him.

The ground lay low, netted over by ancient bent swamp trees that spread their branches beneath a thin moon. Below the branches, the world was dank and black. When they had walked much of the night, the ground sloped even lower than before. The trees cleared for a moment, and the moon showed a basin of sorts. Waist-deep water surrounded an island. Two figures had entered the water and were climbing out now, little more than shadows in the night. One carried a child, the other a goat. Kardas almost smiled at the sight of them.

Beside him, Borden drew his sword. He started forward.

He stopped. Gasped. He began to tremble, and Kardas saw his knuckles go white as he gripped his sword. His eyes stared, not at the water or the island, but at something in the darkness no one else could see.

From his other side, Doublin cursed softly. Kardas kept his eyes on Borden.

What is it? He nearly asked. *What do you see?*

Before Borden's eyes, the fens had melted away. A great man stood before him, armed, a naked blade held at the ready. The man stared down at him with great dark eyes, murderous eyes. His hands were covered in blood, and it had dried on the sword hilt so that his hand was stuck fast to it.

Time began to move. It slipped past him like water, carrying pictures with it. He saw himself on the castle parapet; Mirian coming to him in the fading light.

The girl looked up at Borden's words but did not answer. She did not have to. Borden could see her eyes burning in the darkness, with nearly as much force as his own. She was angry with him.

"Come here," Borden said. She came. "What am I?" he asked.

"A tyrant," she answered.

"You do not admire me for that."

"I have never admired you.

Adrenaline pumped through him as he faced the giant in his path. Fear and regret. The sharp edge of vengeance, urging him forward. He looked down to see his feet shrouded in the darkness of the fens, to see only faint traces of moonlight reflecting off the water below. In the dark, a baby was crying.

The great, dark, bloodstained man stood still in his path.

Behind him, he heard the sound of someone rushing. He whirled around. Annar was coming through the night, rushing forward, sword drawn to attack. Borden raised his hand and caught his brother by the forearm, twisting his arm, forcing the sword to fall out of his hand.

The apparition pushed back. He was too strong. Borden's own wrist would break. His eyes widened in surprise.

"My lord," a voice whispered. Borden stopped pushing. He found himself standing hand-in-arm with Kardas. The nightmare visions were gone.

Borden had dropped his sword behind him. He didn't even know when. He turned away from Kardas, breathing hard, and sheathed the sword.

He could still hear a baby crying. That, at least, was not part of the nightmare. He narrowed his eyes and tried to see the refugees on the island, but nothing would reveal itself to his eyes.

Abruptly, he turned away.

"My lord," Kardas said quietly. "Let us go home."

Borden stared at him. "Not until my work is finished," he answered.

He looked back at the island. A great shape seemed to waver before his eyes, blade still naked, hands still bloodstained. Blocking his path.

He whispered the words. "However long it takes."

*　　*　　*

Two weeks of walking east brought them to a place where the ground began to rise in ridges and the land was thickly forested. Game grew more and more plentiful; Mirian's goat yielded milk enough for the baby and his guardians. Two weeks of walking— and on the fourteenth day, Taerith saw through the trees a ridge he knew as well as the contours of his own hands.

They camped in the woods that night and talked by the fire.

"It's hard to believe it's so close," Taerith said. His eyes were on the ridge, outlined by the moon that shone clearly above it. "All this time I've been close enough to go home if I wanted to."

"Why didn't you?" Mirian asked.

Taerith smiled. He looked down, stirring ashes with his stick. "I didn't know I could," he said. He shook his head. "No, I couldn't have. I had to find a home somewhere else… make one myself."

"Did you?" Mirian asked.

He looked up. The firelight danced in Mirian's hair as though it belonged there. Bundled beside her, Isaak slept soundly. The goat moved behind her, pulling against her tether. Behind them, the moon shone down: pure and distant like Lilia, a dream high in a starry night. The stars called up other memories. He saw Kardas on the standing stones, fighting for the loyalty of his people, and Joachim the priest. He remembered the dark eyes of the unicorn and the rumbling wheels of the circus. And above them all, hovering, fathering them, Deus with wings.

"I think I did," Taerith said.

In the flickering firelight a shadow passed over Mirian's face. "I'm afraid," she said, and stopped. Taerith waited for her to continue. Strong, fiery Mirian—the words didn't belong in her mouth.

"Corran was my prison," she said, "but it was also my home. I can't go back—I know that. But I have no where else on earth to call mine."

"I understand," Taerith said. He thought of Mirian's tree with her family buried at its roots—and Lilia. He understood the fear in her eyes. "My brothers and sisters and I—we all left home feeling as you do. Our guardian forbade us ever to come back or see each other again. We thought he had taken our home from us forever."

"And now you're going back," Mirian said.

"Yes," Taerith said. "I'm not sure what I'm going back to."

"Is your guardian still there?" Mirian asked.

Taerith gazed up at the ridge again, wishing his eyes could search out the wooded darkness. "If he's still alive," he said.

*   *   *

Doublin had run away a week earlier. Borden, in his lucid moments, was aware that the mercenary had gone, but said nothing of it. Kardas wondered what reports the coward took back to Corran with him. Reports of a mad king—of a ruler who sat and stared at nothing, who tracked a quarry but would not take it, who held something terrible in his eyes.

They had fallen far enough behind Taerith and Mirian to keep their presence entirely secret, but not far enough to lose them.

Kardas hunted and gathered what food he could. They made no fires; cooked no meat. Borden would not allow them to give away their presence.

Once, late at night, they spoke to each other.

"Loyal one," Borden said. He spoke the words with irony;

making a mockery of them.

"My lord?" Kardas asked. He had not slept. He had been staring up at the moon, wishing Taerith far away.

"Can you see it?" Borden said.

Kardas looked into the darkness. There was nothing there—nothing but the night. Yet it seemed to him that something did stand in their way. Something intangible.

"No," he said.

"It won't let me go forward," Borden said. He smiled, a twisted grimace. "My own mind is destroying me."

Kardas did not speak his answer out loud. *Your heart is destroying you, my lord.*

Borden stared into the darkness. He could see it: the giant, who he had come to recognize as himself. Standing silently and impassably in the way. He would overcome it. He was determined to.

"Turn around," Kardas whispered. "Go home."

Borden clenched his fist. "That is the one thing I cannot do. I have to finish what I started."

*   *   *

The sound of rushing water reached them before they came upon the river. The woods were a nursery of budding green in a damp tangle of saplings and old trees, grey and dark brown branches forming an elegant weaving above and around them. Taerith led the way, his feet eagerly finding old paths again. This was familiar ground—familiar woods—a spring he had not known since banishment. Behind him, Mirian stepped carefully through the green-world with Isaak in her arms and the goat trailing behind her.

They stepped out of the woods and found themselves on

the banks of a swollen, raging river. Beyond it, the ground swept up into the ridge, and adorning its sides like a glistening emerald coming into light, Braedoch Forest.

Taerith swallowed a lump in his throat. "Home," he said.

Mirian's voice came from far away. He turned. She was still at the edge of the woods, wrestling with the goat as it tried to stay where it could eat the new shoots of the underbrush. Isaak was in his makeshift sling on her back.

She looked at him pointedly and repeated herself. "That river's going to take some crossing."

*   *   *

Taerith spent an hour collecting kindling and firewood while Mirian perched herself on a rock by the river, feeding Isaak from one of the special flasks Marta had given her and talking to him in a low voice. The rush of the river drowned out even that sound—Taerith smiled as he watched her lips moving.

He could feel spray from the river on his face as he paced in search of the best place to build a fire. His mind raced as he worked. They would be camping here for some time unless he could find a way to cross the river.

He arranged sticks in the shape of a tent, wishing as he did that he could find drier wood. Clouds over the ridge spoke of more rain coming. Perhaps they should think about building a shelter as well.

Something nagged at him—some understanding he couldn't bring to roost. He stopped his work and tried to focus on it.

The image rose up suddenly before him, one in spirit with the river and the greening slope. A boat.

He smiled and jumped to his feet. Mirian looked up at him, questioning. He grinned at her and headed for the woods.

Fifty paces, through a copse of silver-barked trees, over three white boulders. He knew the landscape perfectly. The ground dipped into a bowl-shaped hollow, the base of it muddy and slick with clay deposits.

A sapling was growing over the hole he had dug in the side of the hollow all those years ago. He pushed it aside, and there it was—the hull of the boat, just visible in the dim light that filtered into the woods.

He propped his back against the sapling, holding it away as he pulled the boat out. It came with little effort. The end he grasped was damp, but the rest of the boat—a long, thin, light craft made for navigating rough water—was dry. The shelter had done its job.

When it was out, laying on the ground like a youthful dream made tangible, he examined it quickly. It needed some repair. The damp end had rotted partially away. The boat had been designed to carry only one or two people—Aiden had taken it out with him to hunt, he remembered, and Ilara had stolen it once—but Isaak hardly counted as a third person.

The rushing sound of the river was clear even in the hollow. Taerith hauled the boat up over his head and trekked back to the riverbank.

Mirian looked up at his approach. It took a minute for the sight to register, and she broke into a wide smile. Isaak was in his sling on her back, awake and alert. She stood and helped Taerith lower the boat to the ground.

"It needs some repairs," he said, "and we won't take it till the river calms just a little more. But it will take us home."

Home. Something in Mirian twinged at the word. For her it was still a hurt, an aching word. She turned away, glad for Taerith and the happiness in his eyes but suddenly lonely again.

Taerith disappeared into the woods, reappearing not long after with several long slim branches. Mirian watched as he stripped them and began to fashion them into arrows, arsenal for the makeshift bow he'd made on the journey. An hour later he was off on a hunt.

*   *   *

Mirian looked up from milking as a shadow fell over her—a curious shadow, one that felt to her eyes like light, shot through with traces of silver. She broke into a smile.

"What are you doing here?"

Zhenya, his hand as ever on the unicorn's shining back, smiled. "You left too soon," he said. "I always meant to go with you."

Mirian finished squeezing a last shot of milk into her small bucket and stood, wiping her hands on her skirt. The goat bleated and wandered off, seemingly unaware of the unicorn.

"Where is he?" Zhenya asked. He was looking around the camp site, his strange, childlike eyes searching.

"Taerith went hunting," Mirian said. She wanted to step forward, to greet Zhenya properly, but the presence of the unicorn awed and quieted her. She waited where she was.

Zhenya looked back and smiled. "I meant Isaak."

"Oh!" Mirian skirted around the unicorn until she reached the patch of new-sprung clover where Isaak lay in his blankets. The baby's eyes were open. Mirian smiled at him as she lifted him into her arms. His eyes, dark for so long, were changing colour now. They were grey like Lilia's.

Zhenya reached for him. "May I take him? Only for a little while," he asked. There was a curious, wistful look in his eyes. "I want to take him wandering."

She wasn't sure how to reply, and so she didn't bother. She handed Isaak over instead. Zhenya took him as tenderly as any mother, with a delighted smile. The unicorn turned its magnificent head and looked on the babe with eyes as deep as the night sky.

Zhenya cradled Isaak with the baby's head in the crook of his arm, and, absorbed in him, walked toward the woods. The unicorn went along, a part of Zhenya, a part of his constant delight. Mirian smiled as she watched them go. A wave of exhaustion hit her as they disappeared in the woods. She hadn't really slept in weeks.

*   *   *

Taerith bent his bow as he crept toward the sound. Whatever his quarry, it was just beyond a clump of bushes. He saw a flash of brown fur and tried to peer through the branches.

A hand clamped down on his shoulder. He spun around, bowstring taught, ready to let the arrow loose.

It was Aiden.

For a long moment Taerith stood with his arrow still at the ready.

His brother. The eldest Romany, he whose impetuous temper and prodigious strength Taerith had so often balanced in his youth. Aiden, playmate and fellow hunter; Aiden, also-banished.

It couldn't be.

"You look well, Taerith," Aiden said.

He lowered the bow. Aiden was looking at him through eyes

that were not what they had been—eyes that were hard, harbour-ing pain and guilt and cynicism. His face was different, too, older and marked with the same bitter scars.

"You look awful," Taerith replied.

Aiden laughed. It was much the same laugh, if emptier than it had sometimes been. "I should," he said. "I'm a failure."

"Why are you here?" Taerith asked.

"Why else?" Aiden asked. "I'm here for revenge. To kill Duard—and I've failed."

*   *   *

More than once, in the chase, Borden had heard the baby crying. He couldn't hear it now. The nearby sound of the river drowned everything else out. He could only imagine the sound now, and that made it worse. Imagination made everything worse. He was so close, and if he did nothing, the child would grow up—would come after him—would take everything.

Imagination came to its head. Borden stood and drew his sword. He stared up at the apparition that had held him back so long.

"Let me pass," he said.

The apparition stared back. There was life in its eyes—vi-tality, conviction. Borden knew in the instant that he had been wrong. This was no creature of his mind. It came from outside of him.

The giant did not speak, but it stepped forward. As it did, it changed. Great, dark wings spread up from its back and stretched themselves to the sky. The man's form changed and became that of a bird: a bird in which even the darkness was somehow like light—shining, powerful, blinding.

He knew it for what it was: his last chance.

The darkness, so long a part of him, the obsession that had held him captive for years, broke out of him like a torrent. Borden drew back his sword and threw it into the heart of the creature.

It looked at him once with human eyes and disappeared.

The ground around him came up in ragged pieces and then took wing. A flock of doves, birds of peace. They rose all around him with a clatter and a cry.

At his feet, another form appeared in the dust. It twisted and writhed and became, before his eyes, a serpent. It lifted its head from the dust and looked into his eyes.

The day returned to itself. Vision over. Madness gone.

Nothing now stood in his way.

*   *   *

Mirian sat by the river and watched it rushing and roiling in a white-lashed foam, its tearing force the last obstacle to the end of Taerith's journey. Where her own would end she didn't know—could hardly imagine. The cold stone that had settled in her throat when Lilia died was still there. It nearly melted each time she looked at Isaak, but at night it returned—fear, and uncertainty, and the still-fresh sorrow of her truest friend's death.

She shivered.

Behind her, a stone shifted. Someone was there, not three feet behind her. She stiffened.

Slowly, Mirian turned her head.

It was Borden.

Chapter Twenty-Eight

Thunder rolled over the ridge. Mirian stood slowly, her eyes not leaving Borden's face. She was frightened—afraid because she had declared herself this man's enemy, afraid because she was alone—but her fear gave place, as she looked into his eyes, to horror—not of him but for him.

He had come to her last with blood on his hands, and there had been fear and guilt and pain in his eyes. After the loss of so much, she'd thought his eyes would be empty—but they were so full.

She took a step toward him. She hadn't meant to, but his eyes held her.

So full—of something tormented, inhuman.

She expected him to speak. He said nothing. Thunder rolled again, and a wind began to blow, and then she was afraid in earnest.

The Borden who had been was gone.

The man who had—had what? Had wanted her, needed her somehow—was not the same man who stood before her now. That man might have killed her. This man surely would.

"Come back," she whispered as a cold rain began to patter

against her face and the stones on the riverbank.

He moved too fast. He grabbed her by the throat.

"Where is he?"

"Where is who?" she answered back. She took his arm with her hands, trying to push him away. His grip tightened.

"Where is the child?"

Somehow she managed to pry his fingers loose enough to allow herself to breathe.

"Let me go," she said.

He shook her. "Where is he?" he roared.

She broke loose and roared back, as much as she could between involuntary gasps for breath. "Gone! Why are you hunting us?"

She backed away from him, toward the water, desperately scanning the beach behind him for some place to run. The sky was darkening on every side, the water behind her white and wild, and Borden stood black like an iron wall in her way.

"My brother…" Borden began. Lightning tore the sky behind him.

"He's dead!" Mirian screamed over the rising wind. Borden drew his sword and dealt her a blow to the shoulder with the flat of it that sent her sprawling on the wet stones.

"Where is the child?" Borden demanded.

Body resounding with the pain of the blow, Mirian rolled onto her back and started to push herself up.

The tip of Borden's sword, held against her heart, stopped her.

Fear, if it was still present in her, receded where it could hardly touch her. Other emotions took its place. She still couldn't tear away from his eyes. She could weep for the hatred in them.

It was raining harder. Another bolt of lightning forked over the forest behind Borden.

Of everything in this wilderness, it was Borden who had always been a part of her. Borden who was her home.

A girl's home should not hold her at the point of a sword—should not have murder in his eyes.

But then, neither should a girl rebel against her home.

He asked again, pushing the sword down so she could feel the sharp point through her clothing. "Where is he?"

You should have been his home, she thought. She swallowed and wished away the tears in her eyes. The pressure on the sword lessened. Something in him was faltering.

"Answer me. Don't you want to live?" he asked. For a moment he sounded like his old self.

She shook her head. Slowly, she reached up and touched the sword. He didn't move. She pushed the blade aside, her eyes still on his face.

"Not at such a price," she said.

He looked back at her. The raging hatred in his eyes flickered a moment, gave way to remorse. She got to her feet slowly, wishing that somehow she could touch the part of him that felt regret—could make him come back.

"You should have been mine," he said.

She stood tall. Still. There was spray in her hair, nipping at her, freezing her heels and the backs of her hands. The rock beneath her feet was slick with water. The river rising, trying to take her…

His eyes changed, and she saw it. He lunged. She turned on one heel and grabbed his sleeve, throwing off balance. And even as she did, as his foot slipped on the wet rock and he fell, even then she tried to undo it. She reached for him, tore at his sleeve, tried to catch him and keep him back.

But the river had him now, and the river was truly wild. On her knees on the slick black rock, rain pelting at her, she watched him go under and screamed.

"Borden!"

*　　*　　*

Aiden's words were too much to process all at once. His sudden appearance was itself enough to knock Taerith off balance, but it did present a problem of its own—or the answer to one.

"You went home?" Taerith asked.

"If you can call it that," Aiden answered.

"Then what are you doing on this side of the river?"

Aiden looked at him in surprise, then threw back his head and laughed. "Trust you to ask a question like that at a time like this!"

Thunder rolled alone then, mingling its deep voice with that of the river. Taerith half-smiled at himself, but the image of Mirian and Isaak at the riverbank—cold and soon to be wet, coupled with a sharp memory of a fire under the wooden circular roof of home—demanded an answer to the question. He asked it again.

"I'm hunting," Aiden answered. He recognized the quiet frustration in Taerith's face and nodded upriver. "There's a bridge up that way. Where the river narrows."

Taerith frowned. He could picture the river in that direction where it narrowed and cut through rock so sheer it was almost a chasm, but no bridge.

"There never used to be," Taerith said.

"Well, there is now!" Aiden burst out.

Taerith reached down and picked up his arrows. He had dropped them at the sight of Aiden. He tucked them into his belt now. "I need to get across."

"Well, come then," Aiden said. He started in the direction of the bridge. Taerith didn't follow.

"Not alone," he said.

Aiden stopped and regarded him. "So you brought someone too, did you?" he asked. "Good God, what is wrong with us? Didn't you learn the danger of attaching yourself to people when Duard sent us away?"

Corran was the only answer to that question—Corran, where he had stayed because of caring and not regretted it. But there was no way to put all of Corran into words. "I learned how dangerous it can be not to care. The price is too great."

Aiden looked a long time at Taerith. But for their faces and the unspoken experiences that somehow deepened their voices, they might have been boys still.

Aiden smiled. The old, cocky, ironic smile. "This is a strange way to talk," he said, "for long-lost brothers now found. Hello, Taerith. It's good to see you."

Taerith smiled. His eyes clouded, and he and Aiden stepped into a warrior's embrace.

Aiden slapped Taerith on the shoulder as they separated. "Tell me," Aiden said. "What brings you back home to Braedoch? And please tell me you didn't bring those other three with you— you have more sense than to attach yourself to that."

Taerith was about to answer that he had when he realized Aiden had said "three." His fist tightened involuntarily, so hard that had he still been holding an arrow he would have snapped it. "Who?" he asked.

"Dark men," Aiden said. "Warriors; they smell like trouble."

He hadn't finished speaking before Taerith was on his way, running, back to the riverbank.

*   *   *

Straining to see through the trees, Taerith saw Mirian first: standing at the riverbank, long red hair streaming with the wind and rain, and Borden close enough to touch her. He willed more speed into his legs and drew his sword as he ran.

His advance was stopped cold as he burst through the tree line. Kardas stood in his way. Taerith had not seen so much anguish in his friend's face since the night he had gone to fight the wild men and return himself to bondage.

Taerith eyed Kardas a moment and turned back to the drama at the water's edge. He rushed forward—and found himself locked, steel to steel, with Kardas.

"Kardas, let me go," Taerith said. Warning mixed with sorrow made his eyes intense.

"Orders," Kardas said. "A few things bind the wild men. This is one of them."

Taerith pulled his sword away; started forward again. Again

the clash: the way blocked. Anguish in Kardas's eyes.

A battle yell split the air. Surprise pulled Taerith and Kardas apart, and between them a living whirlwind sprang up: Aiden. The speed of it forced Taerith to the side, as before him a conflict faster and more powerful than anything he had ever seen arose. Everywhere Kardas turned, Aiden was. Everywhere Aiden could attack, Kardas repelled him. One thing became clear in the minutes—the seconds—he watched: Kardas, defeater and king of the wild men, just might not be good enough to defeat Aiden Romany.

"Aiden!" Taerith cried, seeking out some way to get between them. "Aiden, don't kill him!"

Something pulled his eyes away from the fight to the edge of the trees just beyond them. A living, muscle-bound streak of lightning burst from the trees and drove forward, hooves pounding the ground, horn pointed at Kardas's chest. The unicorn split the fight with a grace more than any earthly thing should possess: the grace of power and beauty united. Kardas held his hands up in surrender, his dark eyes full of the lovely death that breathed hard before him. "Don't kill him!" Taerith shouted again.

His eyes were drawn back to the forest edge. Zhenya was there, the baby in his arms, standing on tiptoe in the pelting rain. He was looking to the river. To Mirian.

Taerith whirled around just in time to see Borden lunge at her—and then something happened, and Borden disappeared from view. Mirian fell to her knees behind him, narrowly avoiding a plunge into the water herself. They all heard her scream out Borden's name.

Taerith stripped off his sword as he ran. Somehow he managed to loosen his boots without slowing. He reached Mirian and took her shoulders for a moment. He scanned the water. There—already swept far downstream, the dark form of the man he had once followed. Taerith ran along the edge of the bank and dove into the river.

The surging current pulled him forward and dashed his shoulder against a rock. He fought to get control of himself as the water pulled him down. The water was a mass of white bubbles and swirling debris. He struggled to see through it and keep himself from being driven against the rocks along the bank.

Thunder crashed as he surfaced for a breath. He whipped his hair out of his eyes and searched for Borden. There, again—dark clothes, the vague outline of a form in the water. He wasn't far. Taerith dove under again and swam with all his strength.

He reached him. He hooked his arms underneath Borden's and tried to drag him up to the surface, but the current kept sucking at them both, hurtling them forward. Taerith nearly cried out as another rock smashed against his back, driving precious air from his lungs. Borden was too heavy. Taerith tugged; Borden wasn't moving.

Through the underwater spray Taerith saw the branch—Borden's cloak, heavy with water, was caught. He groped for the clasp at Borden's chest and undid it. He needed air desperately, but he was so close… still holding on to Borden, fighting against the ceaseless push of the current, he found Borden's belt and undid it. A knife and ax fell away.

Something was still holding them down; still keeping them under. His lungs were straining to the breaking point. He felt his hands growing weaker; losing their grip. He needed air; he knew, with what was left of his consciousness, that he needed it now.

But not without Borden; he couldn't let go; couldn't leave

him to drown; couldn't…

The current was carrying them both with it. He could see the surface above him, no calmer than the water beneath, could see the darkness above that was sky and clouds and thunder.

Hands reached down and caught him.

He came up struggling, coughing, trying to free himself. "Taerith!" The voice broke through a crash of thunder. Mirian. He was fighting Mirian.

He stopped struggling and found something hard and rough beneath his feet. Hands were still hauling at him from above: Mirian, her skirts soaked, half in the water, and Kardas holding both of them.

He turned before he'd even left the water completely. Aiden was dragging Borden out. Taerith joined him, taking one of Borden's arms and pulling him up over the rocks. Wind and rain lashed at them as they laid the one-time crown prince down.

Mirian knelt by Borden's head and brushed his long black hair from his face. She drew her fingers away covered in blood. It ran thickly down one side of his face, flowing from a wound she could not see. She rocked on her heels and began to cry.

Taerith knelt on his other side. Rain turned the world around him grey. His helplessness was a physical pain, an ache that grew with every second Borden did not open his eyes. He felt a hand on his shoulder and looked up. Kardas stood beside him.

"You did all you could," he said.

"Help me bury him," Taerith said. "After the rain."

Kardas nodded.

Chapter Twenty-Nine

They crossed over the bridge as the sun came up the next morning. The new grave lay beside the river, marked not with stone but with Borden's sword, driven halfway into the ground. Its hilt formed a worn cross.

Trees arched out over the river, their branches forming a green canopy over their heads. Raindrops kissed with sunlight dripped down from the newly-budding leaves. Taerith and Kardas led the way. The bridge rocked and swayed beneath their feet, but the boards held. Mirian crossed behind them with Isaak in her arms. She paused once and looked down the raging river as it widened. Tears came to her eyes, but she ducked her head and kept going.

Behind her, Zhenya and the unicorn brought up the rear with brightness.

Braedoch Forest welcomed them into its green arms. Every sight, every smell was at once new and familiar to Taerith, like a waking dream of childhood. They came to a well-worn path, and it seemed to him that the dust of it was still stirred by their leaving—Romany feet and horse hooves as each of the nine children of Isaak Romany went into banishment alone.

When the slope of the ridge leveled out and Taerith smelled the smoke of the hearthfire, tears stung his eyes. He stopped.

Mirian appeared at his side, bouncing an awake and beginning-to-squawl Isaak. "That's it?" she asked.

He smiled. The Romany home, surrounded by forest—built of wooden, circular chambers, every board hewn by his father, every peg carefully shaped, with a roof he and his brothers had re-paired every spring—it was a long way from the castle in Corran.

"That's it," he answered.

*   *   *

Aiden stood at the door, his dark head bowed, arms folded across his chest as he leaned on the doorframe. He looked up at Taerith's approach. His blue eyes were startling as they had always been, but they seemed clouded over now.

"He's inside," he said. "She's with him… Kristalyn."

Taerith didn't wait to ask. He pushed gently against the door. It opened to him. The fire in the center of the room was smoking; the room was filled with the peculiar smell of wet firewood. A cot lay near the fire, and on it an emaciated form. Taerith's heart caught in his throat.

A girl was seated next to the cot. She was beautiful. She wore the clothes of a forester from lands to the east. Golden hair spilled down her back. Her eyes when she looked up were green and compassionate. A great black cat—a panther—lay curled near her feet. It lifted its head at Taerith's entrance.

"Easy, Kurio," she said, and the panther relaxed.

"My name is Taerith," he said.

"Aiden told me," she answered.

His feet moved forward of their own accord. He dropped into a crouch beside the man whose rasping breath filled the silence. Duard turned and regarded him. His eyes were bloodshot; if he even recognized anything around him Taerith couldn't tell. The side of his head was bruised where Aiden had tried—and failed—to take his vengeance.

The cracked lips opened. "Taerith," Maeron Duard said.

Taerith reached out and took the old man's hand. "It's me," he said.

"You haven't come to kill me," Duard rasped.

"No," Taerith said. The druid's fingers tightened around his.

"I knew that," he said. "You were always the thoughtful one. You knew… I never really wanted to hurt you."

Taerith blinked back tears: bitter tears, angry tears, and yet tears also of pity. Maeron Duard: the man who had held the Romany children in fear and neglect; the man who had almost certainly killed their parents; the man who had banished them. He had done more to destroy them than anyone alive.

And yet, here on the threshhold of death, blame seemed more futile than it ever had in life.

Even then, Taerith had not really blamed him. Duard had been a man caught in old feuds so much bigger than himself— bound by curses old and acrid.

Taerith closed his eyes. Tears slipped past his eyelids. Old feuds, old curses: like the animosity that drove Borden to murder his brother and to die a useless death himself, a great man lost to his own bitterness. Like the cruel triumphing that enslaved Mirian and left her with nothing but a tree to love. Things so much bigger than one person—like the quarrels and struggles and political battles that used Lilia until she died.

"You were wrong," Taerith said. He opened his eyes. The

bloodless face stared up at him. Kristalyn, who had retreated to one wall, looked at him with surprise and perhaps accusation. But he had to speak.

"You were wrong," he repeated. "It could have ended with you. Had you refused to kill my parents—had you chosen not to send us away—it could have ended with you."

Duard made a sound like laughing. "It does end with me," he said. "It dies with me."

Taerith shook his head. "No," he said. "It has already ended—with me. With Aiden. We—we choose to let it end."

Something dark flickered in Duard's eyes. "That's the coward's way out," he said. "You ought to strike me down now. Take vengeance."

Taerith thought of the sword over Borden's grave. In his mind's eye he saw it rusting over the years, breaking away and being swept into the river.

"I am heartily sick of vengeance," he said. "We release you, Duard. We forgive you."

He stood and released the old man's hand. "You are going to have to find a way to deal with that."

Kristalyn was still watching him. There were tears in her eyes. Taerith motioned toward the fire. "Is there no dry firewood?" he asked.

She shook her head. "There was none when we came, and it has hardly stopped raining since our arrival."

Taerith nodded. "We'll make do, then. If you would, please, put a pot of water on. I'm going to see what old herbs still linger in the stores here."

He looked back down at Duard, answering the question

the old man was too weak to ask. "I'm going to heal you," he said. "If I can."

*　　*　　*

Taerith stepped out of the smoky house into the clear air. It was still morning. The air was clean as rain, washed into newness. Aiden still stood near the door. Taerith faced him.

"No vengeance, Aiden," he said. "It's over now."

Aiden nodded. There was still, in his eyes, a terrible hardness—but something in it moved in acquiesence to Taerith's words. "I know," he said.

Taerith slapped his brother on the shoulder and moved on, his head bent. It took him a moment to remember that he was searching for herbs. He moved automatically toward the root cellar when a loud bleating interrupted his thoughts.

He looked up, startled. Mirian was chasing the nanny goat with a bucket in her hand. Zhenya, seated nearby, laughed and jumped up to join the chase. He limped faintly—very faintly.

Taerith smiled as he watched them catch the goat and wrestle her into submission. Isaak lay on a wide stump nearby, wrapped up in Mirian's old shawl. Taerith picked the baby up, looking into the grey eyes so like Lilia's. He meant to say something about all the trouble such a little one could cause, but the eyes caught him off guard and he could only smile, willing away a lump in his throat.

Far away, wind stirred a bundle of feathers on a grave beneath a tree.

*　　*　　*

Taerith leaned against the doorframe, listening for Duard

Rachel Starr Thomson　323

with one ear while he picked through herbs. Aiden sauntered up.

"So…" Aiden said. He rubbed the back of his neck. "She's beautiful."

Taerith frowned. "Who?" he asked.

Aiden laughed. "Your wife," he said.

"Who—" Taerith stopped and cocked his head. "Mirian?"

Aiden bent an eyebrow. "How many wives do you have, little brother?"

"None," Taerith answered. He laughed at the look on Aiden's face. "She was in trouble… I helped her escape."

"And Isaak is…"

"An orphan," Taerith said. Not for the first time, he realized how much time it would take to explain everything… and even then, some things couldn't ever really be explained.

"Oh," Aiden said. "Well. Forgive me." He turned to go, and looked back with a twinkle in his eye. "She's still beautiful."

He left Taerith deep in thought.

Mirian was standing on a knoll nearby, looking down over the ridge. The deep blue sky above her was streaked with high, thin clouds. Her hair was blowing in the breeze, as he had seen it do so many times. She stood hugging herself—cradling something, cold or painful, and hers alone.

Taerith approached her quietly. He stood next to her for a time, looking down on the wooded valleys below. Far in the distance, the world flattened out—into a land of fens and moors, a lonely stone castle and a tree.

"Home is not what I thought it would be," Taerith said. "I should have known."

"Things change," Mirian said. The words came too quickly; she hadn't thought them out.

"No," Taerith said. "They haven't, really… I've changed. Aiden's changed. When the others come back—they won't be the same either."

Mirian turned her head and looked at him. She didn't smile. The loneliness in her eyes was so clear it made him ache for her.

"Mirian," he said, "do you want to go back to Corran?"

She stood still for a moment, then shook her head and hastily wiped at her face with her sleeve. "No," she said.

"Then I think you should make a new home," Taerith said.

She cocked her head just a little. It was a familiar gesture by now. "Where?" she asked. Her voice was faint.

"In the same place I make mine," Taerith said. He didn't wait for her to answer. "Mirian, you and I have loved the same loves and felt the same hurts without ever really taking hands. Someone told me recently that belonging is a choice, so…"

He stopped and looked away from her, out at the wide world. He smiled. Turned back.

"So if you're willing to belong to me, I'll gladly belong to you, and we'll both have a home. And Isaak will have one besides."

Mirian blinked. A smile tugged at the edges of her mouth. Slowly, she held out her hand. He took it.

"All right," she said.

He entwined his fingers with hers, lifted her hand, and kissed it. "Welcome home," he said.

*　*　*

That night, as they gathered around a fire on the knoll under the stars, Taerith still had hold of Mirian's hand. He sat on a log and she on the ground in front of him, and he held her hand and stroked her hair with his other. Zhenya sat across from them, holding Isaak—he had held him most of the day. The unicorn stood outside the circle, stamping its hooves in the dust, shining under the stars. Zhenya watched the creature, its light reflected in its eyes.

Aiden sat on the ground near the fire, poking at the flames with a stick while Kristalyn watched from the shadows beyond the circle.

It was Kardas they watched—Kardas they all watched, except for Zhenya. He had spent the day wandering the ridge; coming to grips, Taerith knew, with his freedom. Now he sat with the fire behind him, his face in shadow but his eyes full of power and light. The barbarian king crouched on the ground facing Taerith and Mirian and listened in silence as they spoke.

"He should have the throne one day," Mirian said, "but we don't want him to grow up there. There are too many tangles— too many threats still."

"But Corran shouldn't be abandoned while it has a king," Taerith said. "You know that."

Kardas nodded slowly.

"Master Grey will be guarding the throne now," Taerith said. "Waiting for us to return. He would accept you—would help you."

"I am a king," Kardas said. "Why should I act as a steward?"

He smiled in the darkness. Joachim's words were there in his ears, as they had been since the day they were uttered.

The loyal one. It takes a very loyal heart to sit a throne without claiming it.

Kardas stood. He stretched to his full height in the starlight, as much a creature of the night as the unicorn that tossed its head to dance with the stars. He reached down and took Taerith's hand, and then Mirian's hand, and smiled down on both of them.

"I would be honoured," he said. "I am only sorry to leave without you two."

*　*　*

Taerith spent the night in the central chamber next to a pot of simmering herbs. He tended the fire and kept the concotion brewing, feeding it to Duard every hour.

When the sun began its ascent, Taerith awoke suddenly because Duard was not breathing.

A moment later he heard the raspy intake of breath, more laboured than ever, and then his name, faint but clear. "Taerith."

He went to Duard's side immediately and looked down at the pale face.

Duard opened his eyes. They were bleary, but they could still see, and the old druid smiled.

"I bless you, lad," he said. "I bless you all."

Two hours later he was dead. Taerith poured the herbs onto the cot before they burned it. He and Aiden took Duard's body deep into the woods and burned it on a funeral pyre there.

When they came back, Mirian and Isaak were sitting in the doorway waiting. Isaak was awake, propped against Mirian's knees as she played with his hands. Taerith smiled at the sight of them. Mirian looked up and smiled back. The sun was bright overhead, though off in the distance rainclouds were gathering again.

Taerith walked into the house. It was quiet. The fire was still smoking. He crossed the main chamber to Duard's room and pushed open the door. Cobwebs pulled away from the wood as he entered.

In the far corner of the room, a table sat. Paper and ink lay out on it. Taerith lowered himself into the chair and took up the feather pen.

My dear brothers and sisters, he wrote.

Come home.

About the Romany Epistles

The Romany Epistles are a nine-author series of interconnected novels. Written by a group of online friends calling themselves the Wayside Inn Writers Society, the books follow the adventures of the nine banished Romany siblings: Aiden, Taerith, Daelia, Arnan, Ilara, Wren, Aquila, Zoe, and Sam. The project was informal and not all books were completed; however, the adventure lives on as some novels are still being serialized and others are moving to publication.

The original Romany Epistles can be found online at: http://romanyepistles.blogspot.ca.

Rachel would love to hear from you!
You can visit her and interact online:

Web: www.rachelstarrthomson.com
Facebook: www.facebook.com/RachelStarrThomsonWriter
Twitter: @writerstarr

The Seventh World Trilogy

Worlds Unseen   Burning Light   Coming Day

For five hundred years the Seventh World has been ruled by a tyrannical empire—and the mysterious Order of the Spider that hides in its shadow. History and truth are deliberately buried, the beauty and treachery of the past remembered only by wandering Gypsies, persecuted scholars, and a few unusual seekers. But the past matters, as Maggie Sheffield soon finds out. It matters because its forces will soon return and claim lordship over her world, for good or evil.

The Seventh World Trilogy is an epic fantasy, beautiful, terrifying, pointing to the realities just beyond the world we see.

"An excellent read, solidly recommended for fantasy readers."
– Midwest Book Review

"A wonderfully realistic fantasy world. Recommended."
– Jill Williamson, Christy-Award-Winning
Author of *By Darkness Hid*

"Epic, beautiful, well-written fantasy that sings of Christian truth."
– Rael, reader

Available everywhere online or special order from your local bookstore.

Novels by Rachel Starr Thomson

Available everywhere online or special order from your local bookstore!

Angel in the Woods

"A mastery of storytelling"

"a beautiful tale of honor and heroism."

Lady Moon

"Laugh-out-loud funny"

*"reminiscent of Patricia C. Wrede and
Terry Brooks's Magic Kingdom for Sale."*

Reap the Whirlwind

"Haunting."

Theodore Pharris Saves the Universe

"Imaginative and hilarious."

Short Fiction by Rachel Starr Thomson

Available as downloads for Kindle, Kobo, Nook, iPad, and more!

Butterflies Dancing

Fallen Star

Of Men and Bones

Ogres Is

Journey

Magdalene

The City Came Creeping

Wayfarer's Dream

War With the Muse

Shields of the Earth

And more!